HOKEE WOLF III
THE MASSACRE SHOSHONE

CLARK VIEHWEG

Black Rose Writing | Texas

The author grants the final approval for this literary material.

First printing

This is a work of fiction. Names, characters, businesses, places, events, and incidents are either the products of the author's imagination or used in a fictitious manner. Any resemblance to actual persons, living or dead, or actual events is purely coincidental.

ISBN: 978-1-68513-278-1
PUBLISHED BY BLACK ROSE WRITING
www.blackrosewriting.com

Printed in the United States of America
Suggested Retail Price (SRP) $21.95

Hokee Wolf III is printed in Garamond Pro

*As a planet-friendly publisher, Black Rose Writing does its best to eliminate unnecessary waste to reduce paper usage and energy costs, while never compromising the reading experience. As a result, the final word count vs. page count may not meet common expectations.

THE
HOKEE WOLF SERIES

Hokee Wolf

Hokee Wolf II: Satanic Rituals

While the massacre of the Shoshone Indians at Bear River provides the backdrop, this story is about human trafficking, a modern evil equal in depravity to the massacre.

PURE EVIL

BACKGROUND

History

The Shoshone Indians dwelt in a large area, including Utah, Idaho, Wyoming, and Montana, for *fifteen thousand years*, living peacefully on the abundant game and fish.

The white man coming west was initially greeted by friendly Indians and welcomed to the bountiful life in the region. Cache Valley in Utah and Idaho (Where Jim Bridger cached his furs for the winter) was flush with deer, elk, geese, ducks, and rabbits, while the creeks and rivers were full of fish. Westward migration by eager land grabbers, history uses the polite term *pioneers*, killed so much wildlife that the Native Americans began suffering starvation.

Facing starvation, Indians began raiding the farms and towns for livestock to eat. This led to hostilities resulting in deaths on both sides.

The Paiutes lived peacefully alongside the Shoshone in the same territory for eleven thousand years. And like the Shoshone, the tribe faced severe starvation as the settlers killed off all the wild game. This also forced the Paiutes to raid the white man's settlements for cattle to eat.

Abraham Lincoln alternated between seeking friendly relations with the Indians and allowing their extermination. In 1863, with the Civil War sapping his thoughts and energy, the President supported killing the Native Americans. Early in the morning of January 29th, a cold wintry day with snowdrifts covering the ground, Colonel Patrick Edward Connor led two hundred bounty-hungry California Volunteers (called soldiers) on a surprise raid to massacre the peaceful Shoshone camped by hot springs close to the Bear River.

Brave Volunteers slaughtered over five hundred warriors in what is now called the Bear River massacre. The government had placed a bounty on male Indian scalps, turning the Indians into nothing more than a wild game with a price on their heads to be hunted and eventually exterminated. The California volunteers, who were untrained military men under Connor's command, eradicated Native Americans not living on a reservation. Several hundred Indian tribes ceased to exist. These volunteers were eager to take part in the Bear River massacre for the Indian scalps. In central Idaho, the Paiutes were hunted and killed by these same bounty hunters called soldiers. Only about one hundred and fifty Shoshone warriors escaped the onslaught at Bear River by swimming in the freezing river and hiding in the bushes on the other side. While over five hundred women and children were slaughtered with bayonets, two hundred and fifty women and children were spared the massacre, as there was no reward for their scalps, and bullets were expensive. These survivors were rounded up and placed in a camp with no food. After the soldiers left the area, the surviving warriors returned to the camp only to be marched later to the Fort Hall Indian Reservation in Idaho, a desolate lava plain with no water or trees, meaning no food for the Indians who were forced to live there. Soldiers also marched the few surviving Paiutes to the Fort Hall Reservation.

Now

Today, a cool northwest evening breeze swept across the hot lava flats by Fort Hall, carrying a hint of the Snake River 15 miles to the west. The sun had set behind the undulating plains, turning daylight to dusk and ushering in the cool evening air, the favorite playtime for the Indian children living on the Fort Hall Reservation. Although several children had gone missing over the past few months, the parents of seven-year-old Diwali Tukurika were not concerned. Their small clapboard hut was close to the police station, only two miles away.

As darkness approached, a small man in black clothing crouched behind a boulder one hundred feet east of the hut. When the dark figure was sure that no one was watching, he stood and walked up behind Diwali, placing a chloroform rag over his nose and mouth, clamping it down tight so the child could not make any sounds. Then, taking an envelope from his back pocket, the man placed it on the ground with a rock on top to keep it from blowing away. Inside the envelope was a message, *DEATH TO THE SHOSHONE.* The man threw the unconscious child over his shoulder and slipped into darkness. That night, another young Indian child went missing.

Like most Indian Reservations, the Fort Hall Reservation today is under the control of the Indians, who manage all government activities on the reservation, including law enforcement. So, when Indian boys and girls between the ages of five and ten turned up missing, with messages of death to the Shoshone, only the tribal police would investigate their disappearance. After several months of failures by tribal police to find their missing children, the tribal leaders went looking for Hokee Wolf.

HOKEE WOLF III
PURE EVIL
THE MASSACRE SHOSHONE

CHAPTER ONE

Hokee Wolf was in his office on a strikingly beautiful sunny summer afternoon when his office manager, the widow Hilda Worthmyer, ushered in three council members from the Fort Hall Indian Reservation, seeking an audience with the legendary investigator.

Sitting in a custom-made chair with shoulder-length black hair held off his face by a white headband, the handsome investigator looked relaxed, reading a white paper on modern bank robbers with his size ten Tony Lama cowboy boots resting on the desktop. Hokee alternated between boots and handmade buffalo skin moccasins, which he wore whenever in the field. Hokee made these moccasins of natural leather with no artificial preservatives to remain grounded, a condition essential for his work. Today, his shining black boots reflected rings around the office from the sunshine streaming in from the window. When the three men from the Shoshone-Paiute Indian Reservation arrived with Hilda, his lady Friday, Hokee put his boots on the floor, killing the reflections.

The three reservation council members introduced themselves using first names only: Atohi, Onacona, and Waya. Perhaps they only had one name; Hokee knew a little about how reservation Indians identified themselves. Half Indian himself, the Navajo Reservation where he was born, rejected the mixed-blood baby after his mother committed suicide. Hokee, the Navajo name for abandoned, was the name they gave the unwanted kid

1

before dumping the boy only six out by the highway. The young boy went north looking unsuccessfully for his white father when a Blackfoot Shaman living on the Shoshone-Paiute Fort Hall Indian Reservation noticed the homeless young boy in Pocatello, Idaho, and made him an apprentice.

Atohi, named for the woods, wore antelope skin leggings and a woven woolen serape with a traditional Shoshone pattern in yellow and green. He was short, only five foot four inches tall, but he had a tall man's attitude as he looked down his nose with a dark unfriendly eye at everyone and everything, not Shoshone.

Onacona, the leader of this delegation, was a Paiute aptly named after the white owl. Although not a tall man, at five foot ten, he towered over the diminutive Atohi. Dressed in council clothes, dark woolen pants with a beaded long-sleeved woolen shirt, his withering brown eyes with a golden tint like a real owl left no doubt in anyone's mind who held the power in this group. He was not so much imperious as quietly serene, with a confident leader's powerful presence that filled the office.

Waya, another Shoshone, was the warrior. Dressed in the white man's garb of Levi's and a long-sleeved Pendleton shirt, he also wore cowboy boots and a white Stetson, like he dared anyone to take offense. That he was a warrior showed in how he moved with cat-like stealth and restless eyes, forever moving to assess any potential threats. And, like his two companions, he never smiled.

Onacona spoke quietly in an authoritative tone. "Mr. Wolf, your reputation for locating the missing is legendary. We hope you can help us with our problem."

Not one to miss the subtle nuances his three visitors promoted, Hokee asked, "What is it you are missing, councilman?"

Nodding his head towards the man from the woods, Onacona showed he wanted the short man to do the talking.

As though talking to his inferior, Atohi responded quietly, imperiously. "In the past six months, eleven boys and girls between the ages of five and ten have disappeared from our reservation. Our tribal police have had no success in determining what happened to these children, and, of course, the

United States Government is not interested in what happens on the reservation. So, you are our last hope to find our children."

"What can you tell me about these missing children? What time of day did they go missing? Do you suspect anyone who abducted them, and did anyone see someone who looked suspicious on the reservation?" Hokee looked at Atohi, but it was the warrior Waya who answered.

"No, Mr. Wolf, no one witnessed anything unusual. The children all disappeared in the late evening hours, shortly before their bedtime.

"Have your tribal police turned up any leads? And please call me Hokee."

The council members looked at each other until the quiet leader, Onacona, finally responded. "Last year, a man named Lkal (pronounced El-kay-ahl) broke into our tribal office and stole several thousand dollars we kept on hand for emergencies. Our tribal police caught the thief in Blackfoot and recovered most of our money, but unfortunately, Lkal escaped before they could return him to the reservation. We believe he is stealing our children and selling them into slavery. A written note saying death to the Shoshone is left behind when the children are abducted. He is a Shoshone, and why he hates his people is unknown. And before you ask, our beliefs are purely speculative, based on what we know of the man."

"Is anyone friendly with this man, either on the reservation or in the surrounding towns?" Hokee asked.

Now it was Atohi who responded. It seemed like the council members were talking to Hokee as a tag team. "The thief was always a loner, not on friendly terms with anyone we know. Rummers are that he had a girlfriend outside the reservation, but we could not confirm the rummer, nor do we know where to look for any such woman."

This case was shaping into the kind Hokee hated, a nasty disappearance with little or no helpful information. "Do you have a picture of Lkal? Can you describe him to me?"

The warrior, Waya, answered, handing over a picture he had removed from the pocket of his Pendelton. "Unfortunately, this is the only picture we have. They took it when Lkal was a young boy, around twelve or thirteen.

He is about five-five, brilliant, and muscular. Lkal isn't a handsome man, as you can see from the picture."

"Okay, gentlemen. You haven't given me much to work with, but I can help. My fee is a thousand dollars a day, plus expenses. My guess is that this case will take a few days, perhaps a couple of weeks. If I have been unsuccessful by then, we will waste no more time. Lacking information, I must resort to unconventional methods. If they are alive, I will find your missing children. Please pay five thousand dollars as a gesture of goodwill. I will charge you no more, regardless of the time and expense involved."

With a heavy countenance, Onacona asked, "we were told you accepted charity cases and did not charge. Is this true?"

"If a parent loses contact with one of their children and they are poor, I often take their case without requesting payment. I know your reservation is not flush with money, but five thousand is not a fortune, and you do not appear to need charity. During my search, I expect my expenses to be at least that amount. I don't need your money, but I want your commitment to focus on returning your children. The payment to me reflects your intention to support the search in every way possible. I'm primarily talking about your mental support. Now, I don't mean just thinking about finding your children *once in a while*. What I mean is for you to spend considerable time and energy dedicated to this project. You understand that my search involves considerable energy, and your dedicated energy significantly enhances my chances of success. This five thousand will help you focus more on the problem."

Now it was the warrior who spoke. "Hokee Wolf, we can find the five thousand, but how do we know you don't just take our money and forget about the missing children?"

"If you think that, you are welcome to leave. I don't need your problems or your money." Hokee also did not smile as he stood, inviting his guests to go away.

"Okay, Hokee," Onacona jumped in, "we will give you the money, and I'll lead the effort to get our entire tribe focused on finding our children."

"Thank you Onacona. Your efforts will help considerably."

Atohi dug a buckskin bag from under his serape. He counted five thousand dollars in soiled, crinkled bills onto Hokee's desk.

Then, without saying goodbye, all three men turned and left the office, never looking back.

Hokee waited a couple of minutes for the men to clear the building, then called for Hilda.

When she entered his office, Hokee pointed to the stack of money. "Would you take care of this, please? It looks like I will spend a lot of time in the sweat lodge for the rest of the day. Leave a message on my phone if I don't answer, and be prepared for another one of my absences. This job may require me to do some serious traveling, but I will let you know before leaving if that becomes necessary."

With a shy grin, Hilda responded, "Well, it couldn't take more traveling than you did on that contract swindle job last year."

Responding with his own sly smile, Hokee said, "Yeah. You make a good point, Hilda. Hopefully, this time, I won't get shot."

Then Hilda responded with a rueful smile, "Hopefully, you won't attract a roomful of killers who tie me up with duct tape."

"You know I'm sorry that had to happen. I'll try to keep the bad guys away from the office."

Neither one suspected that this case would threaten them both in ways neither could imagine.

CHAPTER TWO

Hokee drove home to be with Shilah and prepare for the sweat lodge he had built next to his cave house. It was only partially a cave, but he called it the cave house. Years ago on a vision quest suggested by his mentor and surrogate father, Why-aẏ-looh, Hokee stumbled across the undulating lava plain on bleeding feet when he found a deep hole in the lava plain. Two hundred-feet-deep lava walls surrounded this small area with an overhang on the north end, creating a small cave. Hokee could see some wet earth and plants, near one lava wall suggesting water, and dying of thirst, Hokee crawled down the lava walls to the bare ground at the bottom. The partially hidden cave was behind lush foliage growing from an underground river. The water saved Hokee's life, and he built his home using the cave for his master bedroom.

Shilah was Hokee's wolf, given to him by Why-aẏ-looh, when Hokee decided to become a private investigator using his shaman training to solve crimes. Shilah means brother in the Navajo language, and the few people who visited Hokee's home wondered how the wolf and Hokee Wolf were related. No one knew how Hokee got his last name.

After playing tag with Shila, Hokee settled in a lounge chair on his wide veranda, drinking Dos XX from a bottle. He missed his girlfriend Glory, a television investigative reporter for a news station in New York, who was called back to help cover growing scandals in the mayor's office. Hokee called her number in New York, but the call went to voice mail.

'*Damn,*' he thought. He missed her company, not to mention the help she could provide.

Before building a fire to heat the stones for his sweat lodge, Hokee sat and concentrated his thoughts on the current problem. '*Who was Lkal? Was he responsible for the children's disappearances? Where were the children now? Were they still alive? Where was Lkal's girlfriend? Who were Lkal's associates?* Before beginning his search for answers to these questions in the sweat lodge, Hokee sat for several hours in meditation. A successful hunt always begins by placing oneself in harmony with that which is being hunted. Every cell in our bodies is conscious. By aligning one's thoughts and energy with the problem, the cells in our body respond by becoming more sensitive to all life. This allows the hunter more freedom during the hunt in ways only a shaman can understand.

Hokee collected mesquite wood from northern Idaho for his fire. Mesquite burns hotter than almost any other wood, heating the lava stones much faster. Only pure lava rocks will work in a sweat lodge, as other rocks will explode when they become white hot and then doused with cold water. With the fire heating his stones, Hokee went inside the house and into the underground river that flowed at the back of his cave. The water was icy cold, but Hokee found that a quick dip helped cleanse the body, mind, and soul.

After the river wash, Hokee brushed his aura with an eagle's feather, followed by a sage smoke cleanse. Anyone watching this strange behavior might think the man insane. Still, when performed with intention in a sacred ceremony, these seemingly simple acts provide the warrior with a solid protective coat. The sweat lodge is used to dive deep into the inner universe, searching for answers to these seemingly innocent questions. Lurking in man's mind are the most vicious killers imaginable. Many shamans have lost their lives or their minds in these depths. Hokee's preparations provide armor to help survive these battles.

Would-be healers and fake Shamans use the sweat lodge more to entertain than accomplish anything worthwhile. Individuals who undergo this experience leave the hot sweat lodge and douse themselves in a cold shower, believing they have accomplished something valuable. Of course, feeling good about yourself is usually a sufficient reward to keep the uninformed happy. A sweat lodge is a tool for an authentic shaman to investigate the unknown and unknowable. To go there, strict attention must be paid to the initial preparation. Anything less than one hundred percent concentration could mean death or permanent insanity.

After his cleanse and using *real* magick to provide added protection, Hokee shifted the hot rocks to the pit inside the sweat lodge. He had stashed his herbs and water inside the lodge's opening flap, then crawling inside, Hokee closed the flap and began his journey.

Four hours later, after replacing the hot rocks twice, Hokee crawled from the lodge a humbled man, facing an evil never suspected in any of his previous journeys into the vast unknown. He was happy that Glory wasn't with him today. Glory lost her mind on an earlier case which, while challenging, did not compare to the danger of the current situation. Hokee was not a man who allowed fear into his life; however, today's sweat came as close to breaching his defenses as he had experienced. He was not confident about his chances of surviving if he continued his pursuit of the missing children. The fear of death held no power over Hokee. We all die when our time arrives. Dying for a noble cause is the warrior's prayer.

Hokee often walked with Shilah in the lava fields surrounding his home whenever he needed inspiration. This was a treacherous walk, as thin crusts created by cooling lava often cover twenty or thirty-foot drops onto the jagged lava rocks on the bottom. Such a fall almost certainly meant death. Even if the fall didn't kill him, the chances of being rescued were virtually zero.

Then the undulating terrain could twist an ankle or cut the shoes from his feet. Hokee had to let his unconscious mind control where he stepped on this walk. This exercise allowed him to concentrate on his problems as long as he could maintain discipline and trust the process. Nobody walked these plains besides Hokee; it was much too dangerous. Shilah bounded around like a six-month-old puppy, looking for a rabbit to score for his dinner. If you could see Hokee, you might think he was sleepwalking, which wasn't far from the truth. The inherent danger sharpened his concentration to the point required for the inspiration he sought.

It was times like this that made Hokee wonder about his choice to become an investigator. He could be a shaman like his mentor, living an ascetic life instead of hunting dangerous animals like those in his searches. James Baldwin, among many others, described man as the most dangerous animal on earth. They make a wolf pack seem like Sunday school teachers when they roam in packs. And it was just such a pack that now confronted Hokee.

He found the key to locating them during his sweat. The immediate task was to figure out how to stay alive long enough to end their reign of terror for the Shoshone-Paiute on their reservation.

CHAPTER THREE

The Shoshone Indians are a comely people. The head of a Shoshone warrior could replace those of the most respected Grecian or Roman leaders found on statutes. They have well-proportioned faces with sharp angles and straight noses. Besides their skin color, nothing separated the Shoshone men from the most revered historical figures. The same could be said for their women, which might be why their children had been targeted for abduction.

Lkal was an exception to this description. Not mentioned by the council members who visited with Hokee, Lkal was physically and socially deformed. He had a pancake face, a button nose, and ears that stuck far out from his head. Uncommonly intelligent, he hated how the reservation Indians teased and shunned him and vowed at an early age to make them pay. When he met Cicely Holliday at a dance club in Blackfoot, the idea of revenge took hold.

Cicely was a Gypsy, a race without a country. Gypsies traveled throughout the Mideast and Europe for thousands of years, hated and scorned by every nation. The Gypsies adopted the local language and often married into the local population, yet somehow, they always kept their identity wherever they lived. And foremost in the mind of every Gypsy was the desire to make humanity pay for their abominable treatment.

In many of America's small towns, the legend or myth is that the Gypsies would steal your children. Whether this happened didn't matter; regardless of the truth, the belief prevailed, and the Gypsy caravans were viewed as a nuisance. Cicely was a beautiful woman with a full figure and a sultry look that almost begged for male attention. When a local gang of bullies set upon the caravan, which was her home, most of their wagons were burned and several individuals suffered severe injuries. Marauders raped the eighteen-year-old beauty repeatedly until she became unconscious. Local law officials ignored the Gypsy's pleas for help. Fed up with the life of a Gypsy woman traveling with the caravan, Cicely struck out on her own. Away from the tribe, her lustful beauty scored big time with the male population, who cared little about her nationality. Instead, the men bought her drinks, paid for her meals, and offered her gifts and their bodies, which she almost always rejected. Cicely knew all they wanted was to fuck her, and until that happened, they would continue to pursue her, paying for her way through life until she met Lkal. When the lovely Cicely, with long curly black hair and smoky dark eyes, met another recluse from society, they formed a partnership, of sorts.

While the legend of kidnapping children was primarily a myth, Gypsies who traveled the world invariably established relationships with societies who made their living by smuggling, and in today's world, the smuggled product with the most profit were people. Statistics show that there are 30 million people[1] who are being trafficked worldwide. Human trafficking is a billion-dollar business. Headlines typically feature stories about women kidnapped for prostitution, but these women are only a tiny portion of those trafficked. Cicely had connections with some of the world's most brutal and successful human traffickers. Kidnapped Shoshone children were precious commodities in this sick world, providing Cicely and Lkal with a lucrative living.

Mauritania is a small country on the west coast of Africa responsible for much of the world's human trafficking. Mauritania is culturally and politically part of the Arab world, with Islam as the principal religion.

Today, the country has one of the worst human rights records in the world with modern day slavery. Their most prominent city, Nouakchott, is

---

[1] https://togetherfreedom.org > trafficking-facts-statistics

on the Atlantic Ocean, providing convenient access for smugglers. Once a French Provence, the country is multiethnic, often run by dictators who are not immune to enslaving their own population. However, foreign nationals make up the most significant proportion of enslaved people. Mauritania slavers dealt in all forms of human trafficking, including selling women and children to other countries to line their pockets.

Houston, Texas, is the primary distribution point for trafficked individuals in the United States. Teeten is the Mauritanian leader of the local slave gang, responsible for most of the trafficked individuals from across the country. A short chubby non-practicing Muslim man with dark skin, long braided black hair, one eye lost in a knife fight as a young man back in Mauritania and a perpetual scowl on his face, he is fearless. Teeten is a wicked, dirty fighter with almost inhuman strength in his arms and legs who obeys no rules and laws. His dark skin lets him pass as an American black man who uses the race card to buy immunity from much of the havoc he and his gang cause in Houston.

Houston is the central location for human trafficking in America because of the many interstate freeways, both north-south and east-west, plus the several U.S. and Texas highways, not to mention its closeness to international shipping lanes. Teeten's gang owns a sizeable multi-acre estate in south Houston featuring a 6500-square-foot mansion with a swimming pool and several outbuildings, including a warehouse for storing smuggled goods, including people. The villa is built in the southwestern style with many graceful arches and a red-tiled roof.

Cicely's Gypsy caravan trolled the northern states in the summer and spent winters in the south. She was fourteen when they were in Houston and she met Teeten. Cicely already displayed the beauty she would carry as an adult and Teeten was tempted to have his way with her, except there were too many Gypsy men who carried long curved knives, as did most of the women, including Cicely. Still, the one-eyed bandit lusted and remembered the girl with the smokey eyes, so when she showed up with Lkal, she was remembered.

Cicely and Lkal met with Teeten in a warehouse next to Pier 8 near Kemah, Texas, the paramount shipping and receiving port for smuggled goods, including people. The warehouse was a long dark building, 20 feet from a 400-foot weathered wooden pier. Inside the dilapidated warehouse were several cages constructed of sturdy chain link fencing you would need a bolt cutter to cut through. The cages had buckets for the humans, who were housed there until the ship became available. Cicely was informed about the warehouse location by one of Teeten's wives, hoping that perhaps this dark-skinned witch would kill the bastard for her, as she was tired of his constant beatings. Kemah, while offering access to the Gulf of Mexico via Galveston Bay, was off the Coast Guard's grid, making it a smuggler's haven.

"Greetings, my beautiful Gypsy; who is that ugly freak you brought with you?"

Teeten smiled what he thought was a charming smile revealing a gold front tooth. To most, his smile was chilling, made more so by his one very black eye, which looked like the blackest thunderstorm clouds. His smile was also distorted because of his customary facial scowl. Teeten was wearing black pants that were a little tight over his stubby legs and a black silk turtleneck shirt. His two companions wore the same clothes, almost in uniform.

"Hello Teeten; I see you are as handsome as ever and with the same friendly greeting to strangers." There was no smile on Cicely's face. She wore a white form-fitting jumpsuit accentuating her voluptuous figure and long, straight black hair. Her oval face didn't need any makeup, but he had painted her lips with an orange glow gloss.

"Don't tell me that this turd is your husband. I would have to kill him." This time, Teeten didn't bother with the awkward smile.

"We're business associates looking for someone interested in buying young girls and boys." She said this, indicating Lkal by her side with the sweep of her arm. So far, Lkal had said nothing, although the insult did not go unnoticed, and he prepared to shoot the squat little man and would have already done so, except there were two other men nearby with the same dark complexion.

"Weeeellll," drawled Teeten, trying to imitate the Texas speech pattern. "Why didn't you say so?"

"I just did," she responded, still unsmiling. "We're here on business, so forget any other thoughts you have in your devious little brain. I am still not interested in becoming another one of your wives or concubines."

"What, not even a quicky for old time sakes? You're breaking my heart." Again the attempt at a charming smile which fell as flat as his first miserable try.

"Come on, Teeten, we all know you don't have a heart, just a beating blob of flesh harboring nothing but hate and greed." This time she did smile, but it never reached her eyes and, seemingly as though by magic, there was a compact little automatic in her hand pointing at a spot right between his eyes. "And if either of those Neanderthals by your side even cough, I'm going to plant a 45 slug in the center of your forehead."

Teeten was familiar enough with Gypsy's, knowing they never joked about this kind of shit, and one look into those smoldering dark eyes convinced him that this was no fooling matter. "Okay, guys, don't make the lady mad. I've already done that. What kids are you talking about, Cicely?" Now he was all business, recognizing that this was all that interested the pair standing before him. He looked at Lkal seriously for the first time, studying the Indian carefully. He saw the same meanness he recognized within himself and decided to give the pair a hearing. The Indian wore a pair of new Levis and a dark blue tee shirt. A pair of black running shoes were on his feet. Although Teeten doubted they had much to offer, kidnapped kids brought premium in certain circles, and he was a businessman. "Reservation kids from Idaho," Cicely responded, dropping the pistol to her side. Both boys and girls, preferably one at a time. These are Shoshone kids, some of the most beautiful people in the world." She said this with a hint of pride in her voice, although the reason for such pride was a mystery, even to herself.

"How many kids are you talking about altogether and what are their ages, and when can you deliver?" He asked this as a businessman. Straight up with no hint of the Texas drawl.

Cicely looked at Lkal as though saying, '*okay, it's your turn to talk.*'

Looking straight at the smuggler in his good eye, Lkal answered. "We want to start with one kid in two weeks. Either sex you prefer. We can deliver two kids monthly for a year before it gets too hot for us to continue. All

14

together, we can promise twenty kids ages five to ten. Ten boys and ten girls. We will deliver them here or to your place in Houston. The price is

$5,000.00 for each child, payable upon delivery." There was no humor in the Indian's face or voice. It was all business.

Teeten looked at Lkal as though he came from another planet, with his perpetual scowl firmly in place. "$5000.00 is too much. $2500.00."

"Bullshit," Lkal exploded, showing emotion for the first time. One look into his mean eyes was all it took to understand there was no negotiation. "$5000.00 is cheap. These kids will go for over fifty grand each on the open market. Five grand is our price for assuming all the risks and delivering the goods. Take it, or we're going to your San Diego competitor." He didn't bother to explain that they came here because Cicely knew a little about the man and his business. One of the distinguishing characteristics of Lkal's condition was that his enormous ears sticking out from his head turned bright red when he became angry.

Teeten noticed the bright ears and being intelligent, recognized the significance. "Okay, five grand upon delivery." Mentally, he decided that the man and woman would die upon the final delivery, but the woman, only after he had the fun, denied him all those long years in the past.

CHAPTER FOUR

The Fort Hall Reservation comprises over 800,000 square miles in large tracts covering significant parts of four southern Idaho counties. While less than 6,000 Indians live on the reservation, the council permits six individuals from other races to hunt and fish on reservation grounds with daily passes. Fort Hall is the largest community on the reservation, with small villages of only fifteen or twenty families in each location scattered over the large area connected by dirt roads. Hokee's first order of business was to visit the reservation police.

Hokee was familiar with the reservation, having lived there for twelve years with his mentor Why-ay'-looh, a Blackfoot shaman. Although Fort Hall was not the home for Blackfoot Indians, Why-ay'-looh found himself stranded there as a young man and stayed, welcomed by the reservation leaders, eager to have a medicine man in their community.

The Fort Hall Police Department is housed in the new Shoshone-Bannock Tribal Justice Center in the community of Fort Hall. The Justice Center is a long flat-roofed building made of sand-colored bricks. Three flags on tall white poles guard the double-door glass entrance. The Indian Chief of Police is a Paiute responsible for their forty-member staff. A beautiful Indian girl who looked like a princess ushered Hokee into the chief's office. The chief was studying a girlie magazine and smoking a cigarette at his desk when the comely Shoshone receptionist ushered Hokee into his office.

"Mr. Wolf would like to have a few words with you," the smiling beauty announced. The reservation poster girl was dressed in a soft white deerskin dress with colored beadwork along the sleeves and down the front.

Chief Wahvevah put the magazine down face first and wobbled to his feet. The fat, flat-faced Indian wore a ridiculous costume he assumed made him look official while doing just the opposite. Not even Hollywood would dress an Indian Police Chief in such an outlandish outfit. On his feet were shining black combat boots into which were tucked his gray trousers with black silk ribbons running down both sides like tuxedo pants. The effect was that of sausages stuffed in horse guts. His bright red polyester shirt had fringed sleeves with tiny blue gems dangling from the ends of the fringes. Over the shirt was a black silk vest with a big shining star the size of a softball pinned over his heart.

"Welcome, Mr. Wolf. How may I help?" he asked with a fake smile, thrusting out a fat hand pointing to a chair. "Please have a seat. I remember you from when you lived here on the reservation."

Thanks, Chief. I'll make this quick," Hokee said, taking a seat. Dressed in his hunting outfit, black jeans, polo shirt and cowboy boots with a black Stetson in his hands, the detective didn't want to spend any longer with the obsequious chief than was required.

"Who can show me where the abducted children lived and provide the dates they went missing?" He asked in a friendly tone, not wanting to make an enemy of the incompetent chief who got his position by relationship, having nothing to do with his mental or physical abilities.

The chief flopped back into his oversized desk chair, still huffing from having to stand and greet his visitor. "Well, let me see, I think Shoda is leading the investigation. Today, I believe he is following the Snake River into Caribou County." The chief gasped for air as though answering the question demanded more oxygen than the room contained, "I can have one of our deputies drive you over there if you would like," he continued.

Having walked over every squire mile of the reservation with Why-ay'-looh, looking for herbs now lining the walls of his mentor's one-room shack, Hokee declined the offer. "Thanks, Chief; I believe I know the way." Having had his fill of the ridiculous police chief, Hokee stood, showing the meeting was over.

"Don't bother standing," Hokee said to the relieved chief. "I know the way out."

Hokee went back into the lobby lined with colorful Indian rugs on the walls with glass front display cases showing collections of arrowheads, tomahawks, pottery, and Indian clothing. The beautiful receptionist was behind a carved wooden desk flanked by war drums. A discrete name tag shaped like a Sego Lily blossom blended into the top of her dress and announced her name as Zoey.

"Zoey, would you have a current map of the reservation showing the network of roads.?" Hokee asked, giving the girl what he believed was his killer smile.

"The receptionist glanced at the tall, handsome mixed-blood man, nearly fainting at the attention with a shy smile of her own. Few good-looking men were living on the reservation, and she didn't want to waste an opportunity to get acquainted. Everyone knew Hokee Wolf's reputation and there were few women who didn't seek his companionship.

"Why yes, Mr. Wolf," she responded, blushing. "Let me show you what we have," she said, getting to her feet.

"Please call me Hokee if you don't mind, Zoey. Mr. Wolf sounds like a character from Little Red Riding Hood." Hokee favored the receptionist with another of his heart-stopping smiles.

"Well," she said with a grin, regaining her composure, "you have those dark eyes."

Zoey led the way to a beautiful wooden cabinet with labels on the drawers; the labels had names like WATER LOCATIONS, POPULATION CENTERS, RESERVATION ROADS and MAPS.

Pulling open the drawer labeled MAPS, she retrieved a map and handed it to Hokee. "Here you go, Mr. Wolf, I mean Hokee," she said, blushing again.

Hokee studied the map for a few minutes, then asked the receptionist, "Do you know why I am here, Zoey?" He had a pretty good idea of the answer but asked to be friendly.

"Of course, Hokee. I was here when the chief met with the council before they went to see you in Pocatello. You are searching for our missing children."

"That's correct. Now, would you also know the locations where the missing children were when they were abducted?"

"Certainly. Everybody knows. Even though our reservation is large, gossip still travels; we have telephones, you know."

"Yeah, I should have guessed that. Now, would you have the dates when the children turned up missing?"

"Sure. Let's go over to my desk and lay your map down. I can pinpoint where each child lived who has been abducted and the date it occurred."

Zoey sat at her desk and motioned for Hokee to pull up a side chair so he could watch as she drew a small circle on the map where each child had been kidnapped and the date it occurred.

Hokee's day suddenly got much more manageable. He would not have to roam all over the reservation searching for a policeman named Shoda. Instead, he could visit each location without help. Having lived here and walked over a good portion of the reservation, he recognized most of the places where the children had been abducted.

He studied the map and discovered that every abduction occurred near roads intersecting Interstate 15 or 86. U.S. Highway 91 runs parallel to I-15 and five miles to the west, providing convenient access to many of the remote small villages on the reservation where children went missing. Sometimes there were only thirteen days between kidnappings, and sometimes, it was fifteen or sixteen days, but about two a month. The kidnappers were on some kind of schedule.

So, he started asking questions to himself. *Why only one child at a time? Is there any significance to that? And why every two weeks? What does that mean? Why not take all eleven kids at the same time?* As the questions ran through his mind, answers came right alongside.

Lkal knows the reservation and all the abducted kids. He has only one ally. So if a crime syndicate was responsible, they could come in with a caravan of vehicles and get all eleven kids at once, so it must be just two people, maybe three. And the timing? What if they take the kids a long way away to sell them? Perhaps Texas. Yeah, Texas. I remember reading that they are the American capital of trafficked individuals. And the time is about right. It might be San Diego or Houston. A slow week drive down with the kid and another week back to get the next one. I wonder who is helping him?

Zoey studied Hokee's face as he checked the map and saw the wheels turning, so she was not surprised that he asked another question. "Do you know who the woman is that Lkal was seeing off the reservation?"

"No, I don't believe anyone knows. About a year ago, he started spending weekends off the reservation. Since the kidnapping began six months ago, no one has seen him, so everybody believes he is involved. Shortly before that, someone heard him talking over the phone. It sounded like he was talking to a girl based on his language, and he mentioned a club in Blackfoot. Also, Blackfoot is where the police caught him with the stolen money. But that's all we know."

"Well, that's a lot and I appreciate your help Zoey," Hokee gave the young lady another big smile, "thanks very much."

"Ah, Mr. Wolf, I mean Hokee, would you like me to go with you to see where the children were kidnapped and talk to their parents? Some don't speak English much, and I could translate for you." She had a wistful look combined with a hopeful expression.

"What about your job here at police headquarters? Won't you be missed?"

"Nah, I'll tell the Chief you need me to scout the reservation. We rarely get any calls, and he has nothing to do anyway but answer the phone if it rings. It's always for him, besides. I often take off to run errands."

"Well, Zoey, I would appreciate your help. Thanks, if you're sure it will be okay." Hokee didn't need anyone showing him the reservation, but he looked forward to spending a little time with the beautiful young lady, and it would be nice to have a woman along to help ease the pain of the parents with missing children. And, of course, Hokee didn't need a translator, but he didn't mention that to the girl.

Zoey couldn't wipe the big grin of happiness from her face as she left to run into the chief's office to let him know she would be gone for an hour or longer. Her message wasn't one you gave over the telephone.

CHAPTER FIVE

Among those who keep track of such things, Nouakchott, Mauritania, is considered the worst capital city in the world. Home to over 1.2 million residents, with the majority living way below the poverty level, which says a lot in Mauritania. Desert sands bound the city to the east, which is forever encroaching on the poorer city areas. Mauritania is considered the worst violator of human rights on the planet, where open slavery is everywhere, and smuggling is its principal business. While the Atlantic Ocean is to the west, water is scarce, especially in the poor neighborhoods where residents line up daily to get a liter of water for ½ cent. The slave workers are paid five dollars weekly, barely enough for food.

Mauritania's principal port, Port de l'Amite, is about 7 miles southwest of Nouakchott and home to the three prevalent smuggling gangs. Habib, the Moor, runs the gang responsible for smuggling container goods stolen from the docks. Khalid's thugs steal from the farmers, bringing food to the markets, while Shabib and his ruffians handle human smuggling. This makes Shabib one of Mauritania's wealthiest men as his cargos fetch the highest price. Slavery is big business. Shabib is also a psychopath who enjoys human suffering with no sense of right or wrong.

Shabib Ghulam is a white, black man, one of the Moors with a checkered history. Ghulam means servant of God, the cruel leader's image he uses to control the largest assembly of murdering thieves in Mauritania, Arabs professing some relationship with Islam. These days Shabib no longer wears the dock-front clothes of dark pants and a black polo shirt but dresses his lean hard six-foot body in white cotton pants and matching silk shirts. Although he has fair skin and sun-bleached hair, his deep brown eyes glisten like polished obsidian when angry. He carries a riding crop in his right hand with six-inch leather strips at the end colored dark reddish-brown from the dried blood of victims who have experienced the leader's wrath. Some victims, including his 'wives,' who have displeased him. Shabib never marries the women he calls wives. Instead, he grabs one or more of the trafficked women he finds appealing. Behind his back, tucked under a belt, is a black 9mm Glock automatic that has killed more people than almost any other single weapon on the planet. His willingness to use the gun keeps his other murderers in line.

Of the 30 million trafficked people each year, Shabib handles more than almost any other trafficker in the business. Teeten Irfan, the black Houston trafficker, is a distant cousin of Shabib, providing the white Moor with many of his trafficked humans, including many of his wives. There is friction between the two men because Shabib doesn't pay Teeten for those women he takes as wives. They continue to do business together because Shabib is the most reliable trafficker in the business. He promptly pays for those he sells to others, including the Indian children Teeten buys from Lkal and Cicely. The handsome Indian kids bring top dollar from a French madam who runs the largest brothel in Paris.

The two men maintain contact with burner phones, Teeten supplies to his hated cousin, along with shipments of human cargo. They know several countries can listen to satellite phone traffic, so the men speak in Zenaga, a Berber language that is almost extinct and rarely heard or understood by others. They say very little on their phones and use code words to insulate themselves even further from potential listeners.

Shabib was trying to get Teeten to send more of the Indian kids as they were fetching top dollar, and Teeten was attempting to get Lkal to provide over two kids a month without success.

"Look, Lkal," Teeten snarled, exposing his yellow teeth, "my contact is refusing to buy any more Indian kids unless you can provide at least twice the number each month."

It was Cicely who responded. "And we're telling you that the risks aren't worth it. Snatching one child at a time is risky. Trying for over one at a time is just begging to get caught." She was standing well back with her right hand hidden in the folds of the yellow serape she was wearing. It didn't take a genius to know what might be in that hand.

Not one to give up easily, Teeten responded, still snarling, "well, unless you can deliver me two at a time, I believe our business has ended." There was no hint that he didn't mean every word.

Teeten knows this is the wrong course of action, but unless he can satisfy his greedy cousin's demands, his threats to discontinue a relationship with the kidnappers unless the pair provided kids in greater quantity sounded final.

"That's fine with us, Teeten. I'm sure we will have no problem making our arrangements with those crooks in San Diego."

Seeing that this was a fight he would not win, Teeten relented, "okay, try it once. If it's too risky, I'll see if I can talk some sense into my buyer."

"We will look into getting more children on our next run," Cicely responded. "But don't expect miracles, Teeten." Along with Lkal, Cicely knew the reservation police were stepping up surveillance, and grabbing two kids at once posed a risk they were unwilling to take.

Had the pair known of Hokee Wolf, they would have known better than to plan for more abductions. They both knew that Teeten was a cruel, undisciplined man with a short temper and superior strength. They didn't know someone with even greater power was on their trail.

Cicely could see beyond the lust in Teeten's expression when informing them of his demands and knowing his reputation, she knew that in the future, when Teeten felt the time was right, the Houston flesh trafficker would force himself on her while his crew made Lkal watch, then he would execute them both. Chills ran down her spine as her guts clenched in spasms. Nodding to Lkal, Cicely backed away, and Teeten watched the pair leave. He knew about the lady's little derringer and didn't want to get gut shot. Well okay, they would disarm her when he felt the time was right. For now, his cousin in Mauritania would continue paying, even for one at a time, if that was what the pair could provide.

As the pair drifted away, Teeten felt like someone had stepped on his grave. Fearless, with ungodly strength and no enemies who dared get too close, he couldn't fathom what could provoke such a feeling. Shrugging the feeling away, he led his two followers back into the warehouse to prepare their shipment.

Chapter Six

Hokee and Zoey stopped at seven different homes where a child went missing and heard the same sad tale at each location. Unfortunately, the houses lacked air conditioning and were too hot during the day to stay indoors, so the kids played outside until dark when they were called inside to eat dinner. Unfortunately, these children did not possess electronic games or cell phones; they had no money for that foolishness.

When a child didn't come in to eat, the parents went out looking for their wayward offspring, only to discover that they were missing. No one ever saw what happened to the child who had vanished. The children were all playing, some running off chasing grasshoppers or looking for a missing ball or something when they heard the supper call. The kids ran off to their separate homes, and no one noticed that one child had disappeared until the parents called.

Hokee drove back to Fort Hall with Zoey and found a drive-in that served cold drinks. Buying them both a cold Pepsi, Hokee sat in his Explorer, studying the maps Zoey provided. He made time notations on the map where Zoey had already pinpointed the houses where the missing children had lived. It became apparent that the kidnappers would take turns kidnapping children from homes close to I-15 and then I-84. If this pattern held, the next child to go missing would live close to I-15. While that narrowed the field, it was still a mighty large territory. Hokee needed something to help narrow the search down. The next child was not due to be snatched until at least three days from now, which gave Hokee time to look into other avenues.

"Zoey, don't take this the wrong way, but how old are you?" It wasn't until the words were out of his mouth that he realized the question would be taken the wrong way. He had noticed her infatuation with him. *Shit,* he said to himself.

With glistening eyes, she responded, "I'll be 23 next month." She said it with hope in her voice.

Hokee ignored the girl's high expectations. He was simply unaccustomed to handling this kind of situation. "Well, I'm thinking about visiting some bars and strip joints in Blackfoot and wondered if you were of age. I didn't want to get you arrested if you were a minor." He tried to ignore the disappointment in her eyes.

"I'm legal and have my driver's license with me in case I get carded." Hokee could see she was trying to recover from her high expectations. Not that he wasn't tempted. She was a beautiful young lady.

"Okay then, we might be gone two or three hours if you want to go with me. Do you need to let anyone know you will be gone that long?"

"No," she blurted out. "I mean, I have my cell phone in case someone is looking for me, but I rarely get any calls. The police provided me with the phone in case they had an emergency. Shoda or some other police officer calls me to go with them to talk with the parents when we have a kidnapping."

"I want to see if I can find out if our kidnappers hang out in one of the Blackfoot bars. And having you along will make it seem like more of a friendly inquiry, just two people looking for their companions." Hokee could see the sparkle return to the girl's eyes as he spoke.

There was a significant age gap between the pair, although Hokee had one of those hard-to-read faces and was in excellent shape. Zoey looked young for her age, but she acted with the maturity of a much older girl. They could make it work, but Hokee was leery of giving the young lady the wrong impression. He wouldn't let himself seduce the unsuspecting young lady, no matter how desirable she might be.

"Oh, Hokee, this is turning into a real adventure," Zoey gushed.

She was enthusiastic and excited, but Hokee let it ride for now. Fortunately, the Explorer had bucket seats, keeping the young lady at a safe distance. Hokee wondered what she would do if automobiles still had bench seats. So it was with sincere relief that he wouldn't find out.

The Snake River is just west of Blackfoot, with I-15 running alongside. Hokee searched for someone who might know Lkal at the Golden Crown Lounge. This bar was more upscale than Hokee believed Lkal might frequent, so he kept dropping into the bars along W Bridge Street, then he and Zoey began looking at bars along W Jackson Street. At the tenth bar, they struck gold.

The Hitching Post, also known as the Tumbleweed Saloon, is a real dive. According to internet reviews, the women at this bar can't keep their tongues out of your man's mouth. One of the posters on the wall sums up the place perfectly.

"MAY THE FLEAS OF A THOUSAND CAMELS INFEST THE CROTCH OF THE PERSON WHO SCREWS UP YOUR DAY, AND MAY THEIR ARMS BE TOO SHORT TO SCRATCH."

A touch of real class.

The bartender was a short, fat lady wearing a pink polka-dot dress with black dots. She had a red-bloated face like she sampled too much of the bar's products and had legs in black leggings that looked like railroad tie fence posts. The back of the bar was handsome for such a seedy place. It looked like polished mahogany, and the bar, which ran almost the room's length, was white marble. In front of the bar were drugstore stools with stuffed black Naugahyde tops. Hokee and Zoey sat at the bar and ordered a Johnny Walker scotch and a White Russian for Zoey.

Elvira, the bartender, was friendly and liked to talk, even if it was only to hear herself yacking. The floodgates opened when Hokee mentioned they were looking for their friend Lkal.

"Oh yeah. He comes in here every ten days or thereabouts with the black-haired woman, Cicely. She's a real purty lady, and I don't know what she sees in that short dumpy ugly mutt. God only knows how they ever got together." Elvira stopped to catch her breath.

Hokee asked, "would you remember the last time he was in here?" Elvira got this squint on her face as though thinking was difficult. "Well, lemme see, it's been several days, maybe ten or thereabout."

Hokee studied the lady bartender, looking for the right angle to pursue his next question. "Elvira, this young lady by my side comes from the reservation where she and Lkal grew up together. They want to surprise him with a birthday party next week, but nobody knows when he will be back in town." Then, reaching into the back pocket of his pants for a wallet, he slipped out a hundred-dollar bill. Then, holding the money out to the bartender, he said, "here are a hundred dollars if you will call me without him knowing it the next time he comes into the bar."

Elvira's face lit up, making her ugly mug almost pleasant. "You betcha," she said, snatching the bill from Hokee's hand. "Got a phone number?"

Hokee grabbed a cocktail napkin from a stack on the bar and jotted down a number using a borrowed pen. Then, sliding the napkin across the bar, he said, "I have another hundred for you; if you don't let anyone know, you called me."

"You got it, sweety," she grinned. "It's just between you and me." Hokee nudged Zoey to finish her drink and downing his scotch, thanked Elvira, and the pair left the Tumbleweed Saloon, hopefully only to return once.

Hokee dropped Zoey, who seemed reluctant to leave the Explorer back at the reservation police station, and just before slipping out, she reached over, kissing Hokee on his cheek.

"Thanks, Zoey, you've been a big help today. You made the parents of those missing children feel better with your presence. Enjoy the rest of your day."

As she got out of his vehicle, she asked, "will I see you again, Hokee?" Her wistful expression almost made Hokee regret his decision, but he tried to ease her hopes.

"Zoey, I've learned in my business that each day brings new opportunities to experience life, and we never know what the new day offers.

I've enjoyed being with you, and hopefully, we'll meet again soon." At least the first part was the truth. And who knows, stranger things have happened.

Hokee saw Zoey standing by the road, watching him disappear as he drove away.

CHAPTER SEVEN

Hokee was staining a new hand-carved kitchen stool three days later when he received a call from Elvira. It was fortunate timing, as he wasn't busy searching for a missing student from Idaho State University. Elvira reported that Lkal and Cicely were there drinking, having arrived twenty minutes earlier. She apologized for waiting so long to call Hokee but explained that she could not get away earlier without being observed.

"Thanks, Elvira. I'll be in shortly to give you the other hundred dollars I promised."

Not wanting to miss the pair of kidnappers at the bar, this was one of the few times Hokee cursed his ten-mile-long driveway. It took ten minutes to reach I-15 but only fifteen more to travel the twenty-two miles to Blackfoot. Then, parking in the back of the saloon, Hokee entered through the rear door, hoping to spot Lkal and Cicely without being seen. He wanted to make sure they were still inside before waiting outside to watch the pair leave and see what kind of vehicle they were driving.

Stepping inside, he spotted Elvira, who noticed him standing in the hallway on the way to the washrooms. Then, waving another hundred- dollar bill, Hokee signaled her to come to get it while he could remain partially screened from the bar stools.

"Are they still here?" he whispered while handing her the money.

Snatching the bill from his hands and stuffing it inside her bra, she whispered back, "yeah, they're sitting on the stools near the center."

"Thanks, Elvira," Hokee whispered before slipping back out of the rear door.

Hokee drove around to the front into the main parking lot, inspecting the vehicles. Finding a spot where he could watch the door while monitoring a Ford Conversion Van, he parked and waited. The Ford van was an upscale conversion with a raised roof and dark tinted windows along both sides and rear, making it impossible to see inside. It was the perfect vehicle to transport a stolen child sixteen hundred miles.

playing a hunch, Hokee watched it in case the pair slipped out of the door without him noticing. All he wanted to do tonight was establish the make and model of their vehicle.

After almost two hours and an empty thermos bottle of coffee, Hokee saw the man and woman leave the bar heading for the Ford van. Watching the couple's interplay, Hokee concluded their relationship was purely business; they were not lovers. The pair did not hold hands or glance at each other affectionately like they might have if headed for a night of sexual bliss. Instead, they shook hands like business partners and separated about halfway to the Van. Lkal headed for the Ford and Cicely started towards a dark blue Cadillac CTS.

As the couple separated and got into their vehicles, Hokee concluded that his earlier assumptions about their kidnapping schedule were wrong. It doesn't take a week to drive to Houston, two or perhaps three days if they had to stop to let the kids loose to eat or go to the bathroom. And it surely would not take a week to drive back to Blackfoot from Houston. So if the kidnappings were purely business for the pair, they wouldn't want to spend any more time on the road with each other than necessary. They may even have separate motel rooms on the way back home. So, what required another four or six days for the kidnapping cycle?

Thinking about his earlier excursion around the large reservation with Zoey, Hokee decided that this extra time was so Lkal could scout out their next victim. He would more than likely spend his evenings on the reservation watching the kids play while seeking the right opportunity to grab a child without being seen. The more he thought about it, the more convinced he became that this would be how they planned their next operation. Lkal would have to sneak around the reservation in the near dark without being seen, which would take some time. Now that Hokee believed their operation was scoped out, he needed to plan his next moves. Thinking as he drove, Hokee returned to his home in the lava flats.

Back home, relaxing in one of his handmade chairs with Shilah at his feet and a tall scotch in his hands, Hokee reviewed what he presumed was the kidnapper's method of operation. If his assumptions were correct, it would take Lkal three to five days of surreptitious scouting before claiming their next victim. In the meantime, Hokee needed to prepare his trap. Getting to this point in his ruminations was easy, developing plans for the trap, not so much.

Hokee needed to discover the next link in the kidnapping ring. He could catch Lkal and force the information from him or follow the pair to Texas and see where they took the next kidnapped child. If he did the latter, it would mean one more child would suffer from being kidnapped. This was not an option in Hokee's book. He would have to catch Lkal before the next kidnapping. Okay, that was the easy part. What about Cicely? If it were up to Hokee, he would just kill the bitch and dump her body down a hole in the lava flats. Alternatively, a better solution would be to turn both kidnappers over to the reservation police after an encounter to get the required information from Lkal and or Cicely.

The next night, Hokee parked on the reservation close to the -15 off-ramp waiting for Lkal's Ford Conversion Van to appear. Shortly after the sun sank behind the Sawtooth Mountains in the west and before full dark, Lkal's van appeared. Lkal drove about four miles towards Bonneville Peak before dousing his headlights and continued for another two miles on an unmarked dirt road before parking at a switchback on Lower Rock Creek Road. They were only a few hundred yards from one of the small villages scattered about the reservation. Hokee followed in his Explorer with the lights off. There was barely enough light in the dusk to see Lkal's vehicle half

a mile ahead. Unless Lkal was highly vigilant, Hokee's vehicle should not be visible. The van came to a stop in a shallow gully.

Hokee waited for a couple of minutes before walking towards the Conversion Van. He wore all black clothes except the Antelope Hyde moccasins on his feet. These were colored dark brown by the oil Hokee used to cure the leather. On his right hip, Hokee carried the old Colt 45 rescued from the ledge by the underground river a long time ago. He had placed the gun on the ledge to keep it dry before braving the river after deciding that the cougar guarding her cub on a higher shelf across the river posed no danger. Hokee also carried a large skinning knife in a black sheath on his left hip. He crept up to Lkal's van, checking to ensure it was unoccupied. Having seen no light come on when Lkal opened the door to go about his evening's search for another kidnapping victim, Hokee eased the rear door open, careful to make no noise while hoping that the interior light would stay off. He climbed into the back seat, closing the door but not securing the latch. He didn't want the door to click shut, never knowing how far away Lkal might be, and Hokee didn't want to warn the kidnapper that he was inside his vehicle. Unknown was whether Cicely was with Lkal, but Hokee didn't think so. Tonight was more than likely just another scouting expedition by the man. The van was parked about five miles from the nearest dot Zoey had placed on the reservation map showing the previous kidnappings. And, as Hokee recalled, this reservation area had very few dwellings.

It took a long thirty minutes of stressful waiting before Lkal loomed up in front of the vehicle, heading for the driver's door. As soon as Lkal was seated, Hokee placed his hands on the kidnapper's head and neck, holding tight while pushing his thumbs on nerves that rendered the man unconscious immediately.

Hokee pulled the man into the back of the van before binding his arms and legs with the thin nylon zip ties Hokee carried in his pockets. Then he leaned back against the front seat, waiting for Lkal to regain consciousness.

When the man stirred, Hokee began speaking.

"Lkal, my name is Hokee Wolf." He spoke, but with no inflection in his words. The mention of Hokee's name caused the bound man to squirm. Hokee was well known on the reservation.

"I haven't taped your mouth shut because you will talk to me. This conversation can be painless if you tell me what I want to know. If you refuse to talk without torture, you will become a cripple, a eunuch, a man without a tongue, and you will wear diapers until the day you die. The choice is yours."

Lkal wiggled around until he lay facing Hokee, their faces four feet apart. "What do you want to know?" There was a snarl in his tone and no fear in his eyes."

"You can't see too well in this dark but let me show you this knife up close so you can get a feel for how this will go if I don't like your answers." Hokee brought the shining thin-bladed knife close to Lkal's eyes. The light reflected off the silver blade, which got Lkal's attention.

With a slight quiver, he spoke, "There's no need for that man; just ask me what you want to know."

"Okay, we know you and Cicely are stealing reservation kids and selling them in Houston. I want to know who buys the children and where they are located." Hokee spoke without emotion in his voice. The effect was chilling.

The wheels were turning around in Lkal's mind. He could tell everything he knew about Teeten and his operation, but Teeten would kill him if he ever found out. But Hokee Wolf was hunting bearskins, and old Teeten might not be wearing his skin much longer. More than likely, his kidnapping days with Cicely were a thing of the past. He knew Hokee's reputation and had learned that many people who crossed the mixed breed were never heard from again. "If I tell you what you want to know, what will you do with me?"

"I'll turn you over to the reservation police. I'm told you escaped from them once before. You may not be so lucky this time. Who knows? If you escape again, no more kidnapping or I will kill you. Now tell me what I want to know."

Lkal talked for several minutes, with Hokee interrupting him occasionally for more clarification on specific issues. When Lkal had divulged all he knew about Teeten and his operation, Hokee asked about Cicely. "Where can I find your partner?"

"Look, Hokee, I've told you all about the Houston operation; leave Cicely out of this, please." There was the sound of desperation in Lkal's voice.

"Lkal, the woman is a kidnapper, like you, and you both steal children. I have no love for kidnappers but children; that is beyond any sense of morality. I want the woman, and you give her to me, or I'll start cutting."

Whimpering like a whipped dog, Lkal told Hokee where Cicely lived, "Is she expecting a call or visit from you tonight for a report?"

"No, we were supposed to meet in the morning, but please do not put her in a prison cell by me. Gypsy women also know how to use a knife." Lkal spoke of Cicely almost in reverential tones.

"Lkal, if I find out you have lied to me about anything, you will never walk again."

Hokee then turned on the interior light to check Lkal's arms and leg bindings. Satisfied that the ties were holding, Hokee fished another rope from his pocket and tied the kidnapper to the side of the van. Not knowing what the man had stashed in his vehicle, Hokee didn't want him squirming around to find something sharp and cut himself loose. It was only a few miles to the police station, but there was no need to take any chances.

Hokee drove the kidnapper's vehicle to the police station, which was all lit up, but could see no one inside. Then, hustling inside, he could see no one, so he shouted to get attention. Eventually, a sleepy-eyed deputy wandered into the reception area to see about all the fuss.

"Is the jail here?" Hokee asked, disgusted at the less-than-professional behavior of the man and the entire police department. No wonder these clowns couldn't find the kidnappers.

"Yes, jail is here," the man said, pointing down a hall.

"Let me see your jail," Hokee demanded. He didn't leave the deputy any options.

The man objected, but after seeing the look in Hokee's eyes meekly said, "follow me, sir."

The jail pens looked like every other eight-by-ten cell with iron bars in front, steel walls, a stainless toilet with no lid, double bunk beds against one wall, and green Army blankets on a thin mattress resting on a steel bottom.

"Do you have any prisoners at the moment?" Hokee asked.

"No, mister. No one here now." The man seemed almost afraid of Hokee and what he would ask next.

"Who feeds the prisoners and watches the prison?" This was Hokee's thought, but he didn't ask the question. Instead, it appeared to Hokee that the jail rarely had guests, and the reservation police had no protocol for handling prisoners.

"Biria," Hokee said, reading the man's name tag, "I have one kidnapper outside in the back of a van. He has escaped from your reservation police before. I don't want him to escape again. Can you ensure he stays in jail until tomorrow when you have more help?"

"Yes, mister. Bring him here and I will lock him in the cell." Biria seemed surprised to learn that Hokee had caught one of the kidnappers. Reservation police had been searching for the kidnappers for months.

"Biria, I want you to get on the phone right now and call the chief and some other deputies. I'll be bringing in another kidnapper in a few hours, and I expect to see this place jumping with officers who can process the prisoners and make sure they stay locked up. Okay?"

The deputy looked at Hokee like he wasn't sure who he was, but the orders were clear, and he wanted to do as the man suggested. But no, the man did not suggest; he commanded."

In a timid voice, the deputy asked, "What is your name, mister, so I can tell the chief who is requesting all this activity?

"I am Hokee Wolf, and I do not tolerate incompetence. Do your damn job and get some help in her pronto. I will have their jobs if the chief and more deputies are not here when I return. The reservation council hired me, and I will make sure that they get a full report."

Leaving behind a terrified deputy, Hokee left to go find Cicely.

CHAPTER EIGHT

Hokee sat in Lkal's van for a few minutes considering his next action, then went back into the police station. The sleepy deputy was seated at the receptionist's desk when Hokee entered the lobby. The deputy looked up with fear, surprised to see Hokee again so soon and worried that he might be in for more trouble with the fierce-looking investigator.

"Biria, do you have Zoey's phone number?" Hokee asked politely, but seeing his questioner, the deputy looked like he had swallowed a piece of beef too big for his throat.

"Wh ah, ay" yes," he stammered. "Let me look it up for you." Then, relief showed on his face as he realized he could satisfy the man facing him. He had been expecting another tongue-lashing.

With Zoey's number in hand, Hokee left the police station to make the call outside, as he didn't want the deputy to know what he had in mind.

Zoey answered on the third ring, slightly out of breath. "Hello."

"Zoey, this is Hokee Wolf. Are you busy this evening?" Even as the words left his mouth, Hokee was disgusted with himself for not asking differently. It sounded like he was asking her for a date.

"Why no Hokee," the anticipation was not missed by the caller.

"Zoey, I need a favor. How long does it take you to drive to the police station?" Hokee asked in a professional tone to dismiss a misunderstanding.

"I can be there in fifteen minutes," came the hasty reply.

"I would be grateful if you could drive here now," Hokee responded, leaving no doubt about where he was located.

"Okay, see you soon, Hokee," she gushed, unwilling to forgo a romantic meeting.

Hokee disconnected without saying goodbye, and true to her word, Zoey drove her old VW Bug into the parking lot sixteen minutes later.

Hokee was not in his Explorer but standing in the cool evening air beside Lkal's van, waiting.

Zoey got out of her Bug with high anticipation on her face, which Hokee quickly extinguished. "Zoey, I apprehended one of the kidnappers earlier. You might recognize Lkal's van. I had to leave my Explorer out in the desert, and knowing reservation Indians, I'm afraid if I left it there overnight, there would be nothing left in the morning. So, I'd like you to drive it back here to the police station and leave the keys at the front desk." "Why sure, Hokee, I'd be happy to help." She tried unsuccessfully to hide her disappointment.

As they got into the van and started off, Hokee felt the need to explain. "I'm sorry to interrupt your evening, Zoey, but I didn't know who else to call on such short notice. There was only one deputy at the police station, and I'm in a bit of a hurry."

"Oh, it's no problem at all. I was just watching an old rerun of I Love Lucy. I am happy that you thought to call me," she gushed.

They rode silently for a couple of minutes before Zoey showed her intelligence, "You're going after the other kidnapper, aren't you?"

"Yes." Hokee didn't want to lie but didn't feel the need to elaborate.

"I could help Hokee. Maybe watch the prisoner or something." The anticipation was almost oozing from her pores.

"I'm afraid not, Zoey," his tone left no room for argument. "I don't know how long I will be or who will wait for me when I get there. "

Recognizing his tone, Zoey fell silent. There was no room for argument.

As they approached the Explorer, a group of five teenagers was already surrounding the locked vehicle, deciding whether to break the windows and start stripping. Then, as the van lights approached, the gang stood waiting to see if it was a passing car or if it meant trouble. Being five, they were confident of disabling the driver if the vehicle stopped to investigate.

Hokee drove up behind his Explorer and, leaving the van's headlights on, cautioned Zoey, "please stay here while I send these boys home."

"Be careful, Hokee; I recognize them as a bunch of reservation thugs."

Seeing only one man get out, the five young men flexed their arms and bunched up their shoulders, acting like the brutal thugs Zoey described.

With no time to screw around, Hokee pulled the 45 from his hip, pointing it at the group, "the first asshole who moves towards me dies. You chickenshit thieves go home." To make his point even more explicit, he fired the gun to their left into a dirt bank. In the calm night air, it sounded like a cannon going off. The five would-be thieves scuttled off into the darkness, leaving Hokee standing by the roadside with a smoking gun.

Without turning around, Hokee called out, "it's okay Zoey, you can come out now."

Zoey appeared by his side, and Hokee handed her the keys to the Explorer. "Here, Zoey, I'll follow you back to the police station, then I'll just keep driving. Thank's a lot for your help. It looks like we were just in time."

"How did you know Hokee?" Zoey asked in genuine confusion.

"You forget I grew up here, Zoey. I know reservation rats will devour anything left unattended. I'll see you later." Then Hokee turned and walked back to Lkal's van.

According to Lkal, Cicely lived in a mobile home off U.S. 91 near Firth, about twenty miles north of Blackfoot. The directions were unclear, and Hokee ultimately found himself on a dirt road in the middle of nowhere. It was nearing eleven P.M. when Hokee located the trailer house resting on cinder blocks behind a grove of stunted pine trees. He drove by the place slowly, without stopping. The place was dark and uninviting. A soft light glowed behind a window towards the back. Probably the bedroom, Hokee guessed.

Hokee had little experience with gypsies. Their caravans never came onto the reservation, and by the time Hokee settled in Pocatello, they stopped traveling, having settled in various locations. He read that the men and women all carried sharp knives and knew how to use them, information confirmed by Lkal when Hokee took him to the jail. Elvira, the Tumbleweed bartender, informed him that Cicely was a beautiful woman and haughty.

Now all he needed was a plan to subdue the woman and get her into the van without being gutted by a hidden knife. Knocking on the door at this time of night didn't seem like a good idea. She would be alarmed and on guard before going to the door to see who came calling at this time of night. Trying to devise a plan, Hokee parked Lkal's van a half-mile down the road in the driveway to a farmer's field. He got out, closing the van's door quietly as noise travels a long way in the country, especially late at night when everything but the stealthy night creatures were out hunting. Walking down the road towards Cicely's home, Hokee kept a close watch for anything or anyone who might cry out a warning. Night creatures are silent, but a farmer might be out changing irrigation water, or kids could be out hunting night crawlers for fishing. Some kids collect and sell the slimy creatures to augment whatever tiny allowances they might be given by their parents.

Nearing Cicely's mobile home, Hokee left the dirt road to walk beneath the trees growing alongside. Approaching the trailer, he noticed two vehicles in the driveway, not one, something not clear as he drove past. The car nearest to the road blocked the one in front. GMV manufactured both vehicles, and the Chevrolet Impala by the road looked like Cicely's Cadillac in the quick glance he gave the cars while driving past. She had a roommate or a visitor, more than likely a male. In either case, knocking on the door at this hour was not a good idea. With no other bright ideas, Hokee crept to the trailer home entrance and sat on the ground next to the railroad ties used as steps. He did not know how long he would have to wait, but he was prepared with warm clothing and patience. He had often waited several days to apprehend the person he was chasing. These are the trying times when being a shaman comes in handy.

Sitting on the ground next to the trailer house, Hokee began taking in deep breaths, letting them out slowly until he had slowed his heart rate to forty beats per minute, accompanied by two breaths. This exercise put him in a zone where his senses were heightened while requiring minimal energy. He closed his eyes, blocking out all visual input, so his other senses became paramount. He could hear mosquitos flying and bats' wings beating as they dove upon the insects. Voices from inside filtered out to the night air, although too indistinct to make out the words, one male and one female. He surmised they were not roommates, as no male would like his woman going on road trips lasting over a week with another male, no matter how ugly he might be. So, they were lovers, and perhaps he would leave soon. Hokee could only hope. While he could wait a long time, it would be better to get this over with quickly.

Just when Hokee thought her guest might stay all night, he could hear their footsteps as they walked towards the door. Hokee stood in the shadows with his body flat against the side of the trailer next to the door. Fortunately, there was no porch light, making his job more manageable. The door opened, and the couple bid each other goodnight with a farewell kiss before the door closed and the man descended the creosote steps. Then, just as he stepped off the bottom tie, Hokee grabbed the man's head in a quick lock, pressing his thumbs on the same nerves that put Lkal to sleep quickly. Hokee caught the man under his arms and laid him on the ground in the shadows beside the steps; then, he promptly went to the door, softly knocking, like he was the man who had forgotten something inside.

It took only a few seconds before the door opened, and Cicely said, "Okay, what did you for..."

Hokee grabbed one of her arms before she could complete the sentence, pulling her towards him before twisting it behind her back. He was not gentle, as he did not want her to pull away.

She screamed and began kicking before Hokee clubbed her on the back of the neck with a vicious karate chop, rendering her unconscious. Then, without bothering to shut the house door, Hokee threw her over his shoulder and carried her the half-mile back to Lkal's van before throwing her inside and securing her with duct tape he had picked up earlier on the reservation from his Explorer. He covered her mouth, carefully leaving her nostrils open so she wouldn't suffocate. He then inspected his captive for the first time. She was wearing only a thin red silk robe that had fallen open, exposing most of her body. She was also barefoot and gorgeous. *God, what a waste,* he thought. Under other circumstances, he might have been aroused, but knowing what she was under the skin made her a hideous creature to be detested and avoided.

Hokee had lost track of time while waiting for the romantic couple to finish their lovemaking and it was almost one-thirty before making it back to the reservation police station. While he did not have any feelings for the woman's near-nudity, as a man who considered himself to have a moral compass, he found a blanket in Lkal's van to wrap around the now awake and hostile prisoner.

Cicely's dark eyes blazed with a hatred Hokee seldom experienced. He gave thanks for the duct tape bindings, especially the covering over her mouth. The vindictive, hateful diatribe she would unleash might boil half of the state's legendary potatoes. Once Hokee got the squirming woman wrapped in the blanket, he threw her over his shoulder and marched into the police station.

It was no surprise to see Zoey sitting at her desk in front. Then, as soon as she saw Hokee come through the door, she was on the phone, and within seconds, the chief came shuffling out of his office as two deputies arrived, hurrying down the hall. Hokee dumped the still-squirming Cicely into the arms of both deputies before addressing the chief.

Without using his title, which Hokee didn't think the chief deserved, he said, "this is the second kidnapper. I presume you will keep them both confined for a very long time."

"Oh, yes, yes," the chief gushed. "Thank you for such great service." His jowls bouncing, the chief was almost comical. "They will not escape our jail. I promise you, Mr. Wolf."

"See that you keep that promise. This was the easy part. Getting the children back will take a little more time—several days. Perhaps a couple of weeks or longer. I'm not sure how far I'll need to travel, but I will not quit until each child has been returned to their parents."

"How can you be so sure of your success?" The chief asked. "You don't even know where the children are, do you?" The shallow man was trying to act big, and Hokee had his fill of the bumbling idiot.

Hokee turned and walked out of the station without answering the chief, but with a wink at Zoey. He had not exaggerated; the hard part was still ahead.

CHAPTER NINE

The next day, Hokee took a leisurely hike with Shilah, swam and soaked in the underground river, followed by a cleansing sweat in his lodge. Then, feeling like he had scrubbed the negative energy picked up from Lkal and Cicely, Hokee had Shilah jump into the Explorer for a trip to the office.

There were few messages of importance, and thankfully no kids had gone missing from the University. Hokee called his friend Curly, the deputy sheriff, and asked him if he would please drop by for a few minutes.

"Why shore, partner. We civil employees have nothing better to do than serve our State's distinguished investigator."

"Thank's Curly. See you soon." No goodbye, which Curly didn't expect.

Hokee had tea with Hilda, his office manager and girl Friday, informing her of his plans. While waiting for Curly, he called Grant Olson, one of the largest construction contractors in the world who Hokee had served on two occasions.

After getting past the gatekeeper's, he heard Grant's gruff's voice. "Hokee, how ya doen, man? Haven't heard from you in a while." "Hello Grant. Yeah, it's been a while. I hear you're still building or rebuilding half the world."

"Only the half the needed rebuilding," Grant responded with a chuckle. "What brings you calling on my door or telephone?"

Without wasting more time, Hokee got right to it. "Grant, I need a big favor." Hokee would like to have asked what happened to Gene's fiancée and if they ever got married, but if Grant felt like explaining, he would.

"Whatever you need, Hokee, I owe you far more than you realize."

Hokee had given Grant a hundred million dollars, coerced from a competitor who had been stealing contracts from Olson Construction Company using the information provided by an insider. Hokee identified the snitch and left it to Grant to sort out the punishment.

"Grant, I need an airplane for a few days, possibly a couple of weeks, maybe longer. I'll be traveling overseas and need to carry some items frowned upon by PSA."

"Well, hell. I've got a G650 sitting just outside gathering rust. I suppose you want a pilot and crew?"

"It would be helpful. I'll be happy to pay for the expenses."

"Good God, man! Please don't insult me like that. When do you want it?"

"Would tomorrow be too soon?"

"Hell no. I'll have it in Pocatello by eight A.M. Is that soon enough? "That would be perfect. I am most grateful for the help?"

"What have you got yourself into, boy? If it ain't too personal." Grant was almost a grandfather, and practically every younger male was a boy.

"A kidnapping ring has been stealing children off the reservation, and I have been commissioned to get them back. I believe they are overseas, which is why I need your plane. It will probably get dirty. I'll try not to lose your plane," he concluded with a chuckle."

"That would be helpful. But if you run into trouble, try to dump the plane in a way my insurance will replace the damn thing."

"My fondest hope is that I have no trouble in that regard. There may be some fireworks, but I'll try to steer that stuff away from your plane."

"I don't envy the people you are hunting. Child stealing is beneath any man's dignity. I can get you some hired guns." He sounded eager to get more involved.

"I prefer to hunt alone, Grant, but thanks for the offer. Take care, and I'll stay in touch."

"You do that, son."

Neither man said goodbye. That's the sort of relationship they have and the sort of men they were—no wasted words.

Hokee was still drinking tea with Hilda when Curly strolled into his office like he was attending a Sunday school class. Not anxious but prepared to be bored for an hour.

"Howdy, Curly, Want a cup of tea? Hokee asked, pointing to a vacant chair.

"Nah, but I will take some coffee if you have any." Curly collapsed into the chair proffered by Hokee.

Hilda quickly jumped up to get Curly's coffee. "I can have you a cup in two minutes, Curly," she said, eager to please the deputy. "We like to keep the law happy," she continued with a grin.

"Well, that's mighty neighborly of you Hilda; thanks," Curly responded with a grin of his own. Then, glancing around the office like he hadn't seen it in a while, he continued, "what's up, Hokee? You got another missing kid?"

"No, I have several missing kids, but it isn't what you think. I called you because I need the services of a trained law officer." Hokee had to struggle to keep a straight face. Curly often took himself way too seriously. Although, on their last adventure together, Curly was more than willing to bend or break every law in the book if necessary.

"Well, hell, Hokee, the sheriff's department has nothing better to do than serve the state's leading investigator." Curly would have smiled if Hilda had not returned with a steaming cup of coffee at that moment. How she got it so quickly was a mystery Curly was about to explore when Hokee responded to his quip about the sheriff's department serving him.

"As I recall, Curly, I've saved your life and your department's bacon frequently." There was no humor in Hokee's voice or eyes. While he was on friendly terms with Curly and the sheriff's department, he didn't want to let the deputy pretend that the law had been of service to Hokee when it was the other way around. After allowing the thought to settle, Hokee

continued, "anyway, it isn't anything to do with the sheriff's department. I need a personal favor from you."

Curly was feeling chastised while blowing on his coffee before taking a sip. He made the comment about the department serving Hokee offhand without really giving it any thought. "What's this about a bunch of missing kids?" That sounds like sheriff's business to me, Hokee."

"It's Fort Hall reservation kids kidnapped by human traffickers. Not your jurisdiction. I caught the locals responsible for snatching the kids; now, I need to follow the leads to locate and return the missing children. I don't know how long I'll be away, and I need someone to check in on Shilah occasionally to ensure he has enough food. Grant is loaning me an airplane so I can transport items needed to locate and neutralize those responsible for this barbarism." Hokee sat back, watching Curly's response while he explained his request.

"My God, man, but you could be up against some serious players. You got any help?" It was clear from his expression that Curly wished he could go along as Hokee's partner.

"No. Grant offered to provide me a couple of shooters, but the situation is fluid, and I'm not sure what I'll be running into; besides, I need to move fast. I don't have time to prepare strangers with my methods. As you know, I'm not orthodox in my operations."

"Hell, Hokee, I can take a few days or weeks vacation; it sounds like you could use my help." Curly looked like a young man eager to go on his first deer hunting trip."

"That's a generous offer, Curly, but this could get real nasty. I've seen those I'll be up against in my sweat lodge, and I don't want your wife to become a widow. So if you will watch out for Shila, I'll be grateful. Oh, there is one more thing. Representatives of this gang might visit Pocatello to do me harm, not knowing I won't be here. It would ease my mind if you could drop by my office occasionally to check up on Hilda." As Hokee spoke, a solemn feeling descended on the office. The gravity of Hokee's mission had taken hold of both Hilda and Curly. Neither person could find words to express their concerns or prayers for their friend.

Finally, Curly squeaked out a response. "Why sure, Hokee, I'll be happy to check on the wolf, and of course, Hilda here too," he added with a hesitant grin.

Not one to be left out of the conversation, Hilda blurted, "Hokee, you never mentioned how dangerous this project was. You will not get me all tied up again, will you?"

With a big grin and a forced chuckle to defuse the funeral atmosphere his little speech had introduced into the office, Hokee quickly said, "I'm just projecting the worst case. I expect nothing bad to happen; it's just best to be on guard. So what do you say we close up shop early Hilda and go have a margarita? Can you join us, Curly, or will the sheriff frown on one of their finest drinking on duty?"

"Well, under the circumstances, as I'll be doing dog duty, the least I can do is let you buy me a drink. Although, I prefer a bloody Mary."

Leaving the office, Hokee let Hilda lock the doors before heading downstairs. "I'll see you both over at Ernesto's, Okay?"

They both said okay, following Hokee out to their cars.

CHAPTER TEN

Hokee spent the evening cleaning and inspecting his weapons. First, the trusty Colt 45 automatic that had seen a lot of use over the years. He figures to have shot close to five thousand rounds through the barrel at his local shooting range. The range manager was from the Nimipuu people, most now call Nez Perce Indians, one of the federally recognized tribal nations whose reservation lands include much of the territory they lived on as free people for over 11,500 years. Although Hokee had been going to the range for a long time and considered Chaska a friend, they never socialized.

He wore a compact Ruger model 3750 under his shirt for a backup weapon. Although the clip only held ten shells, Hokee always kept one in the chamber. The extra fraction of a second pulling on the slide might make a difference, which Hokee considered more critical than the slim chance he would make a mistake and shoot himself. He practiced shooting it on the range, but only when alone did he see how fast he could put the gun into action. Hokee practiced drawing the weapon with both hands, never knowing what the circumstances might dictate. And even though he wore the gun under his left arm, by hunching his left shoulder and squeezing his biceps against chest muscles, he could practically dump the small gun into his left hand. Maybe not as fast as drawing it right-handed, but close enough.

The last pistol he packed was a browning 22 automatic with a homemade silencer. This was a professional assassin's gun. Hokee had never been when he needed such a weapon, but one never knows. When carrying this gun, he wore a leather jacket with side pockets modified to fit the weapon if he wanted or needed a silent kill.

Hokee had a picture on his wall featuring a gray wolf that looked like Shilah, something Hokee painted while trying to decide what to do with his life. His few visitors found the painting stunning, an accolade Hokee found embarrassing. Behind the picture was a slide-out cabinet that held Hokee's rifles. It was a modest collection, and their resting place was not so much to hide them as to get them out of the way. Hokee's house was 200 feet below the lava valley floor, accessible only by a nearly hidden, ten-mile one-lane road. Hokee never filed forms or asked for a building permit for his house, which went unlisted in the county data bank. Then there was Shila. If anyone stumbled upon Hokee's property, the territorial wolf was all the guard dog a man could want. Trained to accept food from no one but Hokee or someone Hokee had introduced to him, the only way past the wolf would be to shoot him. And no one who knew Hokee would ever be that foolish.

Included in his modest collection was a Browning X-Bolt Hell's Canyon Speed. Unsurpassed in artistry and accuracy, any competent shooter could place their rounds in a softball-sized target from 500 yards. While he had a few semi-automatics, Hokee opted for accuracy, taking down the Hell's Canyon and slipping it into a gun case.

After finishing with his guns, Hokee sorted through his knives, trying to determine those he might need. An obvious choice was what he called a pig sticker. It had a slender ten-inch blade, not much thicker than a straight razor, and twice as sharp. This knife was sheathed in soft doeskin leather and hung down the back of his neck. He could throw the knife with either hand and hit the eye of a target head from fifty feet. Perhaps his arsenal was not typical for a shaman, but Hokee's practice took him well outside the typical shaman's sweat lodge. His last knife was an eight-inch hunting knife, also honed razor-sharp, worn strapped to his left calf muscle.

Hokee debated with himself about the pharmaceuticals. Working with Why-ay'-looh, his teacher and surrogate father, Hokee learned to concoct several deadly poisons, some to kill and some to induce paralysis. All were in powder form a person could mix with food and drinks or dilute in water for injecting. Erring on the side of caution, Hokee packed the drugs in his ready bag.

Thinking about his mentor, Hokee wondered what the old master would think of his adopted son today. Why-ay'-looh was like a father to the entire Indian nation. He stayed in his old one-room shanty dispensing herbs and advice, plus the occasional sweat lodge to all those who sought his advice. Hokee considered himself more of the sheepdog watching over the herd, or in his case, the wolf pack. That was the reason for focusing his investigative skills on locating the missing kids from Idaho State University, with the occasional side job that came his way. When predators threatened the pack, especially those who targeted the young, Hokee considered these hunters less than human and extended them no mercy.

Now it was Shilah time.

There was no need to call or whistle. Shilah was waiting for his master, knowing that something unusual was happening. Domesticated dogs are far more psychic than people give them credit for, and wolf companions are much more so than even the best charlatan to don a silk turban and gaze into a crystal ball. Shilah knew something powerful was taking his master away, and he was eager to spend as much time together as possible. This would not be one of those dangerous, meditative walks across the lava flats, but a stroll down the long road towards the gate leading to Hokee's house, looking at the stars and feeling the cool evening breeze.

Together, man and wolf climbed up the sloping driveway to the plain's rim while listening to the outdoor fountain splashing its accompaniment to the crickets and a few lonely frogs. Once on the lava plain, Hokee could catch a hint of the Snake River several miles to the west, carried on the refreshing breeze. For once, Shilah was content to pad alongside Hokee, perhaps knowing this would be their final stroll together for a few nights. Usually, he would run off using his fabulous sense of smell to chase rabbits and squirrels or the occasional antelope. He often caught the smaller animals, but never the large ones.

The desert air is clear, and at 4500 feet elevation, the stars are like a bowl of uncounted and uncountable twinkling lights. It felt good to be alive, and Hokee prayed he would return to have many more evenings like this with

Shilah. He had not heard from Glory in several days and assumed the worst. She was a city gal at heart, and the siren's song of the big metropolis called New York was under her skin. It felt to Hokee like Glory couldn't find the words to say goodbye, so rather than try, she just let their relationship die its slow death. As he thought about the situation, Glory was an unusual occurrence in his life anyway. Brought together by circumstances in a case two years ago, the bachelor had allowed himself to get involved with another woman destined to break his heart. Although to be fair, the first one was jerked away by a father who could not tolerate his beautiful little princess being involved with a mixed-race Indian.

Oh well. It was too fine a night to let disappointment spoil the last evening he would have with his one true love for a while. He and Shilah had been bosom buddies for a long time, and hopefully, they would have many more years together.

After walking five miles, Hokee turned and started back home. There was still packing to take care of plans to make. He had some idea about the sort of people he would see tomorrow, but there was always the unknown. Making plans for every contingency he could think of was how Hokee had stayed alive. Not that there weren't surprises, but his careful planning had always seen him through. Although he had faced evil before, several times, if he were honest with himself, the next few days or weeks would present him with another example of an even higher level of man's inhumanity to man.

Arriving back home, Hokee called Shilah. Come on, boy, let's sleep together tonight. An invitation seldom offered but never refused. Shilah, on top of the comforter, snuggled close to Hokee as they drifted off to sleep.

CHAPTER ELEVEN

Olson's company G650 jet appeared at the Pocatello airport exactly at eight
A.M. as promised. Hokee had parked his Explorer in the long-term
parking, as he didn't know how long he would be away, and was waiting on
the tarmac at the general aviation terminal when the plane stopped. After
the pilots killed the engines, the door opened, the stairs dropped, and a
stunning woman with beautiful red hair came out of the plane and stood at
the top of the stairs. She wore a stylish black jumpsuit and a thousand-watt
smile.

Hokee grabbed his bags with clothes and weapons, then headed for the
stairs. Then, as he neared the bottom stair, the vision in black asked
needlessly, "are you Hokee Wolf?"

"The one and only," he answered, climbing the stairs.

"Welcome aboard," she said in a sweet, contralto voice. My name is
Heather. Come in and let me introduce you to the crew.

This was not the first time in a private jet for Hokee, but the grandeur
inside always came as a surprise. A thick beige carpet with an intricately
woven pattern featuring geometrical shapes surrounded a few soft white
leather recliners, behind which were two tables and couches made into beds.
The scene always made Hokee happy he was not flying commercially.

Two men in uniforms that looked like those worn by professional
commercial pilots stood and met Hokee. "This is Captain Hobbs," the

hostess introduced, pointing to the man on the left; this other guy is Captain Jensen," she said, pointing to the one on the right.

Hokee dropped his bags and shook his pilot's hands. "I appreciate the lift, gentlemen... and lady," he amended quickly. "Did Grant tell you we might be away for a few days, possibly a couple of weeks?"

"Yes," replied the primary pilot, Captain Hobbs. "That won't be a problem. Where are we headed so I can file the flight plane?"

"Our first stop is Houston, Texas. We shouldn't be there for over one day-two at the most. Then, if what I have been told is correct, we'll head to Mauretania on the west coast of Africa." Hokee felt like a fool explaining where Mauretania was located, but most people would not know the country's location without a map. "After that, I do not know. It could be one more country, or possibly many countries. Did Grant tell you why we are making the trip?"

"No, he didn't," Hobbs responded. "He told us you would explain everything when we met."

"Right," Hokee said, trying to think of a way to sugarcoat the truth. When nothing came to mind, he continued, "I'm chasing some children kidnapped from the local reservation and sold into slavery. The kids have been disappearing for six months and may have been sold all over God's kingdom. Hopefully not, but the primary human trafficking ring in the world is in Mauretania. I need Houston to tell me who the main man is in Africa. Since I don't know where we will go, there is no need to worry about visas. So we'll have to do this one step at a time."

"Oh, those poor children," Heather said sadly. "I hope we can find them, Mr. Wolf."

'Please call me Hokee, and if I didn't think we could locate the children, we wouldn't be making this trip."

"What will you do when you locate the kidnappers, Hokee," asked the copilot, Jensen.

Not one to dodge the truth, Hokee answered. "There will undoubtedly be some bloodshed. But, with a lot of luck, it won't be mine. I'll go over our plans when we get to the nasty part. What do you say we get this bird in the air, Captain?

"Sure thing, Hokee. Let Heather show you where to stow your gear while I make our flight plans, and we'll be in the air."

"Sounds good. I'm ready," Hokee said, relieved that this part of the introduction was over.

Heather led Hokee to the rear of the 650, showing him where to stow his luggage. "Would you like some breakfast or something else to eat, Hokee?" she asked. Grant had us load the plane with enough food for several days. I guess he was worried you might starve to death." This last comment was accompanied by a blazing smile revealing a perfect set of white enamels,

"A cup of coffee would be great if that wouldn't be too much trouble," Hokee replied with a smile, although his smile was restrained. After wrestling with Shila for a few minutes in the early morning, Hokee started preparing his head for Houston. These preparations didn't go with a smile. "Sure, no problem," she said, disappearing back up front. Heather was slender, about five foot five, with boyish hips and a perfect oval face featuring bright green eyes, the color of ocean water in the early dawn. Then, as she disappeared behind a cabinet, Hokee selected a seat facing front, stretching out his long legs.

He considered various ways of confronting Teeten when Heather returned with his coffee. Noticing the distracted look on Hokee's face, Heather set the coffee down on a table in front of Hokee. "If you want anything else, Hokee, just let me know. I can see you are already in Houston," she added with a chuckle.

"Okay, thanks Heather," and Hokee returned to his planning.

Hokee had to grab his coffee to keep it from spilling as the pilot wasted no time getting the plane off the ground and into a steep climb.

From ground to ground, the flight lasted just under three hours. Before deplaning, Hokee visited his equipment bag, selecting those items he thought might come in handy. Since Texas is a gun state, Hokee wore the 45 on his hip. Everything else was carried in pockets or strapped to appendages in the most accessible locations. Then, going back to the front

where Heather already had the stairs extended; she asked, "do you have any idea how long you will be gone, Hokee?"

"Not really," was his answer. "I don't know how long it will take me to find the men I am looking for, nor how long it will take to get the information I seek. I expect to be back sometime this afternoon, so I would be thankful if Captain Hobbs could have the plane refueled and ready to go. Our next flight might be several hours long."

Captain Hobbs was standing next to Heather as Hokee finished his answer and request, so he responded.

"I'll take care of it, Hokee. There are two of us up front to take turns flying so we can easily make Africa or most places in Europe without stopping to refuel. We'll be waiting here on the plane this afternoon for your return. Here's my phone number if you need to call me." The captain handed Hokee a business card with the pilot's cell number.

"Thanks, Captain. Hopefully, I'll see you in a few hours."

Hokee turned towards the stairs and went down. *Houston, here I come,* he thought as he headed towards the terminal and the car rental kiosks.

CHAPTER TWELVE

The Hertz agent was an overweight Texan lady with the drawl, wearing dark brown cowboy boots on the bottom of fat, stubby legs. "Howdy honey, what kinda car are you looking for, handsome?" She had a wide-open gaze with dark blue eyes that looked like someone staring at the moon.

"Well, beautiful," Hokee responded, playing along, "I want something big and comfortable; what's available?"

"The nicest buggy we got rawht now is the new Buick. Ah reckon that should git cha where you're goen."

"Sold. And if I might say so. That's a fetching dress y'all are wearing." Hokee threw in y'all to show he was one of the good-ole-boys while thinking the dress looked like dyed potato sacks sewn together, but he didn't deem it wise to express that thought. At least until he had the rental agreement in his hands.

"Need to see yer driven license, fore awh finish this rental agreement," she wheezed like someone who had smoked most of her life.

Hokee handed over his license and stood by while the clerk finished the agreement before shoving it over the counter for him to sign. The clerk used her long fake fingernails to point out where she wanted Hokee to sign. "Sign heyar, heyar, and heyar, if ya don't want our insurance. Otherwise, leave it blank, and ahll go over the coverage options."

"No insurance, but thanks." Picking up his license and copies of the rental agreement, he stood while the clerk handed him the key fob instructing him to go out the door to the left and walk down the aisle to row D-14, where he would find a blue Buick Enclave.

"Be careful, honey; that baby has some horses under the hood," she added as a parting shot. Then, when Hokee looked back, she favored him with a wink

The drive from Houston to Kemah is just over 27 miles, but according to the instructions Lkal provided, Teeten's warehouse was another two miles along the waterway next to the commercial docks. Hokee didn't know that Teeten would be at the warehouse; it wasn't like the man kept business hours. The man might be off selling or buying or shipping or even at home beating one of his 'wives. Hokee hoped the warehouse was empty and the purveyors of human cargo were off busy making their mischief someplace else, but he had prepared for either eventuality.

The warehouse was more extensive than expected, but as Lkal had described, it was a weathered building near the dock with two sliding doors to accommodate a large truck or van, plus a pedestrian door by its side. There were no vehicles by the building, which didn't mean the building was vacant. Instead, Hokee chastised himself for not asking Lkal what vehicles Teeten drove. He probably had a regular car, plus a cargo van or large truck to haul the various items he and his gang gained by mostly illegal means for shipment to his contact in Mauretania. Lkal was unfamiliar with Teeten's relationship with Ghulam, the white-black man.

Not wanting to spoil a surprise if such would be the case, Hokee parked the Buick down the block in front of a crab shack advertising fresh seafood. He found the pedestrian door locked, which he assumed meant that Teeten and his gang were elsewhere, so like any good investigator, he pulled out his lock picks and opened the door to a God-awful odor. Then, going inside, he found the wall switch and turned on the lights, illuminating the source of the smells.

There were rows of cages along one wall, and each pen held ten to fifteen people. Men, women, and children were all grouped with no privacy. They had no toilet facilities, only a bucket for human waste, which accounted for the odor. There was a soft mumbling; then, the room became quiet as the caged individuals tried to size up their new intruder. That he had entered the locked door showed he was a friend of their jailers, perhaps a buyer looking over the merchandise. It was more than likely bad news. Seeing a toilet in one of the rear corners, Hokee went to work.

He found a steel bar leaning against the wall and going to the first cage, sprung the lock releasing the door. "Okay," he said. "Everybody listen up. The first person who disobeys me will be in serious trouble. My name is Captain Largo and I will set you all free. Hokee didn't use his given name as he didn't want anyone to know he was in Houston. You may leave your cages one at a time to use the toilet in the rear if you need to use the facility or wash your hands and face. Otherwise, I would like you all to remain in your cages until I have dealt with the smugglers. Then you will be free to go. If you need help, I'll see what I can do, but my time is limited, so expect little. Are you all prepared to do as I suggest?"

There was a general chorus of "Yes, captain."

"Okay, good. I'll spring the locks on the rest of these cages so you can all be free. Does anyone know when your jailers will return?

As Hokee went down the line, springing one door after another, it wasn't until the next to the last cage before a young black man about twenty, who looked like some rapper Hokee had seen a picture of but couldn't remember the name, as rap wasn't something he enjoyed. "I heard one man say they were waiting on some ship to dock this afternoon. We were to be loaded on board this evening. I'm afraid I don't know when they will be back."

"Thanks. What is your name?"

"My real name is Clarence, but everybody calls me Champ because I won a chess trophy in our local chess club." He smiled for perhaps the first time in a long time as his face didn't take to the expression willingly. Like it had been a long time since he had any reason to be happy.

"Did everybody hear what Champ said?" Hokee asked, then before anyone answered, he continued, "that is why I don't want you leaving your cell before they come back. If you are seen outside, your jailers will know something is wrong and may not enter the building. I need them here inside to ask a few questions and put them out of business forever. Please be patient until they return and then you will all be free to go wherever you desire."

There was some grumbling, which Hokee expected, while many changed cages to be with family or friends. Then, as the people settled back down, a constant stream of people headed to the bathroom. They each muttered a thank you to Hokee, who finally turned his back on the caged people and stood by the door, listening for Teeten and his gang.

Several hours elapsed while the people planned what they would do after Hokee gave the word for them to escape. Their murmured voices were no longer sad, but joyful in the happy expectation that their lives as enslaved people would never happen. It was almost five o'clock when Hokee heard a vehicle sounding like a truck outside the big sliding doors, then the quieter sound of a regular car or SUV stopping near the pedestrian door. Hokee had relocked the door to avoid giving himself away. Footsteps sounded coming towards the small door after a car door slammed shut. Keys rattled before the door swung open, and a short, stout black man entered, turning on the lights that Hokee had turned off. Believing this was the scary Teeten, Hokee, creeping silently in moccasins, slipped in behind the man, then hit him on the side of his neck with a syringe filled with a potent homemade tranquilizer. The man collapsed, and Hokee hoped he hadn't killed the bastard. Then, pulling the man to the side out of the way, he laid him on the concrete floor while pushing the button to open the door for the truck idling outside.

A large green army-colored truck drove inside, and two men jumped out of the cab. Hokee stood by the side door, waiting for the man on the passenger's side to join the driver. When both men were together looking for their leader, Hokee shot each one in the head with the silenced 22 magnum. The magnum has a more extended shell than a 22-long and does maximum damage with almost no noise. The two men collapsed straight down without a sound. According to Lkal's descriptions, these were only the

helpers. Teeten, lying unconscious, was the leader and the one Hokee wished to interrogate before he killed him.

Shouting to the victims in the cages, Hokee told them it was safe for them to leave now. "Don't mention this shooting for an hour, please. Does anyone need help?"

They all screamed thanks as they rushed past the open truck door. Not one person stopped to ask for help. Then, when the last person was gone, Hokee checked to see if anyone was outside who could see him before carrying the unconscious Teeten back to the man's vehicle, a Lincoln Navigator. Opening the rear door, Hokee threw him on the floor in the back, got in the driver's seat, and pushed the starter button. The key must have been close because the Lincoln roared to life, and Hokee drove off to interrogate the human trafficker. He didn't want to stick around the warehouse because, sure as hell, one of the kidnapped people would blurt out to the wrong person or the police where they had been held captive and how they were freed. And Hokee didn't want to interrogate Teeten in front of a hundred witnesses.

Driving away from the warehouse, foremost in his mind were the thoughts, *Teeten, old son, your days of plundering are over.* Hokee couldn't wait to interrogate the criminal.

CHAPTER THIRTEEN

Paris, France, is considered the most beautiful city in the world by many. Museums abound, full of famous paintings, sculptures, and stunning architecture. The city's famous streets feature world-renown sculptures and fantastic artwork. Many of the world's most talented artists made Paris their home, and their residences are museums full of priceless artifacts. Near the mansion where King Louis imprisoned Marie Antionette before the guillotine severed her head is another famous mansion, although this one is not listed in the guidebooks.

Bd Saint Germain is a fashionable boulevard one block south of the famous Quai de la Tournelle beside the Seine, and within sight of the Eiffel Tower, is the home of Madame Claude, France's most famous brothel keeper. Madame Claude died in 2015, but Belle Brezing maintains her legacy. The illegitimate daughter of a prostitute, Brezing, lived her entire life in Claude's mansion serving the famous Madame who bequeathed the daughter she never had, her whole fortune including the mansion. Fortunately, there were sufficient funds to pay the inherent taxes, undoubtedly aided by those politically motivated to keep the mansion functioning. After all, the mansion had served Parisian elites for over a century.

With the auspicious house number 999, the mansion is a stately six-level building considered one of the more impressive mansions on a street loaded with fantastic architecture. The bottom two floors were white limestone featuring chiseled images of Greek gods that had recently been power washed, cleaning two centuries of soot and grime. Above the six double windows on the bottom floor, arched cornices flanked a double-wide polished oak door with inlaid glass windows. Wide white limestone stairs leading up to the doors looked like masons had only recently finished putting them in place. The second floor is also white limestone, featuring seven double-hung windows with horizontal lintels, one directly above the front doors. On the bottom half, these windows featured a black wrought iron grille. Seven windowed gables featuring gray shingles covered the top floor with black shutters beside each window. The upper floors were plain white limestone, with arched windows flanked by decorative black shutters. A steep gabled roof towered over everything like a giant hand, an imposing structure belying its primary function. It could house a great museum or a giant art gallery.

Belle Brezing is a short, trim lady with coal-black hair and dark, flashing eyes. Standing only five-four in stocking feet, she usually wore three-inch heels, giving her more stature. She wore her thick curly hair piled on top of her head, giving her the appearance of a much taller lady. She always wore high-necked dresses above which dangled two-carat diamond earrings. With an oval face and thick dark eyebrows, most would call her attractive but never beautiful. Her mouth was always horizontal; she never smiled to prevent wrinkling her smooth cheeks.

Madame Claude recognized something special in the astute young girl and never put her into service but had her tutored by some of France's most distinguished scholars, most of whom were customers of the house. As Belle matured, the madame instructed her in all aspects of the business.

Another tradition instituted by Madame Claude was acquiring young children she raised to serve the Parisian upper crust. Madame Brezing continued this tradition, acquiring most of the children she 'instructed' from Shabib Ghulam. There are plenty of perverted individuals who enjoy having children service them, and *virgins* command a premium price. Of course, the patrons of the mansion were unaware that these so-called virgins had seen months of service before Belle Brezing began telling her clients that the children were 'almost' a virgin, still a bargain at three times the regular price.

She had received the last Shoshone child from Ghulam and was eager to acquire the children in greater volume. Getting them one at a time was inefficient, as it entailed the same security measures required for more significant numbers. Still, she was happy with her purchases, although she was paying the equivalent of sixty-five thousand dollars per head. So far, she could not coerce Ghulam into supplying the children two or three at a time. Occasionally, a visiting Prince or Shiek would purchase one of her kids for a million dollars. As the Shoshone children were all considered beautiful when cleaned and dressed in fancy clothes, Belle could see selling most of them for several times what she paid Ghulam, hence the greed to get the children in more significant numbers.

CHAPTER FOURTEEN

Back in Mauritania, Ghulam tried once more to call the cousin he hated yet relied upon to supply these special kids. Then, inside a van in Kemah, Hokee heard a phone trill but didn't stop to investigate; he needed to find an isolated spot to interrogate his prisoner.

Hokee pulled up the GPS app on his phone and located a turnoff from Highway 146 about two miles away that looked like it might serve his purpose. He needed to find a place before the drugs he injected into Teeten wore off and he regained consciousness.

He located the site at the end of a short, paved road ending in a gated lot with a large white two-story building that looked like a warehouse. The gate was open, and Hokee drove around to the back of the building. There were no vehicles in sight. A set of blue metal stairs led to a blue door beside two small windows. These were the only windows in the entire building. Hokee could not answer his unasked questions about the building's purpose. That it appeared vacant now was his primary concern. The building was too remote for anyone to walk there on purpose. That the gate was open could mean that someone would return soon.

Seeing no cars or anyone around, he parked and crawled in back with a roll of duct tape. Then, feeling Teeten's hard-muscled oversized arms,

Hokee used extra tape as he didn't want his prisoner to break free. Only then did Hokee take the time to search his prisoner, locating his wallet and two different cell phones. Taking the batteries out of both phones was a precaution in the unlikely event someone would track the phones. He had left two dead bodies back in the warehouse, and the released prisoners might already have talked with the police. Once the arms and legs of Teeten were secured, Hokee injected his prisoner with the antidote to wake him up.

Teeten squirmed around, trying to free his arms and legs while Hokee breathed a sigh of relief. This was the first time he had used this concoction on a human, and he worried it might kill his subject. Hokee let his prisoner squirm for a minute before tapping him on the shoulder to get his attention. "Hello, Teeten. Did you have a nice nap?" There was no friendliness in Hokee's question.

"What the fuck is this?" Who are you? What the fuck you want, white man?" An angry, frustrated, hate-filled fury blazed in his black eyes.

A calm Hokee answered. "Taking your question in the order asked, **this** is you lying in your vehicle being questioned by me. I am the man asking the questions, and finally, I want your honest answers."

"Go fuck yourself, you Indian bastard. I'm not telling you anything," snarled a miserable, unhappy man.

Hokee pulled out the 22 with the silencer attached from a jacket pocket and calmly shot Teeten in the left knee.

"Oh, Jesus! Oh God! You shot me, you bastard, you dumb fuck. Do you know the trouble you are facing? You will be castrated and forced to eat your balls."

"Now, Teeten, I shot one knee, and perhaps a good orthopedist can fix it so you can walk again. I will ask you one question, and if you answer me honestly, I won't shoot the other one. Hopefully, I won't hit a major artery so you bleed to death, but I can't guarantee that. It looks like I hit nothing too dangerous so far. You are bleeding some, but you can probably wash the blood from your van. You're just lucky, I guess. Although we probably should put a tourniquet on before too much longer."

"Where are my men? What did you do with them? Although still snarling, his voice was getting calmer.

"You don't seem to have gotten the memo, Teeten. I'm the one asking the questions, and you are the one who will answer or not. That remains to be seen." Hokee was still talking in a conversational tone, much like you might talk over a cup of coffee at the kitchen table.

"What the fuck you want, Indian? You look like a fucking half-breed." Truculence had replaced the snarl.

"Okay, this is your one chance to avoid being a cripple for the rest of your life. So what did you do with the kids you bought from Lkal and Cicely?"

"What do you think, stupid? I sold them." He managed a tight grin, as though he had outsmarted the stupid Indian. "Oh God, my leg hurts. You got to get me to a hospital."

"Soon, Teeten. We're almost there. I said one question, but your answer to my last question forces me to ask one more question. Who did you sell the children to?"

Teeten squirmed around, yelling as that increased the pain in his knee. Apparently, he did not want to answer the question, but he didn't want his other knee ruined with another shot from the 22. Then, with great reluctance, he forced out an answer between clenched teeth, "I sold them to my cousin in Mauritania." The hatred in his eyes was like black poison. If only looks could kill.

"I suppose you and your family of smugglers and human traffickers have your own ship. You may just nod if you like." Hokee didn't need the answer to his query. Regardless, the ship's captain was undoubtedly privy to the illegal cargo he carried and was part of the operation.

Teeten didn't bother to nod or answer. He simply glared.

"Okay, tough guy, I guess I need to know the name of your cousin in Mauritania."

"I hope you go there, you ignorant half-breed. They will feast on your balls." Teeten would have smiled at the thought if he had not been in such pain.

"Hokee made a point of racking the gun; although being an automatic, it was unnecessary. He caught the unspent bullet in his hand to avoid Teeten noticing the act, then asked casually, "One last time to save your other knee. The name of your cousin."

"Okay, okay. It's Shabib Ghulam, and he is the meanest, most brutal, and sickest man you will see before you die."

Hokee put one between his eyes, then said, "I can be brutal too occasionally." Then crawled back in the front to drive back to his rental. Then he parked the van behind the Buick, leaving it unlocked. Someone might try to steal the van once it becomes dark. They would be in for a big surprise.

Once back in the Buick, Hokee called his pilot to tell him he was returning to the airport. "We'll be flying to Mauritania," he said. "Have Heather prepare a meal for me if you would please. I should be there in about thirty minutes."

"Okay, Hokee, Mauritania, here we come. I sure hope to hell you know what you're doing, man. From what I have heard of that country, it is one nasty hell hole.

"You know it, Captain Hobbs; I read it the same way."

"Seeing as how we're good friends and all, and we might get shot upon landing, you can call me Richard. The other gent up here is Howard."

"Okay, gotcha Richard. See you soon." It wasn't the first time that Hokee wondered if he knew what in the hell he was doing.

It was almost six P.M., but he was in the central time zone, and Idaho was in Mountain time. Hilda would still be at work getting ready to go home if she had not left early, something she rarely did, even when Hokee was traveling.

"Wolf investigation," she sounded sultry over the phone, and Hokee wondered as he often did if that was an effect she tried for or if it just sounded that way over the telephone lines.

"Hi Hilda. Just calling to see if the sky had fallen yet."

"No, it's still standing, boss. Nothing major to report. How's your hunting going?"

"Knocking the bad guys off a few at a time. Still, a long way to go. Make sure you remind Curly to check up on Shila. No telling how long I'll be gone this time."

"Oh, don't worry about that, Hokee. Curly probably loves that dog almost as much as you. You may not know this, but he was awfully proud when you invited him to your home last year."

"No, I didn't know that, and thanks. Go home and have a drink on me." Hokee knew she seldom drank alcohol, and especially when alone. "On second thought Hilda, make it a double." Hokee chuckled as he ended the call. He rarely said goodbye. The real reason for calling Hilda was to see if Glory had called. If anything significant had happened at the office, Hilda would have called him.

It was time to close that chapter in his mind. There could only be one reason he had not heard from the woman to whom he had given his heart a couple of years ago. It was time to erase his mind and get on with thinking about what might lie ahead. Clearing his mind of the past and focusing on the present was one of the first lessons from his old mentor. A gift he treasured and a lesson he now applied. He had not thought of the taunting, teasing, and insults heaped on him as the bastard no one had wanted in many years. His pilot's warning about the hell hole he would visit did not go unheeded. How do you prepare for the unknown?

Hokee subconsciously knew the answer to the unasked question. It was the way of the shaman.

CHAPTER FIFTEEN

Grant's plane was parked near the General Aviation terminal, close to the Hertz rental return kiosk. Hokee returned the Buick and walked to the waiting stairs, where Heather stood with a big, welcoming smile.

"Your dinner awaits, my master," she said, unable to keep from smiling while bowing with the sweep of her hand, showing the open cabin door.

"Why the Cheshire grin Heather? He couldn't help but be curious.

Howard, the copilot for this trip, was originally from Houston and knew where the bodies were buried or, better yet, where to find the best prime rib in Texas. The local Iron Grill prepared the meat and delivered it in a portable oven accompanied by a thermos full of a sensational scotch drink, the rusty nail. Unbeknown to Hokee, Grant had informed the pilot of Hokee's penchant for scotch.

"Our little surprise. Richard and Howard have already feasted and are ready to fly, so it's just you and me, Hokee." She kept the smile all the way to Hokee's seat, setting up the table before disappearing back up front. No sooner was Hokee seated than Richard had the jet engines whining, preparing to take off.

While the plane was still taxiing, Heather returned carrying a large platter heaped with medium roast beef, an extra-large baked potato with all the trimmings and a large glass of a light-brown colored liquid. Setting Hokee's meal down on the table, she hurried back upfront to grab her meal to eat with her passenger.

"Better grab onto your drink for a minute, Hokee, until we are in the air. We don't want to lose any precious alcohol molecules."

"No, Heather, we certainly wouldn't want that," Hokee responded with a grin, grabbing his drink and taking a sip. "Wow, a rusty nail. My lord. I don't remember when I last had one of these. How did you know? Never mind, I'll have to speak with Grant about divulging state secrets."

"Don't be too hard on the man. He is providing the plane and the pilots, and well, little ole me," she grinned, taking a sip from her glass."

Hokee couldn't think of a good retort, so he said nothing.

Taking a bite of his prime rib roast, Hokee said, "My God, this roast beef is fabulous. Don't tell me you cooked this alone in the plane's kitchen?"

"I would like to take the credit, but it all goes to Howard. He has friends and relatives in Houston, and I gather they are food snobs. So enjoy; we won't eat this good again for a while, I'm afraid," she said with a slight frown.

"I gather things went well for you here in Texas," Heather suggested. "You know, I think I could go for another glass of the nail if there is any left," Hokee said, leaving her question unanswered. Heather was smart enough to realize that it was none of her business, and Hokee would say something if he wanted her to know. Then, getting up, she took Hokee's empty glass and came hurrying back with a full one in exchange. Finally, they finished their meals in silence, each absorbed in their own thoughts.

After their meal, Heather bussed their dishes and removed the table. She was not gone long before Richard came by and settled in the opposite seat. It's time we had a little chat, Hokee, if you don't mind.

"No problem at all, Richard. I was just about to come up front for a visit, anyway. So what's our flight time to Mauritania?"

"Commercial flights take about ten and a half hours. We could do it in eight, but I've throttled it back, so right now, I'm figuring about nine hours. You realize we do not have clearance to land in Mauritania, don't you?" Richard did not look pleased.

"Yeah, that's mostly what I wanted to talk with you about. Grant told you to bring your passports, didn't he?

"Yes, and I made sure Heather has hers, but we don't have visas to visit that country or permission to land at their airport."

"Okay, neither of those obstacles will be a problem. Mauritania is undoubtedly the most corrupt nation on planet earth. There isn't a politician in the country who will not accept a bribe. So when we are about two hours out, or whenever you are in contact with their tower, tell the control tower manager that you have a special shipment for Shabib Ghulam. Tell them we left Houston and did not have time to arrange visas, but we have our passports. Tell them we will be happy to pay a fine, and if there is any pushback, tell them we understand the fines for an unscheduled visit will be significant, and we will willingly pay. Also, mention that our stop will be brief, only long enough to meet with Mr. Ghulam and deliver our package."

"Do you have a package for Mr. Ghulam Hokee?"

"No. I will torture Mr. Ghulam, then kill him and anyone else who gets in my way. I hope you can get this plane refueled as quickly as possible and be ready to take off in a hurry. If possible, make arrangements before landing; that would be preferable. Oh, and see if Mr. Ghulam will meet on our plane. I don't want our business to take place here on Grant's airplane, maybe Ghulam's car. If what I suspect is true, he will arrive flanked by four or more security guards. Their large number should eliminate his fears about meeting with a stranger."

"You don't mince words, do you, Hokee? I hope I can remember all of that. Perhaps when I get the tower on the radio, you could come up front and remind me of something if I should forget."

"Sure, I'll be happy to." Just have Heather get me when you get the tower speaking to you."

Feeling miserable, Richard returned to the cockpit while Hokee reclined his seat, preparing to nap, when a telephone began trilling. It was one of Teeten's phones. Hokee had replaced the batteries and tuned them on, hoping they would ring and provide him with some information. He

had forgotten they were still in his pocket. With not a lot to lose, Hokee answered it to see who was calling.

"Hello, who is this, please?"

There was silence at the other end for a considerable time, then a voice said, "who in the fuck is this, and where is Teeten?

"Oh my, such good English and such vulgar language; I presume I have the pleasure of speaking with Mr. Ghulam?"

"That's right, asshole; now, who are you, and why do you have Teeten's phone?"

"I'm afraid that your cousin had a terrible accident. Sorry to be the bearer of bad news, but I think it's best to say these things outright, don't you?" Hokee was playing a dangerous game, but it was the only one he knew how to play under the circumstances. With the slightest miscue, Shabib would meet him with a firing squad.

"What kind of accident?" Forgotten for the moment was his question about who had answered the phone.

"A long time ago, your cousin had designs on the female kidnapper, Cicely. The one who brought the young Indian children to him. But unfortunately, when he set about raping her, he missed the stiletto she carried. Then, just as he was about to climax, the knife went straight into his heart. He died instantly. I'm told this by his crewmates, who stood by watching the whole thing happen."

"What happened to the girl?" I hope the bastards took their time killing her." His voice sounded harsh over the phone, like he wanted to take part in her punishment personally

"Well, they didn't share the details, but I believe they accomplished what your cousin tried before they sliced her up with her own knife. It sounded bloody."

"So, who are you? And what are you doing with Teeten's phone?" Now he sounded angry.

"Oh, I'm Captain Largo with the Houston border patrol. Your cousin and I had an arrangement. I never went below deck to inspect your ship or view his shipments, and he always rewarded me handsomely. Cicely just delivered two new kids, and Teeten told me earlier that each kid was worth fifty thousand dollars. So, I thought I bring you the kids personally, and you could pay me for my troubles."

"What the fuck. I only pay Teeten five thousand a kid. You ain't getting any hundred grand man, forget it." Not only did he sound angry, but he was genuinely pissed off. But, mostly, Hokee thought, Shabib directed his venom against his now-deceased cousin.

"Well, okay. We were flying to Mauritania, but I'll have my pilot change course to Paris. Perhaps I can find a buyer there for the kids. I hate to go home empty-handed. Have to pay for this fuel somehow, you know. Anyway, we don't have a landing permit or visas for your country. I was hoping you could take care of that. So goodbye."

"Wait! Wait up, Goddammit. Just give me a minute. You say you're flying here to Mauritania? How in the hell did you know to fly here, and how did you get my name?" The man now sounded angry and suspicious. Like Hokee's story wasn't holding up very well.

"His crew told me. They missed the ship as it had already embarked before all of this went down. I don't believe Teeten was expecting any more kids today. The other slaves were already on board. Anyway, the crew was all shaken up and didn't know what to do. Teeten wasn't around to give them orders, so they came to me. I was already down by the dock. So they gave me Teeten's phone to get in touch with you about the kids. I was just about to call you, but now you understand the situation better."

"Listen, don't go to Paris. I can arrange for your plane to land and make temporary accommodations for you and your pilots. I will...."

"Bull shit, amigo. I ain't landing for no damn ten thousand bucks." Hokee shouted, interrupting Shabib Ghulam, which rarely happened to the white, black man.

Shabib had had no one speak to him like that in years, and he wanted to kill this smug American in the worst damn way, but he wanted the kids first. The line was buzzing with soft static while Hokee waited. "Are you still there Largo?" He omitted the Captain part, probably on purpose. But his voice was calmer. Sort of like the quiet before the knife slips into your gut.

"Yeah, you got anything else to add, Ghulam?" Two could play the intimidation game, and Hokee loved sticking it to the prick. Hopefully, he would live to have no regrets.

"Let me make some arrangements, and I'll call you back." He was about to say something else when Hokee quickly said, "I told you I would not land for ten grand. I want a hundred grand in greenbacks when my plane lands, or you don't even get to see the kids. And they are beautiful, both girls, eleven and thirteen." Hokee hoped this would entice the bastard. Hopefully, those Arab assholes couldn't resist some tender young virgin girls.

"Alright, Mr., er... ah Captain ah... Largo, one hundred thousand when you land." Hokee could practically hear the man choking on the phone.

"That sounds like we can do some business. We should be there in about eight hours. I'll call you with an update a few minutes before we land. Oh, and could you have the fuel truck standing by? We don't want to overstay our welcome. Thank you." Hokee disconnected the call.

Let the bastard sweat. Hokee would do his own sweating in the next few hours. That Shabib would make his plans to kill Captain Largo was a given as soon as he could arrange for it to happen. The question remained, would he kill the pilots and steal the plane? Hell, do Zebras have spots? Of course, they would kill the pilots and steal the plane. The aircraft was worth upwards of sixty-five million dollars. That plus what he could sell the girls for once, they had satisfied his lusts,

Now Hokee had to do some serious planning. Should he tell Captain Hobbs what he to expect from their welcoming committee? He couldn't see that he had any choice. To pull this off, he would need the help of everyone on board, including the lovely Heather.

Hopefully, he wouldn't get them all killed. Hokee wondered if Mauritania had an airforce with fighter planes. That would be good to know before getting into action.

CHAPTER SIXTEEN

With several hours to go before getting close enough for Captain Hobbs to contact the control tower at Nouakchott, Hokee asked Heather for another drink. He only wanted scotch straight up with a glass of water. "Oh, and ask Richard to come back when he has a chance, and you come here as well." Heather looked at him questioningly but went for his scotch and to talk with the captain.

Heather came with his drink and told him that Richard would be back in a couple of minutes. He was changing altitudes to ride the jet stream and conserve fuel.

"Hokee, you wanted to see me?" The captain asked as he settled in a chair next to Heather.

"Yes, thanks for coming so quickly. I want to talk with both of you, and the cockpit would be a little crowded." Hokee sounded weary, like a boxer who had gone ten rounds with a worthy opponent.

"What's on your mind, Hokee?" Richard sensed the internal struggle Hokee was having.

"I talked with Shabib Ghulam a few minutes ago. I'm afraid we might face a difficult time in Mauritania. We need to think ahead and plan for any contingency that might arise." Hokee spoke with reluctance, as he didn't want to share the bad news.

"Remind me Hokee, who is Shabib Ghulam? I know you asked me to inform the tower about him, but who is he?"

"Ghulam is the principal human trafficker in Mauritania and purchased the Indian children kidnapped from the Fort Hall Reservation. I gather he is one of the wealthiest men in the country and owns practically every politician with any power. I believe he intends to kill everyone on board and steal this plane. So we need to devise a plan to prevent that from happening."

"Well, hell, partner, I'd say that might be a little problem." Richard had a relaxed smile and steady voice when he spoke, like he was Chuck Yeager about to break the sound barrier.

Hokee continued explaining the situation, "He thinks we have two Indian girls onboard, the last two purchased by his cousin Teeten. I told him the female kidnapper killed Teeten when he tried to rape her. Believable, as Teeten did lust for the Gypsy beauty, although Ghulam may have suspicions about my version of what happened. For instance, I have Teeten's phone, and no one on Teeten's crew bothered to call Ghulam."

Heather was looking worried and a little scared. This was not what she signed up for when asked to be the hostess for the handsome investigator. Instead, she had visions of maybe a little romance with Idaho's most famous P I. It was not getting killed by Arabs in some God-forsaken country in Africa. That was not on her agenda.

Continuing with the Yeager impersonation, Richard asked, "what is this Ghulam person expecting when we land?"

"I told him I wanted one hundred thousand dollars for the two young girls, both exquisite. I understand that Ghulam and men like him enjoy deflowering beautiful young virgins. Either sex. I expect him to want to board the plane with his bodyguards, kill us, take the girls, and steal the plane. Mauritania is the smuggling capital of the world, and getting an American-owned private jet like this would be a real steal, so to speak. Sorry, I couldn't help saying it that way. I rarely get to double up on my words."

"Jesus, God, and Mother Mary. I thought maybe there would be some real trouble when we landed. Hell, Hokee, you make it sound like a Sunday walk in Central Park with a policeman standing around about every fifteen or twenty yards." Sarcasm seemed to fit Richard's assumed persona perfectly. "What are we going to do, Hokee?" Heather asked with a worried look. "We surely aren't landing, are we? And we don't have any Indian girls onboard." Heather's fear made her tremble like a leaf shaking in a stiff wind. Taking one of Heather's hands to calm the frightened young lady, Hokee said, "Heather, there is no need to be frightened. I will let nothing bad happen to you, Okay? So help Captain Hobbs and me figure out a plan so we all escape uninjured."

Hokee's calm voice and reassuring grip on her hand seemed to help relax the lady.

Looking back at Richard, Hokee asked, "how much fuel will we have left when we reach Mauritania, Captain? I asked you to have a fuel truck standing by and mentioned it to Ghulam, but that may not be a good idea." Richard thought for only a couple of seconds before responding, "at our current speed and with a tailwind we just picked up, we should be good for another thirty-five hundred nautical miles.

"So," Hokee conjectured, "we could easily make, say, Paris or somewhere in Spain without getting more fuel in Nouakchott?

"Spain would be easy," Richard responded, "and Paris most likely, unless we run into some unfortunate weather. I can check and see what the forecast is if you would like. Morocco is also possible if we need to pick up some gas." "Yes, please do when you get a chance," Hokee said. "I don't trust what the fuel truck in Nouakchott might contain. If we don't need refueling, this simplifies our problems. I don't know for sure where we will go from Mauritania. Europe is a guess, but it could be somewhere in the near east, perhaps Saudi Arabia. In that case, we might want to visit Morocco to refill. It's out of the way, but I don't trust Egypt. My last visit there didn't end well."

Both Heather and Richard looked at Hokee for an explanation, but he didn't offer one. Instead, he explained his reasoning. "I won't know where Ghulam sold the Indian children until he is questioned. There could be over one stop."

In a dry voice without emotion, Richard commented, "this is the questioning you want to take place outside of the airplane?" Although spoken like a comment, it was more of a question.

"Well, I'm primarily thinking about Heather. I ask questions in unpleasant ways if people are hesitant to answer. It saves time and energy. Outside would be preferable if we can think of a way to make that happen." "Damn, Hokee, I can't think of anything right now. Hopefully, something will occur to me before we land."

Hokee looked at Heather, but her face was blank, except for the residual fear in the corner of her eyes. "Well, let's see how it plays out," Hokee said. "When we land, stop at the end of the runway, ready to take off in a hurry if necessary."

"The tower will want me to taxi the plane back to the terminal. What do I say to keep them from bringing in the troops?" Richard seemed to have second thoughts about landing in Mauritania.

"How on earth do you even talk to the tower, Richard? Heather asked in a frightened voice. "You don't speak whatever they use for a language in this hellhole."

Looking at Hokee to see if it was okay to answer, Richard said, "air control towers all over the world speak English, Heather. Otherwise, it would be pandemonium. The tower could not direct air traffic if every captain spoke in their native tongue."

"Oh," Heather breathed softly. "I guess that makes sense."

Looking at Richard to ensure they were on the same wavelength, Hokee answered his question. "Tell the tower we only plan on staying a few minutes and don't have the time to taxi both ways." Hokee couldn't suppress a grin, thinking about how the tower in Mauritania would respond to this unusual answer.

The grin faded as Hokee thought about what might lie ahead. Whatever the man was, Shabib Ghulam could not be taken lightly.

CHAPTER SEVENTEEN

The Nouakchott Airport is just over fifteen miles (25 km) from downtown Nouakchott. The terminal is located east of the runway, on the desert side, to keep the sand away from the airplanes. Planes land from the south into the prevailing north winds. Richard landed as instructed by the tower but immediately taxied the G650 back to the runway's south end, ready for instant takeoff. Per his earlier instruction, Richard informed the tower that they were here for a brief time and were only waiting for Shabib Ghulam to make a brief appearance.

Still in his plush coach seat, Hokee could hear Richard talking to an angry tower control officer when Teeten's phone rang. It could only be Ghulam asking what they were doing.

"Hello." Hokee didn't elaborate on his greeting.

"Largo, what in God's holy name are you doing on the runway? Get back here to the terminal."

"Oh, is this you, Ghulam? And how is your day going?" Hokee wanted the ringmaster to be upset and off his game.

"Look, Yankee dog. If you want your money, have the pilot taxi back to the terminal." You could hear the snarl in his voice. He was not used to anyone defying his wishes.

"Look, you yellow bastard. If you want these two choice girls, you must drive out here and get them." Hokee figured that if Ghulam could not show respect, there was no reason for him to show any.

"The runway is for airplanes, you ignorant peasant. The tower will not allow civilian traffic out there." He sounded truly and totally pissed.

"Oh, come now, your majesty. It is my understanding you own Mauritania, lock, stock, and pig shit." Hokee knew he was playing a dangerous game, but given the circumstances, it was the only card he could play.

"All right, you fucker, I'll be right there. Open the damn door." Apparently, Ghulam could not speak without some derogatory expletive.

Tucking the silenced 22 behind his back, Hokee stuffed the Colt 45 inside his belt in front; then he had Heather open the door and go in the back, out of sight.

It took almost ten minutes before a white Mercedes luxury sedan carrying Ghulam and his goons came to a screeching stop five feet from the plane's stairs. Ghulam and four tough-looking, dark-skinned men exited the car. The men were not carrying weapons in their hands, but they all wore jackets in the hot desert, open in the front. Guns in shoulder holsters were almost guaranteed.

Standing at the foot of the stairs, Ghulam shouted, although Hokee was only fifteen feet away, standing in the open doorway. "Where's the girls, Yankee?" At least he didn't call Hokee a Yankee dog.

"Let me see the hundred grand Ghulam, and I'll give you the girls." Hokee could see the wheels turning in the smuggler's head. *So are there people inside with guns? If we kill this Yankee pig, will others shoot back? And I'm standing here in the front. Shit!*

"I didn't bring the money here. I thought we would make the exchange downtown." You haven't seen our beautiful downtown area by the bank. So bring the girls, and we'll make the exchange in town where it's cool, and we can have a drink together."

"I don't think so, Ghulam. The deal was, you bring the money, and we'll give you the girls." No money, no girls. Besides, there isn't room in your car for me, the two girls, and your bodyguards." Hokee could tell the white, black man was not expecting any pushback. People never refused his requests.

"Look, I didn't bring the money here. I'll have to go get it. You can ride with me, and we'll have that drink. Some of my men can stay here and guard the plane." Desperation was showing. It was all he could do not to order his men to shoot this Yankee pig. He would give the order if he weren't in the direct line of fire from anyone who might be behind the door.

"I'll go with you downtown to collect the money and have that refreshing cool drink. But your men will ride back to town with us. The girls will stay here on the plane until we return."

"But you can't leave your airplane sitting on the runway. Have your pilot taxi back to the gates, and I'll have two of my men stay behind to prevent anyone from causing your pilot problems. The tower is already not pleased with your disobedience to their orders."

"Ghulam, I know you are a big man here in Mauritania, and you can arrange for anything you want to happen. Call the tower and tell them to leave the plane alone. It's fine right here. Now I'll go with you and your men to collect the money, but the plane and the girls stay here until we return. If you don't like that deal, then ride off with your men, and we will take off with the girls." Ghulam was seething, but his hand had been called. It was time to put up or shut up.

Ghulam thought for a couple of seconds. *Okay, we take the Yankee pig with us. Kill him in the desert, then come back and park in front of the plane so the pilot cannot fly off. We'll order the pilots out with the girls, then take the girls and kill the pilot out in the desert with the other pig.* "Alright, Yankee, you win. Come on down, and we'll drive into town, get your money, and have that drink."

"Sure, Ghulam. Wait just one minute while I talk with my pilot." Hokee backed away from the door so they couldn't see the pistol behind his back. Then, going over to Richard, he said, "look, Captain. I know this isn't what we planned, but I have a nasty feeling about these guys and what they might be planning. Look at your watch. If I am not back in fifteen minutes, take off and fly to Casablanca. Wait there for me. It might be a long wait. Maybe a week or more, but wait for two weeks. I'll call if possible. If not, then fly home. Please don't fret about me. I'm a survivor."

"Hell, Hokee, I can't leave you here in Mauritania. Mr. Olson will have my balls if I don't come home with you." Richard was distraught, and Howard Jensen, the copilot, was about to throw a fit.

"Look, guys. I can't take care of business here at the airport in front of God knows how many people, and those in the tower probably have binoculars on this plane. So please do as I have requested. I know it will be hard if you have to leave me behind, but fifteen minutes is probably all the time the tower will give you before bringing in the airport guards and security. Ghulam may not be able to order otherwise. I'll find some way to reach Morocco. Okay?"

The two pilots looked at each other, then at a smiling Hokee Wolf. His smile disarmed any further rebuttal, and he did not seem distressed. "Okay, Hokee," Richard complained, "fifteen minutes, and get your ass back here." "I'm damn well going to try. Otherwise, keep a bottle of scotch ready for me in Casa Blanca. See ya."

Hokee went down the short stairway to join Ghulam and his goons, and no one offered to shake hands as Ghulam motioned for Hokee to climb into the front seat. Hokee climbed into the right rear seat by the door, brushing off the man's hands. His Colt 45 was visible to Ghulam and the other men. "You don't need your cannon Yankee, we're all friends here, and I'm afraid you won't be able to take your weapon into the bar." Ghulam had a tight smile that never reached his eyes.

"Well, I'll tell you what, Ghulam, when your men take out their guns and stow them in the trunk, I'll place my gun right alongside theirs." Hokee returned the tight smile.

Ghulam clapped his hands and ordered his men to disarm and put their weapons into the trunk. One man went around to the driver's side door to open the trunk as each man pulled a 9 MM Ruger automatic from inside their jackets, carefully laying them inside the Mercedes trunk. "Okay, Yankee, your turn," Ghulam cheerfully announced. Hokee climbed back out carefully to not turn his back on anyone as he pulled the Colt from his waistband and laid it next to the Rutgers. He then returned to his seat by the right rear door.

One man sat in the driver's seat and started the car, driving off the runway and out of the airport. Ghulam sat on the far left rear seat by the other back door with one man between him and Hokee. That put three big men crowded in the front seat with no room to spare.

"It will only take about twenty minutes to reach our bank, Yankee," Ghulam suggested." " Would you like to have our drink before or after getting the money?" Although the question sounded sincere, it was far too casual under the circumstances. Hokee expected one or more of the men had stashed a second gun under the front seat or glove box or might even have a hidden ankle holster.

"How about having that drink first, Ghulam? I'm thirsty in all this desert heat.

"Okay, Yankee, we'll drink first." Ghulam sounded almost cheerful as Hokee felt the man between him and Ghulam shift a little. Like he was preparing to ram Hokee to prevent him from moving. They had driven about five miles from the airport. The road was surrounded by desert with nothing but reddish-brown sand in all directions when they made their move. In this desolate region, the man beside him jammed his elbow into Hokee's side as the man in the seat in front of Hokee grabbed a gun from under the seat, turning around to shoot the Yankee pig in the head. "Now you die, Yankee," Ghulam gloated as the gun swung about, pointing towards Hokee.

CHAPTER EIGHTEEN

Hokee was ready when they made their move. As the man next to him started the elbow jab to his side, Hokee leaned forward minimizing the blow while pulling the 22 from behind his back. In blinding speed, he shot the man in front before he could shoot him. Quickly turning the 22, he shot the man next to him with the jabbing elbow, and then, shot the man in the front seat next to the driver. This left Ghulam and the driver as the only smugglers left alive. Pointing the gun at Ghulam's head, he ordered the driver to stop the car. The total elapsed time was less than two seconds.

"Do as he demanded," screamed the horrified trafficker in human flesh. Although a tough man with plenty of killings in his past, he had never been seriously threatened before, and he found the experience chilling. Seeing three of his men shot by the Indian in less than a second had a frightening effect on the man used to killing. Only in the past, he and his men did the killing. The car stopped on the road, and then Hokee calmly shot the driver in the head before ordering Ghulam out of the car with his hands in the air. Then things went downhill as Ghulam took off running into the desert.

Hokee had to get out of the car and, standing on the bottom door frame, rested his hands on the Mercedes roof before shooting at the running man. Hokee aimed for his legs, not center mass; he didn't want to kill Ghulam, at least not yet. Still, hitting a running man in the legs from a distance is difficult, and it took three shots before shooting him in the left knee, tumbling the running man into the burning sand. Hokee ran around the car, pulling the driver out of his seat, then pulling the car off the road. He grabbed the driver, dragged him to the vehicle, and stuffed him in the trunk after retrieving his Colt 45. The Rutgers were tempting, but he didn't think he would need that much firepower, a decision he would later regret.

Ghulam had regained his feet and was hobbling away at a decent clip, forcing Hokee to run to catch up with the man. When Hokee drew near enough to order Ghulam to stop, they were almost two hundred yards from the highway. In the distance, Hokee could hear the wheep, wheep of a police siren coming down the road from the direction of Nouakchott in response to a phone call Ghulam probably made while running for his life. There was a run-off ditch from the infrequent rainstorms close to where Ghulam stopped, so without pausing in his stride, Hokee grabbed the Colt 45 and hit the man on the back of his head, tumbling him into the ditch. Hokee ducked down beside Ghulam before peeking around to see if anyone had seen the pair running across the desert. Seeing no one, he ducked back below the ditch's rim, then tore Ghulam's shirt from his body. Ripping the shirt into strips, he first gagged Ghulam, then bound his hands and feet, pulling his arms up behind his body and typing them to his ankles. Ghulam looked like a trussed-up turkey ready for the oven.

Hokee and his captive were not visible from the road, and unless someone was super diligent, it was unlikely their hiding place would be discovered. The desert was hot, almost a hundred degrees Fahrenheit, and the sand felt like coal from a cooking fire. Ghulam came alive, so Hokee hit him in the head again to prevent him from making any sound that might carry over the blistering sand that looked like dried blood. The damn police took forever, and then another police car arrived, followed by an ambulance. The police and ambulance crew loaded the four bodies into the ambulance, being none too gentle. They were also getting hot standing around in the sun, so soon after loading the bodies into the ambulance, the officers took one long look out into the surrounding desert before one officer got behind the wheel of the Mercedes, and all the vehicles left for Nouakchott, leaving Hokee stranded in the burning sun with an unconscious man at his feet.

Hokee had planned on driving the Mercedes back to the airport, and if he missed the plane, he would go up the coast towards Morocco. That was now not going to happen. Before long, the G650 could be seen lifting into the sky before disappearing to the north. *SHIT!*

Hokee tore off one of Ghulam's shoes, which he used as a shovel to scoop away sand until he reached a place ten inches deep with a cool spot to plant his ass. He then waited for Ghulam to wake up from his second nap. He waited for Ghulam to come fully awake before placing one of his size ten black boots on the body and pushing the man onto his side so he could see Hokee.

"Alright, Ghulam, this Yankee pig has some questions. Are you willing to talk?"

Ghulam squirmed about, testing his bound hands and feet before mumbling into his gag. "Just nod your head if you will talk. Otherwise, I'll leave you and walk back to the airport." There was no way for Ghulam to know that the plane had already left Nouakchott Airport. Instead, the prisoner nodded his head up and down vigorously.

Hokee pulled the knife from behind his neck and cut the gag. He didn't want to get any closer to the criminal than necessary.

"You will die, you Yankee pig, you camel dung. Do you have any idea how much trouble you are in?" Ghulam was practically frothing at the mouth, while Hokee could barely work up a decent spit. Hokee supposed Ghulam's mouth moisture resulted from fear.

In a conversational tone, like he was ordering a hamburger from Jake's back in Pocatello, Hokee responded, "you seem to have neglected the rules, Ghulam. I am the one asking questions, and you are the one who will answer. Or not. I can still tie up your yapper and leave you in the burning sand. By the way, it's much cooler if you dig down a foot or so. Did you know that? You probably do, seeing as how you live out here in this hot, freaking blood-red sand. Although it is my guess, and this is just a guess, mind you, that this is the longest spell you have spent in this heat, probably since you started selling young children."

Ghulam yelled, then fell silent. After a moment, he asked, "what are your questions, Yankee?"

"Who did you sell the Indian children to that you bought from your cousin Teeten in Houston? That is my only question. Answer that, and you are free."

Ghulam would have laughed if his knee wasn't giving him so much pain. "Sure, Yankee, you untie me and walk away after I tell you what you want to know. Please, I am not that stupid."

"No, I won't untie you and just walk away. But I will walk away. I figure you will last one or two more days in this sun. But, of course, it won't be pleasant, unlike your million-dollar villa back in town. Or I could set you free with a bullet to your head. Quick and painless, or so I believe. I've only been shot in the shoulder myself, and it probably felt much like your knee is feeling about now."

"So Yankee, let me get this straight. If I talk, you will kill me quickly. If I don't answer your questions, you leave me to die in the desert. So, are those my only options?" Even though the heat was enough to fry eggs on the hood of a car, Ghulam was shivering, resulting from the shock of being shot but possibly also from fear.

"Yes, that's about it. Of course, I can return to Nouakchott and look up some of your other crew members. I'm pretty sure I can get one of them to talk. What do you think?"

"Listen, untie me, and I'll tell you everything you want to know. So please, just untie me." His voice was cracking, like maybe he was on the verge of tears,

"That isn't how this works, Ghulam. Answer my question, and I may show you some leniency." Hokee still had a conversational tone to his voice, but his mouth was getting damn dry, and swallowing was difficult.

"I ain't telling you shit, Yankee. Go ahead, leave me here to die." Instead, Hokee brought out the 22 and shot his other knee before putting a bullet in an elbow, followed by another to his opposite shoulder.

"Okay, I guess you ain't going anyplace now. And you are too far away to call for help. I hope you last at least one more day. It seems a shame to let someone with your background die after suffering only a few hours. So long, jerk."

Hokee started walking away and got about ten yards before Ghulam called him back. "I sold all the Indian kids to Madame Brezing in Paris. I had other buyers, but she offered the top price and paid for their shipping."

"How many Indian children did you sell to her, Ghulam? I want the exact number." A stern command replaced the friendly conversational tone.

"I think it was eleven. Yeah, eleven. I'm sure. Six boys and five girls." A relieved Ghulam was moaning in pain when Hokee put him out of his misery. Although it was doubtful that the master criminal could escape this burning desert tied up with four 22 Magnum hollow points in his body, but why take a chance? And besides, he had to keep his promise to end this human trafficking ring, at least put a severe kink in the works. Several lower-tier men were waiting to take over Ghulam's business as soon as they got rid of the man.

Hokee thought about walking towards Nouakchott; according to the map in his head, it was about ten miles away. However, a man standing upright in the flat desert is visible for several miles, and walking in the heat with the sun baking his body through the dark clothes he was wearing did not seem like the wisest choice. Besides, he had just killed perhaps the wealthiest man in Mauritania, which would undoubtedly trigger a massive search. Hokee hoped the police would assume Ghulam had been abducted and driven off in another vehicle.

It didn't take long in the heat for the corpse to smell, so grabbing Ghulam's shoe, Hokee crawled a few yards away and dug another pit in the sand for his body. Within a few minutes, a caravan drove up and down the highway, looking for a sign showing what had happened to Ghulam. Several vehicles stopped near where Hokee had parked the car off the road, with four dead bodies bleeding all over the interior. Several men got out and walked along the roadside, looking for some sign. Fortunately, the sand was soft and held no footprints leading into the desert. Hokee felt good about his chances of getting away when a shadow crossed the desert, not five feet from where he was lying in the ditch he had dug. Then, glancing up in the

sky, he saw several giant Egyptian vultures with white breasts circling about two hundred feet in the air. Looking back on the highway, it didn't appear as though the birds had attracted anyone's attention yet, although that could change any second. Hokee assumed his presence near the body kept the birds away for the moment, but that may not last very long. He only hoped that the highway searchers would leave before spotting the birds. The birds were still reasonably high in the sky and had gone undetected by those men on the roadside. If those men spotted the birds, would they be curious about what had attracted their attention? Since they were looking for some clue about their missing countryman, it was a relatively safe bet that someone would trek over to see what carrion interested the vultures

Hokee almost smiled. Stuck in a hot desert with no water, in a country whose language he couldn't speak, two thousand miles from a friendly face, and facing men who would kill him on sight given a chance, his chances for survival didn't look appealing. His near smile resulted from a line he remembered from an old Western movie; '*this sure feels like Indian country.*' Maybe you had to be half-Indian to appreciate the humor. When a hostile environment surrounds you, it is called Indian country. Perhaps it was not a sterling episode in America's history or culture and not kind to the Indians, but it sure as hell wasn't Mauritania. Now that he was here, it felt like a hellhole. If he could only last until he found some water, if those damn birds didn't bring on the bad guys, and if he could figure out a way out of this mess. Then it was only about two thousand miles by road to Casablanca. How in the hell was he going to get there in two weeks?

The sun was burning through his clothes; his mouth was drier than Saraha; oh, that's right, he was in the damned Saraha, and that was when the fucking vultures started screeching.

CHAPTER NINETEEN

All six floors of the mansion at 999 Bd Saint Germain were lit with bright lights, looking almost like the house of a fairy princess. Parked on the street outside were three Rolls Royce's, a Joyce Karina Pin, two Mercedes Benz limousines, and the newest luxury Lincoln limo, the drivers all studiously ignoring each other. Inside the magnificent marble main hall, resplendent in black silk tuxedos with diamond-studded cumber bands, sat the rich and pampered princes, drinking Dom Perignon P3 Plenitude Brut Rose, which sells for $1,909 a bottle if you can find it. A stringed quartet softly playing Mozart's Regina Mas performed behind a silk Chinese room divider framed in polished teak. Holding court in a high-winged back chair covered in padded gold velvet tucked with bright gold buttons sat madam Belle Brezing. The effect was that of a queen sitting on her throne.

Madam Brezing was smoking a cigarette held by a solid gold cigarette holder a foot long. A large black man wearing a white jacket with tails over dark gray pants and a black bow tie stood by her side, holding a carved jade ashtray. By the side of her throne sat a white marble end table with inlaid gold filigree upon which a Riedel Crystal wine glass was holding something red and expensive.

The inlaid parquet floors were covered with only the most expensive Egyptian hand-woven rugs with the moon and stars woven into a blue sky background. Overhead hung brilliant chandeliers from Murano beneath a golden dome with inlaid twinkling lights resembling stars. To say you were in the lap of luxury would be an understatement.

As if summoned by some unseen signal, two courtesans of the most exquisite beauty appeared standing by two large Tiffany double doors featuring inlaid, beveled cut glass. Madam Brezing handed her cigarette to the black servant at her side and spoke in a clear voice, benefitting from hours of lessons. Her voice had a rich musical quality, giving her the persona of someone you want for a friend.

"Gentlemen, if I may have your attention, it is time to begin our evening sales. You all know the rules, but in case they may have slipped your mind given all the lovely distractions, let me state them again briefly."

She had the attention of every man drinking her expensive champagne. "Tonight, we have twenty beautiful young subjects from which you can choose. You may each purchase only one. After all, I must save some for my other customers."

Here madam Brezing allowed herself a small chuckle repeated by the seven male buyers.

"You will be allowed five minutes to inspect the offerings before we begin the sales. Once you find a subject to your liking, show your preference, and I will quote a price. If the price is satisfactory, that subject will no longer be available to another buyer. With our great selection for you tonight, I am confident that you should have no trouble finding someone to match your desires."

Madam Brezing stopped to take a drink from her wineglass; conducting these sales is a thirsty business.

"Before I have the subjects brought in for your inspection, I must remind you that once everyone has made their choice, the subjects will be returned to their rooms, where we will give them their traditional evening drink. This will put them to sleep quickly, so there will be no fuss when you take possession. No one wants a disturbance here at Saint Germain. You may continue drinking while waiting, which should only be another ten

minutes. Our staff will assist you in taking possession of your purchase. Are there questions?"

Questions were not expected; the invitation was merely a formality.

Waving her hand as though signaling a friend, the two courtesans opened the double Tiffany doors and marched in twenty young children ages five to fourteen, shepherded by several other beautiful ladies of the night. The children were all wearing custom-made red jumpsuits and appeared slightly drugged.

As the children entered the room, madam Brezing commented, "the children have all been given small valium tablets to ease their fears. I'm sure you appreciate the precaution."

As expected, each child was beautiful. Besides the eleven Indian children from the Fort Hall Reservation, there were two Chinese kids about ten years old, a boy and a girl, unrelated. In addition, there was a beautiful fourteen-year-old black girl displaying a well-developed figure. Three female children from the Philippines or some other South Pacific island and two blond boys about eight who looked Swedish rounded out the twenty subjects.

The buyers were practically drooling as they looked at the display of children. They had expected Madam Brezing to provide them with an excellent collection from which to make their choice, but she had surpassed their wildest desires. Each man wanted to purchase two or three kids and could afford the tariff, but they could choose only one.

One by one, seven children were sold. Two young boys from the Fort Hall Reservation were among those sold. The average purchase price was one million two hundred thousand. Madam Brezing could afford the expensive champagne.

CHAPTER TWENTY

Focused on the men searching the highway for clues, Hokee had ignored the birds until their high-pitched cawing made him look up at the sky. It occurred to him that the vulture's screeching was trying to drive him away from their meal. Four birds were in the air, now circling only about fifty feet above Ghulam's corpse. Then, glancing back at the highway two hundred yards away, Hokee saw the men watching the birds, curious about what had attracted their attention. It appeared as though the men were discussing the birds, trying to decide whether it was worth a trip across the hot sands to investigate. Both he and the birds were far enough away from the road to make it unlikely that Ghulam's body was the vulture's main attraction. Still, if someone came to investigate, what could he do? Hokee had decided that they would let it pass when one short man in a police uniform began trekking across the burning sands to see what had attracted the bird's attention.

Oh shit! Now what, Tonto? Hokee was in a shallow wash that fed the infrequent rains into the ditch where he had placed Ghulam's body. With no other option, he began crawling along the wash away from the circling birds. The only factor in his favor was the soft sand; it left no trace of his passage. The short policeman trudged slowly across the soft desert sands in

the heat, allowing Hokee several minutes to put almost another hundred yards between himself and the body. The birds were now constantly screeching as the officer came close to their dinner. Hokee had his head down, crawling on his elbows and knees when he heard the shot, which nearly caused him to rise and investigate.

The police officer had fired his gun into the air, attracting the attention of those men still on the highway. Hokee took a quick glance above the rim of the wash he had crawled along to see several men coming towards the short officer who had discovered Ghulam's body. Seeing no alternative, Hokee began scooping away the sand at the bottom of his escape path, creating a place to hide his body. Before the highwaymen had assembled around Ghulam's corpse, Hokee had buried himself under the sand, leaving only his eyes and nose uncovered. At the last instant, he pulled a small creosote plant to cover his face before digging his arm and hand back under the sand. He was invisible unless someone stood practically on top of his hiding spot.

The police came, and one man returned to their vehicles on the road to radio for an amblance. There was no cell phone service out here in the middle of nowhere. While waiting, the men scoured the area, looking for evidence. They walked almost halfway to Hokee's hiding spot but saw nothing of interest; they returned to the body, standing some distance away from the smelling corpse. To further enhance Hokee's predicament, the ambulance brought water to the thirsty officers on site. After dark, Ghulam's body was removed, and everyone left the desert. The police had searched the area, looking for evidence explaining how the riddled body came to be so far from the highway, but ultimately they gave up the search as the sun dropped below the horizon. Hokee waited until it was completely dark before getting up from his shallow grave. Thirsty, hungry, tired, and alone in the now-cooling desert, Hokee felt like he could go no further. Still, giving up was not an option.

First, he undressed, shaking the sand out of his clothing. Then, satisfied that no sand remained to scratch his skin, Hokee pulled a pair of moccasins from his back pocket. He debated whether to dump his cowboy boots but cut the hem from his shirt, making a string he used to tie the boots around his neck. Walking in the sand was easier in moccasins, but not knowing how far he would have to walk, it seemed prudent to keep the boots.

Now what? Across the highway, the Atlantic Ocean was less than five miles to the west. So while it would be cooler along the ocean tomorrow, it didn't promise any water he could drink, which was his immediate priority. The glow of Nouakchott's light could be seen across the desert in the south, maybe five or ten miles away. But that seemed like a risky alternative. The news of Ghulam's death would be all over the city by now, and people would be wary of strangers. Especially a tall, dark man coming out of the desert from the direction in which the body had been discovered. There was nothing to the east except more desert, which left the north, towards the airport.

How far had they driven before Ghulam and his thugs decided to kill him? It couldn't have been over seven or eight miles, maybe only five, but why couldn't he see the lights from the airport? And why are no planes taking off and landing? Was he confused about directions? Yes, he was delirious; excessive thirst will do that, and he suffered mild dementia from heat exposure; still, there should be lights.

Well, hell, he should be able to find a drink at the airport. So, with nothing else to do, he started walking north. The only way he could survive this ordeal was to get outside of his body, which he did. A shaman learns how to live in his head, and Hokee developed this ability years ago during his vision quest when he discovered the underground river by his house. Then, like now, he was dying of thirst and hunger, and like now, he was weak and tired and hallucinating.

Slowly Hokee shuffled across the now-cooling sands. His body was on auto-pilot as his mind searched for a way out of this living hell. He was a half-mile from the airport before he noticed the lights. It took him a moment to get his sluggish mind to focus before realizing that Mauritania was not a hotbed for airline flights. Who in their right mind would want to visit this shit hole? Maybe there were no planes taking off and landing, but there had to be water somewhere around the airport.

That thought encouraged him, helping to revive his sagging spirits. Even a shaman can only push the body so far before it collapses. Coming to the airport from the desert, Hokee first spotted some private airplane hangars. He had to be careful to avoid being seen, but no one seemed to be around. Hokee tried the door to see if it was locked, starting with the first hanger he came across. He didn't want to break in if he could find an unlocked hangar. He got lucky on his fourth try. It was a small hanger suitable for a Piper Cub, but it had a restroom with running water. Heaven on earth for a man dying of thirst.

Cupping his hands, Hokee slowly slurped water into his parched mouth. Feeling a little revived, Hokee looked around the hanger and found a small bucket that might have once held some solvent or other cleaning liquid. Undressing, Hokee filled the pail from the sink and began dumping water over his body, washing off the sweat, grim, and fear. The hanger still held the day's heat, so Hokee sat in the airplane to dry off.

So okay, he found water, replenished the liquid his body had lost, and had a bath of sorts. Then, feeling revived, it was time to move on to his next step. Which was what?

Well, he was at an airport. Surely someone must have left their car in long-term parking. If he could find the right vehicle, he might escape this mess. Food was out of the question. It was too bad he couldn't recall Grant's airplane with the sexy hostess and her cooking. Leaving the hangar the way it was when he arrived, arrived, Hokee flitted from shadow to shadow towards the parking lot.

The parking lot was not well-lit, allowing Hokee to wander around looking for a vehicle he could steal. Security appeared to be one small truck with a man who periodically drove around the airport and parking lot, and from Hokee's view, the driver/guard was half asleep. Apparently, the parking lot didn't pay enough to warrant a fence or a ticket booth. At least Hokee couldn't see one as he searched for a car. Modern cars with all their electronic ignition crap and keyless start buttons were beyond Hokee's expertise. He needed an older car before all the modern safety features. There were roughly one hundred cars in the entire lot, and almost none he recognized. Most appeared to be newer models, but across the lot, covered in sand, was a large black four-door sedan that looked abandoned. Creeping closer, he determined it was a 1959 Facel Vega Excellence. A French car left over from when the French ruled Mauritania. It was a luxury sedan, maybe belonging to the Ambassador or other high-ranking diplomat. Why it was still parked here was a mystery.

Would it even start? How long had it been sitting? It was covered with sand, but many vehicles in the lot were covered with sand. And, given the constant winds, it didn't take many days to gain a heavy coat. Hokee tried the driver's door, which was fortunately unlocked. Then, when he opened the door, the interior light came on, so Hokee quickly climbed in and shut the door, killing the light. Hopefully, the roving security guard didn't notice the sudden light flare from the parking lot. Glancing around, the patrol vehicle was nowhere to be seen. First, he found some water. Now an unlocked car. Maybe his luck was changing.

There was barely enough light for Hokee to see that the car's interior was trashed. The once expensive leather seats were cracked with stuffing spilling out. During the day, the sun must have baked the car's interior with ungodly heat. The dashboard appeared warped, and nothing remained of the floor mats, only bare metal. The rubber pads on the clutch and brake pedals were long gone, along with the one on the gas pedal. The once expensive luxury car was wasted, but would it run, and could he get it started? Whoever parked the car had left the keys dangling from the metal sun visor, the cloth covering gone along with the rubber from the foot pedals. Obviously, the car's owner was not concerned with anyone stealing the relic. Who would settle for an ancient beat-up relic with many newer models in the parking lot?

Holding his breath, Hokee put the key into the ignition switch and turned it, starting the engine. The engine cranked over slowly, and Hokee almost gave up hope before the engine coughed to life with a soft rumble. Pushing the seat back to accommodate his long legs, Hokee put the car in gear and drove out of the parking lot, leaving the lights off. There was no sense in taking a chance that the security guard would notice a car leaving the parking lot. Once on the highway heading north towards Casablanca, Hokee fumbled for the light switch, turning on the headlights. The only disappointment was discovering the fuel gauge registered less than half a tank.

It was twelve hundred miles to Casablanca, and Hokee had less than half a tank of fuel. Driving a stolen car with no passport and unable to speak the local language, how far could he travel before running into another problem? At least the car ran smoothly, and he wasn't walking. Besides a rumbling stomach, he felt optimistic about his chances of surviving a few more hours. He might not have been so confident if he knew what was ahead.

CHAPTER TWENTY-ONE

Two hours into his journey, Hokee was almost falling asleep when he decided to find a spot to pull off the road and grab a few minutes rest. He had passed only one car coming from the opposite direction during the entire two hours he had been driving. It didn't appear as though this was a popular travel route. Still, it didn't pay to take any chances, so Hokee looked for someplace where he could park off the road unseen for a brief spell where headlights from another car would serve as a warning. The road was flat and straight, allowing a person to see approaching headlights several miles away. Then, finding a wide shoulder, he pulled off the road and closed his eyes. Before long, the rising sun in the east aroused him from a deep slumber. The previous day's traumatic events had taken a toll on his body, which needed rest. Fortunately, there had been no traffic to disturb his sleep.

Hokee got out of the car and stretched before doing a sun salute to reinvigorate his body and soul. Damn, but he could use a nice cup of hot coffee, a pound of bacon, a stack of hotcakes, and some fresh orange juice. Back in the car, twenty-five minutes later, still fantasizing about a breakfast he would not be eating, he noticed some obstruction across the road about a mile ahead. Getting closer, there appeared to be a truck parked diagonally across the highway, making it impossible to pass without going into the sand and possibly getting stuck. Still closer, he could see six men standing across the road holding automatic rifles. They didn't appear to be the police, and the vehicle was not a police car. The men were not in a recognizable uniform, which meant they were not in the military. That indicated the men were road bandits. Racking a shell into the chamber of his Colt 45, Hokee laid the gun in his lap as he coasted to a stop. Rolling down the driver's window, he was about to offer a greeting when the man on his side started shouting in an unfamiliar language, gesturing for Hokee to get out of the vehicle. Hokee lifted the gun from his lap and shot the man in the head without hesitation. Then all hell broke loose.

Five automatic weapons began shooting into the car, shattering every window while making an ungodly racket. Fortunately, that old French automobile had thick metal sides and interior door panels stopping their bullets from reaching Hokee, who ducked below the window sills. When the firing stopped, and he could hear the men replacing the clips on their weapons, Hokee shook off the glass fragments from his body and, raising, shot two more bandits in the head through the now missing windshield. Three down, and three to go, except now he was dangerously low on ammunition. The 22 was out of bullets, as Hokee had used them all, killing Ghulam and his men. Damn, he knew he should have kept those guns from the men he killed yesterday.

The three remaining bandits could be heard talking to each other. They couldn't know how much ammunition he had, and they had experienced his deadly firepower. The smart move would be to rush his car, except that in doing so, one or more might get killed. They already knew their bullets were not penetrating the vehicle. They had him pinned down, but to kill him, they would need to expose themselves. The bandits continued to talk to each other before the truck started and appeared to drive off. Did they leave, or was it a feint, leaving one or two behind to shoot Hokee as soon as he poked his head above the windowsill?

Hokee waited several minutes, trying to assess the situation. His options were limited. He couldn't remain here forever. There was no telling when another vehicle might come down the road, and three bodies lying beside a shot-up car might help or not. It could also be a police officer, which might be even worse. With no other apparent opportunity, Hokee opened the driver's side door and waited to see what would happen. When nothing happened, and he could hear no sound, Hokee stuck the silenced barrel of the 22 under his black shirt and raised it above the windowsill, drawing a withering hammering of automatic fire. When the firing stopped, Hokee risked a quick glance above the steering wheel and spotted a man kneeling twenty feet ahead. He promptly shot and killed him with one of his last two bullets. He had one bullet left, one man outside with an automatic rifle, and another somewhere nearby or someplace down the road. At least there were only two killers left to cause him a problem. He didn't hear the truck engine, but it could have stopped down the road outside his ability to hear. In either event, that might give him the opportunity he needed.

The man with the truck was too far away to be a severe threat, leaving only one man close to his vehicle. When he shot the man kneeling in the roadway ahead, he didn't spot the other shooter, which put him off to one side, the passenger's side. The man Hokee shot who had approached his driver's window was lying on the highway not five feet from his open door, his automatic rifle almost within reach. Grabbing one of his boots from the passenger's seat with the improvised string still attached, Hokee threw the boot outside, trying to snag the killer's rifle. He succeeded on his fifth try. Sticking the 45 back under his belt, Hokee grabbed the retrieved gun, then jumped out of the car, crouching behind the left rear wheel. There were no shots. Where was the other shooter? Glancing back towards the road in front, Hokee saw the man running down the road towards the truck half a mile in the distance. With four dead comrades and his partner safely down the highway, the remaining bandit had given up and headed for safety. He wanted nothing more to do with Hokee's marksmanship.

Well, shit! His ride was shot all to hell. There was no telling if the damn thing would still run, and he had four dead bodies lying in the road. He was still dragging bodies off the highway when he heard the truck engine begin, and the truck disappeared down the road. As he finished clearing bodies off the road, he noticed that the car's radiator was leaking fluid, not a positive sign. The engine started, and the car would run, but not for long without water, especially now that the sun's heat was building. Of course, with no

windshield and a body riddled with bullets, the vehicle probably couldn't have gotten him past the border, even if he could have made it that far. He drove the car until the engine froze, coasting it off the highway into the sand. Once more, on foot in a burning desert with no water or food. This situation was getting tiresome.

What to do with his guns and the automatic rifle? He couldn't bear to part with his old faithful Colt 45, and the silenced 22 was handy in certain situations, but he didn't have any ammunition for it anymore, and he couldn't eat the damn gun. The automatic was a cheap Chinese AK-47. The drum had 50 bullets, but the weapon was heavy, and the sun was burning hot again. He kept the 22 but threw the rifle into the desert. The 45 he stuck under his belt in the back under his shirt. He only had one bullet left, but hopefully, he wouldn't need the gun.

How far to civilization if such a thing existed in this part of the world? Surely there would be a petrol station someplace along the highway. And what would he do if a car came down the highway? He could stick out his thumb, but how could he explain his presence way out here in the middle of the burning desert? And what happened to the bandits and their truck? Were they somewhere ahead along the highway?

Hokee put his boots back on and walked for almost two hours before a car approached him from the direction of Nouakchott. He was practically delirious from thirst and hunger, so sticking out his thumb, he prayed for a miracle. The car was a newer model Mercedez which flew past, going over a hundred miles an hour before the driver coasted to a stop nearly a quarter of a mile down the highway. Hokee was too tired and hot to run, but he hurried as fast as possible to catch up with the automobile. The door handle was almost too hot to touch, but he slipped into the passenger's seat. The driver was a young Arab man in his early thirties, dressed in casual white linen slacks and a white polo shirt.

"Do you speak English?" Hokee croaked.

"Most certainment, your excellency. "And how do you come to be out here in this desert with no automobile, dear sir?"

"If I might trouble you for some water, it would be a pleasure to answer your inquiry," Hokee responded.

"Oh, most surely," the driver responded, reaching behind him and thrusting a bottle of cold water into Hokee's hand.

"It is almost certain that you have saved my life," Hokee said, "if I might know your name."

"My name is Aliem, and you are?"

"My name is Hokee; it's an American Indian name." Hokee considered providing a fake name, but he decided that using his real name posed no significant risk, not knowing what might be ahead.

"And where is your automobile, Hokee? The stranger asked again.

"I was traveling from Nouakchott last evening when weariness forced me to stop for a few minutes rest. I pulled off the highway as far as possible and must have dozed off when six men in a truck stopped behind my automobile. They all carried automatic rifles and forced me to get out of my car. They then robbed me of my money and passport, then one of the men drove off in my car, leaving me stranded. I heard them joking and laughing. I believed they expected me to die out here in the desert."

"That is a tragedy, dear sir. Fortunately, I stopped for you, as most drivers along this highway would not stop for a stranger, as the bandits out here are notorious."

"May the blessings of Allah be with you and your family forever," Hokee answered.

"Many thanks, dear sir. And do you follow the way of the Prophet? "No, but I believe the one great spirit is the father of all people." "Yes, so we are also taught."

Hokee was hoarding his water, taking only small sips. He didn't know how much water Aliem was carrying and didn't want to abuse the man's hospitality. The car was once again traveling over a hundred miles an hour, knocking off the distance Hokee needed to travel before reaching his friends in Morocco. His constant worry was if they should pass a truck carrying the two bandits.

"What is your destination, Mr. Hokee?" Aliem asked a few miles south of the Western Sahara border.

"I have friends waiting for me in Casablanca," Hokee responded.

"I stop at Nouadhibou," Aliem responded. "That is a city a few miles south of Western Sahara, primarily administered by Morocco."

"If you could let me off by a bank, I might arrange for some money and perhaps transportation."

"I have connections in the city," Aliem offered. "Perhaps we could assist you in your unfortunate circumstances."

Hokee was getting weird feelings from his driver. That a man of conspicuous wealth driving alone in the desert would stop and pick up a large stranger walking along the highway in the middle of nowhere should have been ringing warning bells. The man's insistence on the *'we can assist you in your unfortunate circumstances'* was too much for Hokee to discount as merely a friendly offer of help. And who was the *we?*

"No, I have abused your friendly help enough," Hokee answered. "I have excellent bank references and should be able to get my needs serviced in almost any bank in your fine city."

When the driver dropped his right hand off the steering wheel, driving with only his left hand, Hokee was ready. Before Aliem could swing the black snub-nosed automatic Glock 32 pistol into action, Hokee grabbed the gun, twisting it away from him in one smooth motion. Hokee's sudden movement caused Aliem to jerk the steering wheel, causing the vehicle to swerve off the highway onto the soft desert sand. Aliem grabbed the steering wheel in both hands, trying to correct their trajectory, but it was hopeless; the car rapidly lost momentum, stopping one hundred feet off the highway. Hokee now held the Glock, pointing it at Aliem.

"Give me your phone, Aliem," Hokee demanded. He didn't want the man to call ahead for help or to warn his *connections* in the city visible ahead in the distance.

Aliem reached into the door's side pocket, picking up a sleek newer model Apple iPhone and placing it in Hokee's outstretched left hand. Hokee dropped the phone and gun in his lap, then grabbed Aliem's head with both hands and, placing his thumbs on nerve endings using a technique taught by Krav Maga, put the man to sleep.

What is it with this fucking country? Is everybody a damned bandit? And why would Aliem pull a gun on a stranger who had already been robbed? The last question was the most troubling. What had motivated the man to attempt such drastic action? The only answer Hokee could come up with was that the man was wary of a strange man walking alone in the desert with no visible automobile. Knowing that the country's wealthiest citizen had been killed in the desert must have triggered suspicious thoughts about anyone alone in the desert. And being armed, the driver must have been overly confident about his ability to control the situation. Too bad, Aliem. Wrong choice.

Hokee used the man's necktie and coat lying in the car's back seat to tie up his arms and legs. The man would be unconscious for maybe thirty minutes, long enough for Hokee to place a few miles between himself and the car. It would take Aliem several more minutes to work free of his bindings. Hopefully, Hokee would be inside the city by then, even without a ride.

Aliem's coat pocket had his wallet with credit cards and a passport. Hokee took the wallet, credit cards, and passport; they and the phone might prove handy in Nouadhibou.

CHAPTER TWENTY-TWO

Hokee had barely made it back to the highway when a late-model white Peugeot traveling towards Nouadhibou slowed down when the driver saw the Mercedes off the road in the sand. He stopped the car and rolled down the driver's side window. Speaking in a language Hokee did not recognize, it seemed apparent he was asking about giving him a ride. Hokee gave the driver a big smile and, speaking English, asked about a ride, pointing to the passenger seat.

The driver, a male about sixty with a full head of gray hair and wearing a pair of sunglasses that looked like Ray-Bans or an expensive knockoff, returned Hokee's smile, pointing towards the empty passenger seat. Hokee wasted no time hurrying around the vehicle and jumping in the plush, cushioned leather seat.

Resuming the drive, the man asked in broken English, "what you need?" Knowing that the French had ruled the country in the past and suspecting that the language would be familiar to someone the driver's age, Hokee answered, "le banc," which was one of the few phrases he knew in the French Language.

The driver gave Hokee a big smile and asked, "Parlez vous francais?" which sounded to Hokee like *par-lay-voo-frahn-say*?

You didn't need to know how to speak French to understand the question. While he didn't know the exact answer, taking a wild guess, Hokee said, "non," which was the right word.

The driver smiled and pulled up in front of the Central Banks of Mauritania within five minutes. He pointed to the building, as it was a bank, with the name in letters a foot high. Still, Hokee thanked him anyway, saying about the only other word in French he could speak, "merci." and returned the man's smile.

Across the street from the bank was a restaurant, and smelling the food started Hokee's stomach to clench. He had a hard time remembering the last time he had eaten, plus he still felt dehydrated. An elegant sign proclaimed the establishment's name in Arabic, but diners could be seen through a large plate-glass window confirming Hokee's nose. He crossed the street and went inside, where the sight and scent of food almost made him faint.

A beautiful older lady with black skin and long white hair wearing a ruby-colored floor-length fitted cloak and leather sandals on her feet greeted Hokee with a smile and guided him to a seat by the window. Then, almost before he was seated, a young girl, maybe eighteen, also in a fitted ruby cloak, set a glass and clay water jug on his table.

The girl said, "Welcome, dear sir," with a hundred-watt smile. "We seldom see an American here in Nouadhibou."

Surprised, Hokee asked, "how did you know I am an American?" Giggling with a shy smile, she responded, "It's your cowboy boots, mister. We don't see them in our country."

"Tell me, please, how you can speak English so beautifully.?"

"My parents believe that if a woman in our country wishes to advance in society, it is essential to learn your language. Since I am ten years of age, they hired a tutor for me."

Pouring himself a glass of water which he downed in one gulp, Hokee smiled and asked, "what do you recommend for this starving American?"

"You must try our couscous; it is the best anywhere in Mauritania." "Alright. That sounds perfect. And some of that delicious smelling bread."

"Yes, mister. That would be our French baguette. A holdover from the time the French were our rulers. An excellent choice." Would you like to try some of our tea? It is Mauritanian sweet tea from China, which goes well with the couscous." Hokee just nodded yes.

"With another smile, the young girl left and Hokee immediately downed another glass of water.

The server returned with a large bowl of hungry, stomach-pleasing couscous and a large baguette in only a couple of minutes. The couscous in this restaurant had lamb and vegetables, plus the pasta in a spicy sauce, perfect for dipping hunks of the baguette. Hokee downed his first large bowl like a man who had not eaten in a while and ordered a second helping. Fortunately, the wallet Hokee stole from the pocket of Aliem's coat held several large bills in the local currency. When his server returned, Hokee held out a bill with a large 50 on it to the young girl whose smile showed that he had chosen well.

Hokee debated his options outside on the sidewalk when the ubiquitous yellow cab drove up by the bank, disgorging two men in business suits. Waving to the driver, Hokee hurried across the street and asked, jumping into the back seat, asking, "do you speak English?"

"It's practically a requirement for a cab driver these days," replied a smiling man wearing a colorful red and white keffiyeh secured by a black headband. "Where would you like to go?"

"I would like to visit the general aviation terminal if that is the correct term here in Mauritania. I want to charter an airplane." Hokee didn't want to part with his weapons and was not confident he could carry them on commercial flights.

"Global Aviation has a facility here in Nouadhibou where you can charter aircraft, including helicopters."

"Perfect, please take me there."

The ride lasted fifteen minutes while the driver, eager to speak English, told Hokee about life in Mauritania. He seemed very distraught about the death of Ghulam, which he heard announced over the radio and who he considered an influential man.

"What did this Ghulam do?" Hokee inquired to get his take on the man.

"He was the wealthiest man in all of Mauritania. His businesses were many, providing several jobs. He was a great man." The driver's voice conveyed read sadness. Hokee wondered if the driver knew about Ghulam's dealing in human trafficking, especially young children. It didn't seem like a question he wanted to ask.

Hokee was still pondering the driver's opinion about Ghulam when they arrived at Global Aviation. There were many hangers with the doors open, showing the bays with several airplanes, plus a white administration building with a flat roof. The business appeared well managed, with everything looking clean and orderly, no small feat given the Sahara Desert and the windblown sand.

Giving the driver another note from Aliem's wallet with the big 50 printed on it, prompting a big smile, Hokee thanked him for the information and the ride.

The front of Global Aviation's administration building featured two glass doors flanked by floor-to-ceiling windows, allowing those passengers waiting inside to watch for their airplane. Inside was a spacious lobby with several oversized padded easy chairs and couches. In front of the chairs and sofas were coffee tables holding colorful magazines, which Hokee assumed were Arabic. Dispersed among the magazines were colorful brochures featuring the airplanes Global Aviation featured in its fleet. Across the lobby was a counter behind which stood two beautiful dark-skinned ladies wearing blue cloaks with sashes across their chests, with the name Global Aviation printed in both English and Arabic.

Going up to the counter, Hokee inquired, "do either of you speak English?"

Both young ladies gave him a warm smile while responding, "yes, sir." Then the girl on the right asked, "how can we help you?"

Here was the question Hokee had been wrestling with for some time. He had credit cards, which would cover the cost of chartering an airplane. Still, he was reluctant to have his name associated with his visit to Mauritania, especially when he left a trail of dead bodies and abandoned stolen vehicles. He also had Aliem's wallet with his passport and credit cards. He was delighted to discover Aliem carried an American Express Platinum card, which Hokee thought he remembered had unlimited credit, but he wasn't sure. Did he dare try to use the stolen card? He didn't want a record of his being in the country and didn't want the beautiful attendants behind the counter to call the police.

"I would like to charter a plane to take me to Casablanca. Do you have an airplane and crew to fly me there?"

"Yes, sir," the smiling girl on the right responded to his question. "We have several planes that can fly you there. I would recommend our Beechcraft Hawker 400XP. It has the range to fly you there nonstop in roughly three hours. The Hawker is our most popular small business jet with luxury seating arrangements. A one-way charter will cost eight thousand six hundred U.S. dollars with a pilot and co-pilot plus a hostess."

"Wow. That's fantastic," replied an amazed Hokee. "Could you please see if I have a sufficient balance on this credit card to pay for this trip?" Hokee handed over Aliem's American ExpressCard and crossed his fingers. He figured a man who drove a new Mercedes and carried the A.M.-EX Platinum card didn't worry about credit balance, but it paid to be sure.

The lovely counter girl put the card into her machine and smiled, "yes, Mr. Dawoud. Your balance is more than adequate. Would you like to pay for the plane now?"

And so, just like that, Hokee booked a chartered flight to Casablanca. The counter girl did not even ask for his passport. Instead, she ran the card and handed it back to a pleased Hokee Wolf.

The next stop was Casablanca, where hopefully, he could meet up with the plane and pilots provided by Olson Construction Company.

CHAPTER TWENTY-THREE

While waiting for Global Aviation to round up his pilots and hostess, Hokee availed himself of a local guide brochure he found in English. He read about Western Sahara that he would fly over on his way to Casa Blanca.

He discovered that Western Sahara has a conflicted history, having been fought over for centuries. Once the Portuguese claimed the barren land, then it became the Spanish Sahara until Morocco claimed the land in 1957. However, the French in Mauritania claimed a part, and Mauritania still fights over the border with Morocco and much of the land. Although, why anyone would want this mostly empty desert confused Hokee.

When the counter girl called him, he was still questioning why anyone would want another million miles of desert sand. Then, looking out the window, he saw the sleek white twin-engine jet across the tarmac with the company name, Global Aviation, splashed down the length of the fuselage in bright blue lettering. Hokee was relieved and excited to put Mauritania behind him finally. While struggling across the burning desert sand in his moccasins with no water, he was not sure his Indian Gods would save him.

Waving at the counter girl on his way out of the general aviation terminal, Hokee was eager to get aboard and leave Mauritania, hopefully forever. He couldn't get out of this country too fast. There was no way for him to know what the search for Gulam's killer would entail or how far they would go to stop anyone from leaving the country. Perhaps they would not be checking general aviation, but it was still a worry that was best left behind. At the top of the short stairway was a stunning hostess wearing a full-length blue Global Aviation uniform tailored to show her figure without being too revealing. Her light-brown skin glowed in the afternoon sun, contrasting perfectly with white teeth exposed to a welcoming smile. She waved at Hokee in a beckoning gesture as though ushering him aboard. The plane's interior was comfortable, with oversized brown leather seats, but it lacked the elegance of Grant's Gulfstream. Inside, the carpet was brown with black swirls that looked like a child's painting project, but to Hokee, it looked like heaven.

Hokee was told to take his choice of seats by the hostess. There were six seats on each side of the plane, with every two seats facing each other. Hokee chose a seat facing the front, settling in for the flight. The hostess wore a name tag that said Amber beneath the Global Aviation logo and told Hokee to fasten his seat belt as the plane began moving, then asked if he would like a beverage.

Since this was a Muslim country, Hokee was unsure if they served alcohol, but decided to take the chance.

"Could I get a scotch?" He asked as the plane began taxiing to the runway.

"Certainly, sir," the girl responded with the same beautiful smile. She was only gone a minute before returning with a small bottle of Glenlivet and a crystal glass full of ice. "I'll be back to check on you after we are in the air," she said, handing him the glass and setting the bottle on the small she pulled away from the cabin wall.

Hokee emptied the bottle into the glass and took his first sip as the plane left the runway. Hokee tilted the glass towards the window as a salute goodbye to a country he was happy to be leaving.

As he settled back drinking his scotch, Hokee thought about his next problem. How was he going to manage madam Brezing? She undoubtedly had excellent security, while the police and city officials were probably on her payroll. He could not just go in with guns blazing and demand that she release the children, and she may have already sold one or more to another buyer. So, he needed to play this one differently than he had with

Ghulam. If Brezing had sold some Indian kids, Hokee needed to find out who the buyers were and where they lived. Even as evil as Brezing appeared, torturing a lady was not something Hokee could do. It was not the shaman's way. Scaring her was a different matter.

Hokee put his seat back down and began shamanic breathing. He couldn't do a sweat lodge, and this was the only tool available.

This exercise begins by taking in three breaths as deep as possible, then exhaling slowly while relaxing all the muscles in the body. Initially, you learn to practice focusing on each muscle group, beginning on the right foot, progressing up the leg and then repeating on the left side. Then, you finish by concentrating on your jaws, neck and temples, where we traditionally hold tension the longest. Once you become practiced as Hokee was, you only spend a few seconds going over each muscle group as you exhale the deep breaths. Once you have entirely relaxed the body, the shamanic breathing begins.

Breathe in slowly through the nostrils, then breathe slowly out through the mouth. Focus on breathing until you reach the Zen state, a state of non-being. Here, time stops.

While Hokee was in this state, Amber came by to see if he would like something to eat, but seeing his unfinished drink on the table and him lying back with his eyes closed, she left and returned quietly to the front.

Hokee used his breathing to take him further into the state of non-being until he became lost to the world of physicality. He had no body; he had no being; it was just consciousness fully immersed in space. Sensing a closeness to his guides, Hokee asked, "how do I deal with this, madam Brezing? How can I convince her to cooperate with me?

Almost immediately, the answer came into his mind. *Discover that which she cannot afford to lose.*

With that, Hokee came out of his self-induced trance and, sitting back up, noticed that the ice in his drink had melted. When he raised his seat, Amber saw and came back to his side, "did you have a nice rest.?"

"Excellent," he replied. Having been out of time, or more accurately, in a timeless state, he asked, "how long did I rest?"

Amber smiled and said, "only about twenty minutes. You seemed so peaceful."

Hokee thought but didn't say, *"man, if you only knew."* Instead, he said, "it looks like my ice melted. Would you mind getting me a fresh drink, please?"

Taking his glass, Amber replied, "it would be my pleasure, sir," going back up front to the bar.

What can't Brezing afford to lose?

Then Hokee thought, *"her reputation, she cannot afford to lose her reputation."*

It was then that Hokee thought of Glory. Did he dare call her? Would she be pissed, or even worse, refuse to take his call?

When Amber returned with his drink, he was thinking about Glory with a distressed look on his face.

"My, you look like you woke up from a nightmare," she said, handing him his drink.

"No, sorry. I was thinking about an old girlfriend, wondering if I should call her. I'm afraid she might not be too happy to hear from me."

"Well," Amber gushed, "I don't know about her, but I would like it if you called me."

With a wry grin, Hokee said, "well, thanks. Maybe I'll call her. The worst that can happen is she lets it go to voicemail.

"While I'm here, would you like a sandwich or something to snack on? We have a variety of good eats on board."

"Maybe later. I better call and see if I can talk the lady into helping me once more. The first time she lost her mind, and the next time I almost got her killed, so I wouldn't be surprised if she told me to take a hike."

Hokee was being chatty, and usually, he was the quiet one. You almost had to pry words out of his mouth, and here he was like an idiot college kid blabbering to a stranger. Maybe it was a reaction to his recent near-death experience, or it could be the lack of sleep. Hell, perhaps he just needed somebody to talk with. Shila was his talking companion more than any one else when he was home. *Better button up your lips, Hokee; you could say too much to the wrong people.*

Heather gave him another hundred-watt smile, saying, "I'll leave you to make your call. Let me know if I can do anything for you. Anything at all." This last statement could be interpreted in many ways, and Hokee's practice was to ignore it.

"Thanks, Amber. I'll let you know."

Hokee took a few swallows of the liquid courage before dialing Glory's number. He had his fingers mentally crossed when she answered.

"Well, hello stranger. I've been meaning to call, but this damn mayor business has had me going twenty-hour days."

There was probably some truth in that, but it was still a piss-poor excuse. It doesn't take long to make a brief call.

"How would you like an expense-paid trip to Paris?"

"What, no greeting. No, gosh, honey, it's good to hear your voice. You remind me of the Hokee I first met when all I could do was get you to grunt." "Hi Glory, It's great to hear your voice... do you have some time to come to Paris?"

"Well, okay, I deserve some of that. What's with the Paris thing suddenly?"

"I'm on my way there, tracking a human trafficking ring and some pedophiles selling children."

"Shit. You're serious about this Paris trip. I thought it was a joke or something. How soon are we talking?"

"How about today or tomorrow? I can have tickets for you at the airport if you give me your schedule."

"Wow. That's quick. Let me check on a couple of things. I assume you are not asking me for my beautiful self and a romp in the hay, straw, or whatever you Indian guys romp in."

"Well, that could be worked into the equation, but I need your reporting skills. I have to *out* the most popular madam in Paris or at least get her to give me some children she purchased, and I need the leverage. The threat of international exposure from one of the leading investigative reporters on the planet could get her to cooperate."

"Yes, I can see where you may need my help. My, my. Well, it's nice to know where your priorities lie. Sorry, I'm just feeling bitchy. My priorities have lacked attention. I'm guessing this is going to happen soon."

"I'm on a chartered plane to Casablanca from Mauritania, the shit hole of the planet. I hope to contact Grant's airplane and pilots in Casablanca and fly from there to Paris. I have a day or two to make my plans, and then it's time to visit the madam. Eleven children between the age of five and ten were kidnapped from the Fort Hall Indian Reservation. The local kidnappers are now in jail. I took care of the Houston connection and the traffickers in Mauritania. There is the possibility that I may have to visit other places to collect all the children the madam purchased from the people in Mauritania. She may have already sold a few of them."

"It sounds like you have been a busy boy. Let me make some calls to see what I can arrange. If it's at all possible, I would love to help tackle human trafficking. Can I call you back in a few minutes?"

"Sure, we have about another three hours before landing in Casablanca."
"I'll call you back in thirty or before. And Hokee, thanks for the call." "You betcha, honey. Bye."

Hokee put the phone back in his pocket and arranged the guns in his belt to a more comfortable position. He didn't want to be without weapons; you never know what might be waiting.

CHAPTER TWENTY-FOUR

Hokee settled back in the seat, enjoying his scotch as much as possible. His mind kept returning to Paris and what he might encounter there. That Madam Brezing was well connected was a given. She could not run the most successful house of prostitution and child trafficking operation in the city without police and city politicians in her pocket. Having a lover in Paris besides your marriage partner was almost a requirement for the residents, but pedophilia was a different matter. Surely the Parisians were not that liberal. There are perverts in any society, but to condone such action at an official level was unheard of in Hokee's world. Undoubtedly, some officials would take part, but they would not want the world to know. Still, Hokee could not afford to run afoul of the police, especially as he would carry illegal firearms.

Amber came back to see if he wanted another scotch or anything else. "Yes, thank you, Amber; another scotch would be appreciated."

He wasn't sure, but it seemed there was a hint of disappointment in her eyes. Maybe it was his imagination. He was about to ask for a snack when his phone bussed.

"Hokee here."

"God, I hope so. Okay lover, I'm all booked for a flight to Paris, leaving in two hours. I haven't booked a hotel room. Do you know where you'll be staying?"

"No, I've been wandering around in the Sahara Desert without phone access or water and just now have rejoined the world of communication. Do you have a preference?" Hokee hoped she would take care of that chore for him.

"I like the Four Seasons, but it's the only one I've stayed in during my only visit. It's pricey, but they treat you like royalty."

"Glory, could you see about booking me three rooms? I need to take care of my pilots and hostess."

"Certainly, and the station is taking care of my flight, first-class, so you're off the hook for plane fare. The station manager is excited about doing a segment or two on human trafficking, especially as children are involved. I'll see about booking rooms in the hotel, then call you back. I suppose that is the best place to meet up with you and your traveling companions?"

"That would be great, Glory, and yes, we can meet at the Four Seasons. I'm unsure when we will arrive as I haven't contacted them in Casablanca yet. I'm hoping they are waiting for me there. I had to abandon them at the airport in Nouakchott."

"I can't wait to hear about your adventures, Hokee. Wandering about in the Sahara without water and being abandoned. And knowing you, I expect a back trail full of bodies. You aren't about to be arrested, are you?"

"I hope not. Steps were taken to leave no trail, but life isn't perfect. Listen, if you successfully book rooms at the hotel, don't bother calling back. I'll see you at the Four Seasons." Hokee was afraid of saying too much over the telephone, as you never know who is listening. He felt he had already said too much.

"Okay," she said, sounding disappointed. "I guess I'll see you when I see you."

"And Glory, thanks for helping me in this situation. I appreciate your willingness to jump back into the fire."

"You will not get me killed or something worse, will you?" She said it jokingly and Hokee could see a smile on her face, but he could sense a trace of fear in her eyes.

"No, hell no. The world cannot afford to lose its premier investigative television reporter."

"Good. I'll see you in Paris. Bye, Hokee."

Hokee disconnected without saying goodbye; he had already said what he wanted, and goodbyes were not part of his lexicon.

When he put away his phone, Amber came back by his seat.

"Well, I see she didn't hang up on you. Were you able to resolve your differences?" It was a personal question, but Hokee had let himself in for that when he talked about calling an old girlfriend. Still, the question irritated, and he was unhappy that he had allowed his feelings to show.

"Yeah, I guess so," he responded quietly, hoping to sound like he didn't want to discuss the situation further. "What do you have in the snack department?" he asked with a deflection.

Amber rattled off a list of food items Hokee had no interest in eating, but when she mentioned corn chips, he stopped her and said, "how about the chips and another scotch?"

When she returned, Hokee said his thanks, then ignored her as he put his seat back and closed his eyes. He didn't want to continue discussing his personal life with the lovely, charming hostess and wanted to think about Paris. He was feeling guilty about involving Glory in a situation that could be dangerous. Despite his assurances that she would come to no harm, he was not entirely sure what they faced with Madam Brezing and her Paris connections. Then there were the people to whom she may have sold some children. God only knows they would not be happy to lose their purchases or reputations. The potential for danger lurked everywhere.

CHAPTER TWENTY-FIVE

As his chartered plane landed at the Mohammed V International, Casablanca's main airport sixteen miles east of the city, Hokee searched the aircraft parked along the runway as they landed, hoping to spot Grant's Gulf, but there were so many parked planes, and they were going to fast plane for Hokee to see if his ride was still parked there. The Beechcraft's pilot parked a hundred yards from the General Aviation terminal, where Hokee assumed Grant's pilots would have landed and parked nearby. Using Aliem's phone, Hokee called Captain Hobbs, hoping he would answer an unknown number. He was reluctant to use his own phone, which would leave a record of his being there if anyone ever bothered to check.

Captain Hobbs answered on the second ring and was delighted to hear Hokee's voice. He had been concerned about their passenger, along with Heather and Captain Jensen, wondering if Hokee was still alive. Hokee assured him that all was well and asked the captain to contact the crew and meet him at the general aviation terminal. They were going to Paris.

Hokee said goodbye to the beautiful and disappointed Amber, thanking her for taking good care of him during the flight and asking her to thank the pilot he had never met. Taking advantage of the flirtatious hostess was not on his agenda. Taking so many lives recently left a scar on his soul, which would require a significant session in the sweat lodge to heal. Until then, he would not impose his aura on another human being, even if he had the desire and opportunity. Explaining his actions to someone he had met just once, only recently, was also not possible.

Leaving the plane, Hokee walked to the aviation terminal and the lounge to wait for Captain Hobbs and the crew for his flight to Paris. The surrounding structures had a Moroccan influence with Moorish arches, white stucco walls, blue roof tiles, and stained glass windows. The terminal's interior featured acres of hand-woven rugs with colorful geometric designs and soft beige leather couches. Roving service personnel were always within hailing distance to supply drinks or food. Hokee was happy to sink into the soft leather and let his body relax for the first time in what seemed like years. Then, shutting his eyes, he allowed himself to catch up on some much-needed sleep.

It felt like only seconds before Hokee felt a soft hand on his shoulder, giving it a gentle shake. Then, opening his eyes, he saw a smiling Heather, who when she saw his eyes asked, "catching up on your beauty sleep?"

"Oh, hi Heather. Yeah, I dozed off here for a few minutes. Guess I needed to catch up on some missed sack time." Then, noticing the grinning Captain Hobbs standing off to the side, he asked, "do we need any special permits to land in Paris?"

"Nah," he answered. "We will still need to let customs inspect our plane and passports, but that shouldn't be a problem. With American passports, we won't need any other documentation. Your guns will have to stay hidden until they finish their inspection. Other pilots have told me that the inspections are cursory unless they suspect we are smugglers. There shouldn't be a problem."

Hokee stood up and stretched before asking, "how about our plane? Is it ready to take off?"

"Captain Jensen has gone to do a preflight check and bring the plane up to the terminal," Hobbs responded. "He should have the plane here in a few more minutes. You probably have time for a cup of coffee if you would like."

"That sounds great. I could use a little wake-up help. The last couple of days were taxing. Will you and Heather join me in a cup? I see a server approaching us now."

"Sure, I love this Moroccan coffee," Hobbs answered. "I don't know where they get their beans, but it has a kick. How about you, Heather, want a cup?"

"I think I'll stick with tea," she answered. "The coffee gives me too much of a buzz. It's okay first thing in the morning, but one cup daily is my limit." They all sat down on the soft leather cushions as their server, a slender, dark-skinned man wearing a bright red tailored uniform, soon delivered their order. Hokee gave the man another of the large denomination bills from Aliem's wallet, telling him to keep the change. He would have given the man everything in the wallet, but that would have seemed too strange. They hadn't finished their drinks before Captain Hobbs received a text from Jensen informing him that the plane was just outside the terminal and ready to leave. As they were leaving the terminal building, Hokee glanced around, and seeing no one was watching him, he dumped Aliem's wallet and phone into a trash bin, keeping the passport and American ExpressCard. Losing the wallet and all that cash seemed a shame, but Hokee didn't dare carry it to Paris. He wanted as little connection as possible with Mauritania on his body as he left Casablanca. A fake passport and stolen credit card might come in handy.

Back on Grant's Gulf, Hokee felt himself relax for the first time in days. Paris was bound to be stressful, but it couldn't be worse than Houston or Mauritania, or so he erroneously thought. But for now, he was in a friendly atmosphere among friends. Paris was three hours away, an excellent nap time if the friendly, flirtatious Heather would leave him alone.

CHAPTER TWENTY-SIX

After talking with Hokee, Captain Hobbs chose to fly into BVA, the Beauvais International Airport, instead of the Charles de Gaulle International or Orly. He reasoned that customs at the BVA would be a little more relaxed than they would encounter at the larger airports. Given the arsenal Hokee had stashed on board, they thought there would be a more relaxed customs inspection with a less rigorous effort spent searching their plane. In addition, Hokee was concerned that even though they were arriving from Casablanca, African officials may have started an international search for the man who had killed one of its wealthiest citizens.

About 50 miles south of Paris, a taxi ride to the Four Seasons from BVA can take 60 to 90 minutes if you're lucky. Besides, Hokee was in no hurry to confront Madam Brezing.

After arriving at BVA, the control tower had Captain Hobbs taxi to the main terminal, where customs officials met their plane. They were asked, ordered, to stay aboard their plane until customs could board and inspect their passports and cargo.

Two bored officials wearing stained white uniforms climbed the stairs and entered the main cabin. As far as these officials were concerned, airplanes arriving from Casablanca carrying wealthy Americans were of little concern. These visitors were obviously not terrorists and unlikely to be smuggling. When the agents asked Captain Hobbs why they chose to land at BVA instead of one of the major airports closer to downtown Paris, Captain Hobbs had a ready answer. This airport is in the town of Tilleé, where the beautiful Cathedral of Saint Peter is found with its famous astronomical clock and fantastic stained-glass windows. Captain Hobbs informed the customs officials that his passenger, mister Hokee Wolf, was particularly interested in studying the cathedral since he had spent time in Paris at the Notre Dame and wanted to compare the two beautiful structures. Like most Frenchmen, this answer pleased the customs officials, who were proud of their village.

Captain Hobbs handed the officials all four passports in a bundle, which were promptly stamped. The officials didn't notice that the photograph on one passport did not match one of the passengers. Both customs officials told the group to enjoy their visit. No attempt was made to search the plane. Hokee left the plane with Heather, accompanied by the two customs agents. Hobbs and Jensen were left on board to park the plane and get it fueled for their next flight. Captain Hobbs had the added chore of transporting Hokee's arsenal, which he carried in a large leather bag that looked like it held a rolled-up painting, a not uncommon sight in Paris. They would later meet in the terminal lounge while Hokee arranged transportation to the Four Seasons.

After finding a limousine driver who was thrilled to transport four wealthy Americans to downtown Paris, a pricy ride, Hokee called Glory.

Her phone rang four times before she answered. No greeting, no prelude to a normal conversation, just, "I was wondering when you would show up. I've been here for hours."

"Hello, beautiful, and I especially love the warm greeting." Hokee was not really upset, but he had to let her know that even though she was here doing him a favor, she couldn't walk all over him as she did almost everyone else. "How come it took you so long to answer your phone? My guess is you're lying by the pool or sitting at the bar, driving all the men crazy who are hitting on you."

'Well, your detective skills are showing, lover. "I'm lounging by the pool, driving the men crazy who keep hitting on me."

Hokee had to laugh at her brazen speech and uncomplicated behavior. "Well, keep it up, but don't let any of them seduce you. We'll arrive in about two hours, maybe a little sooner, depending on traffic." He didn't want to say where they were in case the telephones were being monitored, which was highly unlikely, but when you could be the subject of an international search, you didn't take unnecessary chances. "Were you able to secure the rooms we need?" Hokee didn't mention any names for the same reason.

"I booked two additional rooms using the television station's name and account. You will have to repay the station, or old Levi Morgenstern, my boss, will have a cow, even if he loves my story about abducted children for a porn ring."

"Not to worry. I'll take care of it, but let's leave it under the stations' account for the time being. I don't want my name associated with anything formal here in Paris. Hopefully, I have left no footprints in my travels, but there may be those who could describe my physical appearance. There is no reason to attach a name to that remote possibility."

"I hear you. He who will not be named should find the welcome matt out when he arrives. The hotel has all three rooms next to each other. The rooms are on your favorite floor, and our room number is your favorite girl's age, added to one thousand." Glory had to smile as she visualized Hokee struggling to remember her age. She wasn't sure, but perhaps she had never told him about her birthday.

Hokee responded as though this was a no-brainer. "Okay, lover. Put the champagne on ice, order the escargot, and we'll be there soon." These days Hokee always preferred the first floor wherever he stayed. He didn't like to be confined by stairways or elevators. He saw them as choke points and potential traps since his encounter with the doppelgänger at St. John's Island. They were there chasing the thief who robbed a bread truck carrying money from Yellowstone Park to Pocatello. Glory's age was another matter. He didn't know her age, but he had more than an hour to figure it out. If he couldn't do that, he may as well hang it up as a world-class detective.

In her Paris mansion, Madam Brezing was thinking about the death of Shabib Ghulam. Who could have killed him and left his body out in the desert? Did it have anything to do with their mutual business? She knew that life in Mauritania could be treacherous, with smugglers fighting each other over territory; still, Shabib was a big man in the country with powerful allies. Maybe someone was taking over his business, meaning they would look for her to continue making purchases. Or perhaps someone was angry over something or someone Shabib had traded. So, it would pay to be on the alert just in case. A call to her friendly police captain was in order. It was only wise to be prepared for trouble.

CHAPTER TWENTY-SEVEN

Hokee and Heather were drinking coffee in the lounge when Hobbs and Jensen arrived with two porters carrying luggage. Hobbs was carrying the leather case holding Hokee's rifle, plus a couple of pistols. The Colt 45 never leaves his body when he is working, and even though they were in an airport far from Paris and unexpected by any enemy he could imagine, Hokee was always on duty when engaged in a mission. The silenced 22 was also tucked under his belt.

Their limousine driver, a man named Simon with black hair and the dark complexion of many Jewish males, was pacing in circles by the lounge doors with a scowl creasing his face as though trying to hurry them along. His light gray chauffeur's uniform showed sweat marks under the arms, and he appeared agitated, although there should have been no cause for such behavior. He had been engaged for a lucrative fare to downtown Paris with the implicit understanding of a generous tip. Attuned to departure from the expected norm, Hokee called him over; "Simon, do you have a problem taking us to Paris?"

"No, no, monsieur. I just got a telephone call that my wife went into labor at the local hospital. We need the money from this engagement, but

the round trip could take several hours, depending on traffic. It has me worried, is all. Forgive me."

Without hesitation, Hokee counted out five hundred dollars, which he placed in Simon's hand. "Go see to your wife, and good luck."

"Oh, monsieur, may the God in heaven bless you with safe travels and much good fortune."

Simon bolted for the door and sitting down the case he was carrying, Hobbs asked, "was that our ride to Paris?"

"Fraid so," Hokee responded with a grin. "Guess I'll have to find another limousine."

"That was sooo sweet," Heather cooed.

"Yeah," Jensen added. "At least he didn't say, 'may Allah be with you.' Hey, not that I have anything against the Muslims or anything, but those guys in Africa made me nervous."

"Me too," Hokee quipped. "But it wasn't their religion that scared me nearly as much as that freaking desert. Excuse me while I round up a ride. Do you guys want a drink or something to eat before we leave? He asked, looking around the group. "We aren't in any big hurry."

"Not me," Hobbs answered. "I just want to get out of this monkey suit and into something cool and dry, like a vodka martini."

"You doing your James Bond routine now, Captain?" Jensen asked playfully. "I'm good boss," he added, talking to Hokee. "How about you Heather? Want something from the bar? I'll go get it for you."

"No thanks. I'll just finish my coffee while our chivalrous boss rounds up another ride to Paris."

Hokee went to the flight counter and returned shortly with the promise of another limousine to meet them all just outside the lounge doors in two minutes.

The new limousine driver was a sizeable, swarthy-looking fellow with a body shaped by many long hours in a gym. His long black hair was pulled back in a ponytail, emphasizing his sharp aquiline features. Hokee surmised the man was Egyptian, easing his mind about an African driver who might have been tuned into news about the dead men in Mauritania.

"Hello," the driver greeted his fares with a broad smile. "My name is Bassel, and it is my privilege to be your driver. I understand you wish to visit the Four Seasons Hotel in downtown Paris."

The man's name instantly put Hokee's mind at rest as it confirmed his thoughts about the man being Egyptian. "Yes," he answered, looking Bassel in the eyes with a matching smile. "It pleases us to have such a pleasant man as our driver."

Heather rolled her eyes while Hobbs ducked his head to hide his response to Hokee's over-the-top interaction with Bassel. Jensen stood with a glazed look on his face as though trying to figure out what was happening. "Well, let me help you beautiful people load your luggage and we'll be on our way." While talking, Bassel grabbed two bags and started loading the car.

Heather and Hobbs looked at Hokee, hoping he would not respond with another syrupy quip. Instead, Hokee gave them a brief grin plus an eye wink to let them know he was through talking. He had already said more than he liked. By nature, Hokee was reticent with words.

Bassel kept talking while helping everyone get settled. Hokee watched to ensure that Hobbs cared for the long leather case holding his firearms. "I have refreshments in the icebox for you lovely people, should you like- excellent French wine, champagne, and French pastries. The travel time should be a little over an hour at this time of day, but that could change while we are on the road. I will let you know if that happens."

"Thank you Bassel," Hokee responded. "I think we're all comfortable. I might try some of your fine wine."

"Yes, yes. Please do," was Bassel's answer as Hokee pushed the button, raising the glass partition, cutting off any more dialogue with their driver.

"Thanks, boss," Hobbs said. "The man has his charms, but a little goes a long way."

"Oh, but he is such a lovely man," Heather responded with a wicked grin.

"Yeah," Jensen added. "Such a lovely man."

Hokee closed his eyes and settled back in the comfortable seats, letting his companions chatter to their heart's content.

His eyes were closed, but his mind wouldn't shut down. Hokee was sure Madam Brezing knew by now that her pedophile business could be in jeopardy and would take precautions. He hoped he was in time to prevent her from taking drastic action, like shipping all her children out of the country. Her police and official government connections were his most pressing concerns. Hopefully, Glory's threats of exposure would help contain any exuberant actions from her political connections. He didn't want to get into a shootout with the Paris police.

While Hokee thought about the problems he faced in Paris, his companions drank champagne and snacked on pastries. Unfortunately, they did not know about the troubles ahead.

CHAPTER TWENTY-EIGHT

The first twenty miles went by quickly as the traffic was light. Bassel was driving on A16 which went through farms and vineyards for mile after mile, and although picturesque, it became tedious after a few miles. Twenty miles from Paris, the traffic became much heavier, causing Bassel to reduce speed. By the time they reached Saint-Denis, it had become stop-and-go, with five miles remaining before reaching their hotel. Hokee finally gave in and accepted a glass of champagne, although the bubbly was not something he particularly enjoyed.

The Four Seasons hotel is a tall white multistoried structure that Michael Angelo could have designed. As a five-star hotel, it is Luxury with a capital L. Gilt-framed pictures of French Royalty adorn the long ocean blue carpeted hallways lined with soft cushioned chairs and white marble end tables on which fresh cut roses rest in crystal vases. Exiting their limousine, the four weary travelers looked down the long, blue-carpeted hotel hallway and felt very out of place. Giving Bassel a hefty tip for his long drive and thoughtful drinks, they were met at the door by men wearing long gray tailored frock coats and trilby felt hats. Porters wearing suits of the same color but without the hats picked up their luggage as Bassel deposited it beside the limousine. Captain Hobbs had to wrestle one of the porters for

Hokee's leather gun case as the man insisted on trying to carry it inside. Hokee interfered by telling the porter that the case contained a costly painting that had to be handled with extreme care. This explanation seemed to satisfy the young porter, as Paris is known for its artwork.

At the reception desk, Hobbs, Jensen and Heather were issued keys to their rooms after showing their passports. Hokee explained he was staying with a friend who had already registered, making it unnecessary to show his passport. He didn't want any official recognition of his stay in Paris, just in case. Leaving Captain Hobbs to take care of his gun case, Hokee led the way down the hallway toward their rooms.

Hokee wandered down the long blue-carpeted hallway, enjoying the fresh-cut flowers along the way and glancing at the pictures of French royalty from bygone eras. He briefly wondered what prompted the hotel to feature these pictures of mostly forgotten individuals until he remembered how the French still adored Napoleon Bonaparte, whom most of the world considered an egotistical maniac. Ah well, he reasoned, the French still have great cooking. Before he was ready, he stood in front of room 1035.

It had been several months since he had seen Glory, and she had not answered his calls for several weeks. Yet she had flown several thousand miles to be with him, and he felt a little guilty for feeling churlish about his thoughts until he remembered it was the lure of a great story that brought her to Paris, not the opportunity to renew their relationship. His feelings were on a rollercoaster ride. He was excited to see her again, yet losing his first love had left him wary, knowing that his emotions were an unreliable gauge of a woman's heart. *Would she be happy to see him? Would she pretend to be excited only to get the story he promised? Oh God, stop it, Hokee. Just knock on the damn door and take what comes.*

He knocked on the door and felt his heart rate increase while waiting for the door to be opened. When the door swung open, all of his thoughts went to hell as the woman he loved stood in the open doorway wearing a sheer white baby-doll negligee with a million-dollar smile. Hokee returned the smile and, entering the room, took the vision of heaven into his arms as she gave him the warmest, welcoming kiss he could remember. Hokee's killings and desert experiences were wiped from his mind as he lost himself

in the moment. Later, the time would come to recount his adventures to Glory, but for now, she was in his arms, and nothing else mattered.

Later, lying on his back and Glory sprawled on her side with one leg thrown over his thighs, Hokee said, "nice room, Glory."

That brought a sharp elbow into his side as she responded, "You son of a bitch. My God, Hokee, I screwed your brains out, and all you can say is it's a nice room?"

"Well, it is with you here. But I was afraid to tell you how fantastic you were in case you thought that sex was all I had on my mind.."

"Well, thanks, I guess. And I suppose sex isn't all that is on your mind."

"I've got one of Grant's pilots babysitting some guns which, if found, could land him in a French prison. I've got eleven Shoshone children purchased here in Paris from the traffickers in Mauritania by a French Madam named Brezing. Brezing has to have political connections with city hall and the police to operate, and she undoubtedly knows that the Mauritania connection has ended. So when I show up looking for the missing children, she will connect me to the Mauritania mess and possibly alert the authorities to pick me up for murder. Other than that, sex is all I have on my mind."

"Oh, you poor dear. Do you want to talk about Houston and Mauritania?"

"Not now. All you need to know is that Houston is the hub of human trafficking in the United States, and Mauritania is the world's armpit regarding human trafficking, especially children. I've eliminated one of the major traffickers in the U.S. and the primary dealer in Mauritania. I didn't leave any tracks, but as soon as we confront Brezing, she will connect the dots. It could get messy with her political and police allies here in Paris. I don't want to kill a French madam or a policeman."

Getting up and walking naked over to a kitchen nook, Glory asked, "how about a cup of coffee? This room has the most amazing selections. I've sampled a few, and I love this Malongo Blue Mountain bean from Jamaica. I could give you some Wild Kopi Luwak, which is the world's most exclusive, but somehow I can't drink something that comes out of cat shit."

"The Blue Mountain stuff sounds good, and I would like a cup. But please put on a robe, or I won't be able to concentrate on our conversation."

"Spoilsport. I thought you loved to see me wander around naked."

"I do. Just not when I want to talk about taking down the most famous madam in Paris."

While the coffee was brewing, Hokee went into the glamorous bathroom to shower. The bathroom was more deluxe than anything Hokee could imagine, with the world's softest bath towels stacked in piles of six. There were six soaps with loofas, sponges and washcloths to scrub away the day's accumulation of troubles. By the time he emerged five minutes later fully dressed, Glory had on one of the deluxe white bathrobes provided by the hotel while sitting at a small table set for two with a plate of pastries and two cups of steaming coffee.

"Wow. That coffee smells fantastic," Hokee said, joining Glory at the table. "I can't wait to try this Blue Mountain concoction."

"You won't be disappointed, lover boy. Now, tell me you have a plan for dealing with this French Madam." Glory was now all business as her fabulous face wore a stern, fierce look.

"Madam Brezing must be frightened into giving me the children she still has, plus the names and addresses of the buyers of those children she may have sold. The only thing I can think of that would frighten her would be the loss of her reputation and exposure as a procurer and trafficker of children. If her protectors in the political and law enforcement arena were similarly threatened with exposure, they would also be reluctant to act against us." Hokee took a sip of coffee and smiled at Glory, but then his countenance became somber. Clearly, he had more to say.

"Okay, so how do you plan on frightening this lady and the local establishment?" Glory had her own agenda and plans, but they needed to work together now. Glory needed a story for her New York producers, but she couldn't implicate Hokee in several killings he had undoubtedly accomplished over the past few days.

"Okay, we can visit Houston and get pictures of the warehouse that held the trafficked individuals, and the murders of the local traffickers will be on the news. So when we get the children, you can get their stories starting with their abduction in Idaho, their imprisonment in Houston, their journey by boat to Mauritania, and then, finally, their trip to Pairs and Madam Brezing. For Brezing, I have the statement that she bought the children from

Shabib Ghulam, the trafficker in Mauritania. My idea is that we, or I, initially visit the Madam as a prospective customer and ask to see her inventory of children. I take some pictures, then bring you in to seal the deal."

Glory looked skeptical. "And how do you get the Madam to show you her kids?"

"Well, I do a little bar hopping, maybe starting here in this fancy hotel. There must be a bartender or bellman who knows of the Madam and could get me an introduction for the right incentive." Hokee sounded a bit more sure than he felt. He was more suited to force and intimidation than one of an agreeable comrade full of empathy and friendliness.

"Hell, as soon as you ask about finding someone to provide you with a kid to molest, they will call the cops." Glory liked his plan but couldn't help but play the devil's advocate.

"I don't ask for a kid, for hell's sake. Come on. I might not be a smoother or ass-kisser, but I'm not totally stupid. Let's say I'm just interested in something exotic." Hokee was too serious to see Glory pulling his chain a little.

Knowing Hokee took this seriously and didn't have a great tolerance for unnecessary input, Glory quickly agreed. "Yeah, asking for something exotic or out of the ordinary might work. You're tired of the regular street girls. You want something a little different."

"All I need is someone to get me inside with an introduction. I think I can sell Brezing on the rest." Hokee felt like his plan might work. "Well, what do you think?"

Giving her man a big smile, Glory said, "I think you're a gorgeous man, and I want to see you rescue these kids and maybe a few others. It will be a pleasure to drop the hammer on this bitch."

"Does this mean you think the plan might work?" Hokee wanted to boost his confidence, and he trusted Glory's assessment.

"With you, Hokee, I believe anything is possible. I've seen you do some pretty miraculous things and working over a Paris Madam shouldn't be that difficult."

"Okay, we'll put the plan into operation later tonight. Right after our gourmet dinner at the fine dining room up on the roof. Venimus, Vidmus, Vicimus. Well, Julius said I instead of we, but then he had this big ego."

"Hokee, what in the hell did you just say?"

"We came, we saw, and we conquered. Julius Caesar said Veni, Vidi, Vici, which is I Came, I Saw, and I Conquered. I thought including you in our quest to dethrone the ruling Madam more fitting."

"Oh, that's so sweet, although it doesn't have the same ring to it." "Yeah, it loses a little when you go plural. Let's call the others and see about dinner."

"Gees, I thought you'd never get around to the subject. Let's get moving."

"I need to collect my guns from Captain Hobbs. I'll do that while you get dressed. Be back shortly," Hokee said as he left the room.

That wasn't a promise he could keep.

CHAPTER TWENTY-NINE

Heather had the room next to the one Glory reserved for herself and Hokee, while Captains Hobbs and Jensen were across the hallway. As Hokee left his room, he could hear a commotion in the Captain's room across the hall as the door was cracked open slightly and he wondered briefly if he should knock on the door or pass on by, but the sounds were argumentative and loud. Then, stepping across the hallway, he could hear Jensen arguing with someone about the gun case.

Without giving it another thought, Hokee knocked on the door politely, then entered the room. The bellhop who had wrestled Hobb's for the gun case was inside with another older man dressed in a conservative woolen blue suit with a Four Seasons Hotel logo stitched on the left-hand pocket, just below a colorful pocket square matching his tie. The man was a fit five-foot-ten with eyes darker than midnight on a cloudy night and gray hair in a buzz cut. He had his finger stuck in Hobbs's chest when Hokee entered the room.

It didn't take a rocket scientist to guess the source of the argument. The bellhop had suspected that the leather gun case in Hobbs's possession held guns, not a painting, and had alerted hotel security. "Ah, Captain Hobbs,"

Hokee said, crossing into the room. "I'm sorry to intrude, but I came to collect my painting. I hope this is not an inappropriate time."

"And who are you, monsieur?" The hotel security man asked. He sounded indignant with a scowl, and those dark eyes looked menacing.

"I'm just a man who asked this gentleman to hold my painting while I paid my respects to a lovely lady. You French people are so big on love and have such beautiful ladies. I'll take my painting now, Captain." Hokee said a little forcefully."

"Oh yes. I'll get it right away; I just put it in the other room for safekeeping.? Captain Hobbs left the room to fetch the leather case. When he returned, he went to hand it to Hokee, but the hotel security man reached for it, only to be rudely shoved aside by Hokee.

"I'm sorry," Hokee said, pushing the security man further away so he couldn't grab the case. Hokee used his other hand to take the case from Hobbs, "but your clumsy bellhop already tried manhandling my painting, and I refuse to let another ham-handed idiot touch this case. This painting is much too valuable to be jostled around by imbeciles." You could see the fire in Hokee's eyes.

The hotel security man was thrown entirely off guard. Stuttering to gain face while regaining his composure, the man said, "I must ask you to open the case for inspection, monsieur."

"And I must ask you to mind your own bloody business, mister," Hokee said, poking him in the chest as he had been poking Captain Hobbs. "This case only gets opened at the Louvre tomorrow morning. If you wish to be present, be there at 10:00 a.m. sharp. Otherwise, find someone else to bother with your officious meddling."

With that, Hokee moving swiftly, spun towards the door and left the room..

"Who was that rude gentleman?" The security man asked Hobbs. Hokee's mention of the Louvre had thrown him for a loop. Maybe it *was* a picture for the museum.

"He said his name was Earnest McIntosh. We shared a taxi from the airport. He asked me to hold his painting while he paid his respects to a lady staying here. "I'm afraid I can't tell you any more than that."

"Okay, Captain Hobbs, I apologize for the inconvenience. I'll check with the front desk to get the gentlemen's room number." You could see that the security man was skeptical about the entire affair, but Hokee and the leather case were gone. There was no longer any reason to remain in the captain's room.

When the bellhop and security man were back in the hallway, there was no sign of Hokee Wolf. Of course, there was no one registered under the name of McIntosh, and no one matching Hokee's description was registered either. The desk clerk said someone with that description came to the counter saying something about meeting a lady, and he seemed to know her room number. With no other information, the security man returned to his office, sending the bellhop back to the front lobby.

After leaving the Captain's room, Hokee hot-footed it down the hallway to the first intersection leading outside. He grabbed a cab and had it drop him off at a sidewalk café a few blocks from the hotel. His phone was in Glory's room, but the French were civilized, and his server was happy to bring a telephone to his table along with a double shot of Glenfarclas, a 25-year-old drizzly.

Hokee wasn't too worried about having the café's phone tapped, and there was no reason to be monitoring Glory's room, so taking a stiff drink, and since all local calls were free, Hokee called Glory.

"Where are you, you son-of-a bitch?" No hello, no hi, just a snarling greeting. "You said you would be back shortly and I've been worried sick."

"Hi honey, it's nice to hear *your* sweet voice too. Sorry about the delay. I ran into a wee problem," the language probably the scotch's influence, "but I think it's okay now.

"Okay, I'm sorry for the greeting. But damn it, I've been pacing the room like a caged tiger. And you haven't answered my question. Where are you?" "Reading from the napkin, Hokee gave her the name of the café. Call Hobb's, have him and Jensen collect Heather and meet me here. Please don't come with them as hotel security might watch for you. Go down the hall, slip out of a side door, and catch your own taxi. We'll all meet here and I'll explain everything."

"Sometimes, mister Wolf, you try a woman's patience." But you could hear the smile in her voice.

A few minutes later, all four were gathered around Hokee's sidewalk table. Hobbs and Jensen were drinking beer while Glory had a glass of white French wine, which the server said was a house favorite. Hokee filled Glory in on the events in Hobbs's room and suggested he needed another place to stay. He didn't want to run into the hotel security man again.

"Damn," Glory said, "and just when I thought I'd get to spend some more time with you."

"While waiting for you all to arrive, I booked a room at the Le Meurice. I figured if it was good enough for Orson Welles, it was good enough for me. I'd be happy to share my room with you, Glory. But you have to stop calling me a son-of-a-bitch. My momma wouldn't like it one bit."

"But all of my things are at the Four Seasons." Glory sort of whimpered. "We'll have Captain Hobbs collect your things and check you out,"

Hokee said matter-of-factly.

"Oh no, mister Wolf. Heather can collect my things if she's willing. I don't want any man pawing over my stuff." Now Glory sounded like the tough television investigative reporter she was back in New York.

"I'll be happy to collect your belongings and pack for you, Glory. Do you have anything hidden away that you didn't want anyone to see?"

"No, but be careful with my cameras and recording equipment. They belong to the station, and I think they are expensive."

Hokee listened to this exchange and then added, "the hotel security personnel have probably been alerted to watch for any suspicious activity. I believe they are sure I am packing guns and that Captain Hobbs is involved somehow. I'm pretty sure they do not know I was staying with Glory, just some beautiful woman. Since Heather and Hobbs were seen together during the check-in at the front desk, there wasn't much for the security personnel to find out about Glory.

Heather needs to check out of the Hotel for Glory and recover her passport. In my experience, the desk clerk never looks at the passport as they return it to the owner. The passport is kept in a cubby-hole containing the room number, so when you hand in your key or give them your room number, they grab your passport and hand it back to you. They may question why you are leaving at this time of night, and, of course, you act demurely while batting your beautiful brown eyes, telling them you have made other arrangements. They understand you will stay with a man."

Heather beamed at the compliment and seemed eager to participate in this grand adventure besides serving cocktails on Grant's plane.

They were all ready to eat and ordered food, along with another round of drinks. Hokee switched to the French wine, choosing a classic Pinot Noir to pair with an order of escargot and their famous French sourdough bread. The others settled for the olives and canapes for their L'Aperitif. They had the complete seven courses of a formal French dinner, all choosing the roasted stuffed game hen as their main course.

"Oh my God, Hokee, I hate to say it, but these French know how to cook. I believe their game hen tops your rabbit dish," and seeing Hokee's frown, she added, "but it was close."

Heather and Jensen both said, "rabbit?"

Glory answered. "Hokee cooked me the most fantastic meal at that cave he calls home, and the main course was rabbit. It was incredible. The tastiest meal I can remember eating until tonight. Maybe it was the wine," she added, giving Hokee a big smile.

"It's too late, Glory. You can just let Heather leave your stuff back at the Seasons. There's no room for someone in my life who doesn't appreciate my culinary talents." Hokee had a big smile of his own.

Glory jabbed him in the ribs with her elbow, "don't listen to him, Heather. It's just that his male ego got a little bruised. He'll live."

Knowing it was a good time to shut his mouth, Hokee remained quiet. "What about your painting, Hokee? Hobbs asked. "Are you okay carrying that around Paris?"

"I shouldn't have any more problems, Captain. I'm going to have a taxi take me to a bus station with lockers where I can leave my paintings until needed. But thanks for the concern. I'm sorry about the earlier trouble. I hope the hotel security man leaves you alone. It might be best if you and Captain Jensen, along with the beautiful Heather, joined us at the Meurice

tomorrow. I know it's a hassle, but we have little time to screw around chasing each other down."

"No, that will be fine, Hokee. We'll check out first thing tomorrow."

"Okay, guys, I guess it's time to say goodnight. See you all tomorrow."

They all left with no one knowing that Hokee was about to spend one of the longest nights of his life.

CHAPTER THIRTY

After depositing his gun case at the bus station, Hokee waited in the lobby of the Le Meurice for Glory to arrive and check-in, using her passport retrieved from Heather back in the Four Seasons. He was still reluctant to leave any formal document showing that he was in Paris. He wasn't worried about the others leaving their names at the front desk because they were not carrying firearms. The Paris police would have no reason to question them if gunfire came into play. That was a question Hokee would like to answer. Would he be forced to shoot somebody in Paris before this affair ended?

After Glory had her room, Hokee joined her to collect his medicine bag. He wanted to use the hotel sauna as a sweat lodge to connect with his spiritual guides. Glory was unhappy with this decision as she wanted to spend the evening with Hokee and join him in the sauna, but Hokee refused her request. His explanation for refusing her company was that this time he had to focus on his journey through the ocean of unconscious energy and could not protect her if she ran into trouble. Having had the frightening experience of losing her mind, Glory reluctantly agreed to stay behind and wait for his return. She didn't know he wouldn't return until after sunlight kissed the top of the Eiffel tower.

The sauna was cold when Hokee arrived back in the spa area using Glory's keycard, and no one else seemed interested in getting hot and sweaty.

While the sauna was heating, Hokee filled its wooden bucket with water and dumped some herbs from his medicine bag to infuse the water with their potency. He then began meditating with circular breaths before going deep into the subconscious. During his forthcoming journey into the vast repository of unconscious thoughts and memories, Hokee sought to discover the future. The spiritual guides he would meet could offer clues, but the future has yet to be written. There are probable futures, but there are also several possible futures. That is one of the reasons that so-called psychics have such a difficult time predicting the future. Nature habitually throws in random events that deviate from the most probable course of action. Man still has free agency and there can be a ninety-nine percent chance of an event occurring, but that other one percent can pop up at any time and mess with even the best psychic in the world. All Hokee wanted was to rescue the missing Shoshone children without killing somebody, and he wanted his guides to advise. The sauna was ready, and Hokee entered the hot room naked with his medicine bag and the water bucket.

After breathing in the hot air and feeling the sweat break out on his body, Hokee prayed to his guides for help before sprinkling some sage, cedar, and wormwood chips onto the hot rocks above the heater.

While smoke filled the sauna, Hokee breathed it into his body, feeling the herbs begin their magic. He could sense his resistance to everyday events melting away as though they had never existed. His body seemed to float above the frenetic energy of Paris and the swirling emotions of everyday life. When he felt free from this life, Hokee poured water from the wooden bucket onto the red-hot rocks, sending a cloud of herb-infused steam throughout the sauna. This steam sent Hokee into the far reaches of his subconscious mind, into the Akashic Chronicles and beyond, into the deepest corners of the mental universe. It was there he met Ashanti, one of his spiritual guides.

"I know why you are here, Hokee, but as you know, the future is impossible for the incarnate mortal man to see. You can see possible and probable futures, but not a certainty in any of your visions. You face a great evil. Destruction of your country's future, which is its offspring, leads to the end of your civilization. Now, what is your question?"

Hokee had to think about what he had heard. One never hears with the ears. Instead, the ears merely convey signals to the brain, where the signals are interpreted as sounds. When the spirits speak, it is directly in the mind. Nothing Ashanti said was new information; still, it caused Hokee to spend some time contemplating his questions. Of course, he wanted to know if he would rescue the stolen children and if the Paris police would capture him. But his real question was how to get past the security Madam Brezing was sure to have in place now that she knew the Mauritania connection had been severed with the death of Shabib Ghulam. He was almost certain that she would relinquish control of the children once confronted with the exposure of her sins. Getting to that point without being arrested or killed was the problem.

"Would you show me the faces of evil I will confront?" Usually, Hokee would program this kind of request into his pre-sweat meditation, but tonight he had failed to adhere to this part of his preparation.

The face of Madam Brezing floated in his mind, along with that of several men and a few women he did not recognize. He was surprised to see a palace and a magnificent courtyard in which a smug man walked as though he owned the entire planet. Hokee did not know who the man was or where the palace was located, only that it contained a source of evil.

"Okay, one final question. Will my ruse to gain entrance to Madam Brezing's house succeed?"

"Sorry, my child. You know the answer to that question. Peace be upon you." And then Ashanti disappeared from Hokee's mind and he felt completely drained. Rousing himself, he left the sauna, stepping into what felt like was a freezing lounge. Hokee had also neglected to take any drinking water into the sauna and he was severely dehydrated. Then, after sitting in

the cool air and drinking water, Hokee entered the large shower and rinsed off the sweat and stink he felt after his last vision of the palace and the evil man with the smug look.

Getting dressed, Hokee was surprised to see that it was almost seven in the morning. Glory was going to be majorly pissed. Well, hell, it was breakfast time someplace, and he was famished—nothing like seeing hell to give a man an appetite. Hopefully, Glory would have breakfast with him and not throw a hissy fit.

Hokee was already planning his assault on Brezing's mansion.

CHAPTER THIRTY-ONE

Glory was talking on the telephone when Hokee returned to their room. It was very early in the morning back in New York City, but newsrooms never sleep, especially big city newsrooms with an early morning news show. Levi Morgenstern, her news director-manager-producer-boss and sometimes friend, had been waiting for her call. He was eager to get information about her child trafficking story so he could begin teasing it for their forthcoming series. Glory had been filling him in on events in Houston and Mauritania, leaving out Hokee's manner of eliminating the responsible parties. Without naming names, she told him about the Paris Madam who had purchased the Shoshone children and their plans to expose her if she did not return them to Hokee's care. When Hokee entered the room, she signed off, promising a detailed segment with video shortly.

"Hi stranger. It's about damn time. I love it when you spend our first evening in Paris stuck in a sauna."

"Good morning Glory, you're a vision of beauty. I'm so sorry about last night Glory, but business before pleasure. Before confronting our Paris Madam, I had to get something straight in my head."

"And is your head straight now, sweetheart?" Glory asked in a sweet but sarcastic tone.

"Well, yes. I'm afraid my plan to appear as a customer, even with an introduction from our bellhop or doorman, will not work."

"So, do you have another plan?" This time she sounded serious, without the fake emotion she used earlier.

"I do. But now it is time for breakfast. That sauna drained my energy. Let's call the others and meet someplace for a hearty meal. No damned continental breakfast for this lad."

"Funny you should ask Hokee, but this hotel features a buffet of German breakfast items, including, according to the hotel literature, six kinds of German sausage."

Glory called the Four Seasons and talked with Captain Hobbs, who was just getting ready to check out from the Hotel. He promised to collect Heather and meet Hokee and Glory in the Le Meurice restaurant in thirty minutes.

Wanting a shower before getting dressed for breakfast, Glory headed for the bathroom while Hokee went to the kitchenet for more liquid, hoping for an energy drink but settling for a bottle of spring water.

They all met in the hotel lobby before entering the restaurant for breakfast. Hobbs and Jensen were eager to learn about Hokee's plans, while Heather was happy to be in Paris and take part in what she deemed an adventure.

After feasting on a fantastic breakfast meal, they all assembled back in Glory's room for a conference. Glory got everyone settled with a cup of coffee before Hokee started the meeting.

"I have reasons to change the plans Glory and I discussed earlier for extracting the children from Madam Brezing. We both thought the plan had a lot of merits, but last night I discovered Brezing is too closely allied with the Paris police for that plan to work." Hokee didn't bother getting into the specifics of a plan already abandoned.

"Do you have a backup plan?" Hobbs asked. There was worry in the tone of his voice.

"I do. Unfortunately, getting the children will not be as clean and tidy as I had initially hoped. Captain Jensen, I would like you to fetch our plane from the Beauvais International Airport, bring it to the Charles De Gaulle airport, then ensure the fuel is topped off, and the plane is ready to depart at a moment's notice. File a contingency flight plan for the continental United States, although that may change once we are in the air. Leave our departure time open, but alert the tower that we may have to leave quickly. Please remain on the plane until you hear from us, or we arrive with the children." "Sure Hokee. I'll leave just as soon as our meeting is finished." Jensen seemed relieved to be left out of the action with Madam Brezing. "Heather," Hokee continued, "I would like you to go with Captain

Jensen and check out food stores and emergency medical supplies. We may have a dozen kids to feed on a long flight and some may need medical attention. Hopefully, that will not be the case, but we had better be prepared. Here is five thousand dollars," he said, handing her a stack of bills, "to purchase anything you think we might need."

"Where am I supposed to buy this stuff?" Heather asked with a worried frown.

"Hell, I don't know. Have Glory help you find a supermarket and drugstore. You can rent a cab once you are both back at the main airport." Hokee sounded stern and realized that maintaining a calm demeanor was required with this group; they were not battle-hardened troops. Instead, he needed to show them confidence, patience, and strong leadership.

With a softer tone and a wry grin, Hokee continued. "Captain Hobbs, I need you to find transportation to haul twelve to twenty kids from Brezing's place to the airport. Something like a school bus or an extra-large van. Check out online to see what you can find. Then park the vehicle close to Brezing's mansion. "I'll call you when it is time for you to drive up and load the kids."

"I thought we were dealing with only eleven Indian kids," Glory said with a confused look.

"Knowing that Brezing traffics in stolen kids, I assume she has kids from other parts of the world. I'm only guessing about the twenty-kid number. It could be more, but it may be much less as she could have sold them by now. I think it is better to plan for what I believe is the worst case. Of course, if she has sold them, perhaps that would be the worst case, as we may never find them all."

"My God, Hokee. You are just a bundle of sunshine today," Glory observed with her reporter's sarcastic voice.

"Yeah, I know I am raining on everybody's parade. But this entire rescue effort has been one long, miserable affair, and I think it's about to get even worse."

"How could it be worse than getting stranded in the Sahara Desert without water?" Glory asked.

"You all may as well know what is going to happen. Madam Brezing has a direct line to police headquarters. Any attempt to cause her a problem will bring Paris police officers and probably someone high in command. Besides providing them with young kids to play with, I'm sure Brezing contributes significantly to their retirement portfolio." Hokee paused for a breath and drank some coffee.

"Before I knock on her door, I have to cut the direct land lines to the police department plus activate a mobile phone jammer. Since my jammer will cut off several surrounding houses and businesses, it may not take long for someone to leave the area and report the disruption. I'm not sure how much time I will have before the police arrive, but I guess fifteen minutes is the maximum time I can spend inside the mansion. I hope like hell I have the full fifteen minutes. Of course, any earlier response by the police could get nasty. If some police captain calls for a Brezing special and finds the line dead, he may drive by to see what causes the problem. Several things could go wrong, and we'll need luck to pull this off."

"My God, Hokee," Glory said, sounding worried. "Isn't there something else you can do?"

"Well, I haven't thought of any other way of spending time in that house without the police causing a problem. And you'll be in there with me."
"What? I thought this was going to be a simple blackmail job." Now
Glory was frightened.

"It will be a blackmail job, but first, I have to deal with the inside guards I know she has. I may have to kill one or even several. Then, until I can get the kids downstairs and we get photographs of them with Brezing in her house transmitted to New York, we will be at the mercy of the police. Once we get the pictures and they are safely emailed to an outside account, we will have leverage, even with the police."

"What's this about killing? We never discussed this before. I just thought we would go in, see the kids, get pictures and blackmail the bitch into handing them over."

"That was what I hoped we could do, but I discovered last night that Brezing knows what happened to Shabib Ghulam in Mauritania and has beefed up her inside security. She is expecting a man named Largo and is prepared to kill him with the full cooperation of the Paris police. One of our advantages is that Brezing does not know what Largo looks like, which may buy me a few seconds. I am positive they expect her to call as soon as some stranger knocks on her door."

"So that is what you were doing last night. I'm sorry for causing a fuss this morning. Are you frightened?" Glory sounded contrite and worried at the same time.

"Ah, dear Glory. You know better than that. A few things frighten me, but nothing on this earth. No, Madam Brezing would do well to be frightened. I plan to raise hell for her, hopefully costing her dearly."

"Now that's the Hokee Wolf I remember meeting in that Idaho desert when you found the empty grave." Hokee's confident statement gave Glory the confidence she needed to carry on with the plan.

"Okay, now that the housekeeping part has been covered, here are your final orders. Captain Hobbs, you will be parked close to Brezing's mansion. If everything goes to hell and the cops show up before Glory and I come out with a bunch of kids, you head to the airport, find Captain Jensen with the plane, and take off for home. Please don't get caught up in my mess."

"But what about Glory?" Hobbs asked.

"If any killing is done, which I suspect will be the case, it will be me and me alone doing the shooting. As an investigative reporter on an assignment, Glory has a legitimate reason to be there investigating leads she gained in working on a story. Her boss in New York knows about her actions and where she is right now. Glory has evidence that Brezing is involved in trafficking stolen children and is prepared to make this public knowledge. If any harm comes to Glory, the story and the complicity of the Paris police will be broadcast worldwide. Glory should be able to leave with no damage to her physically. Since I will undoubtedly have killed a French citizen or two, I may not be so lucky. Glory can fly home commercially, the same way she arrived. With the three of you aboard, you get Grant's plane safely back to Nampa."

Everyone seemed a little shocked at their assignments and the ramifications. Hobbs, Jensen and Heather found looking into Hokee's eyes difficult as they left the room. It was possible they may never see him again, and to some extent, they experienced a prenomen known as survivor's guilt. They knew they didn't face any real danger, and their boss and comrade could be killed.

Hokee had a big smile as he wished them success in their assignment.

Glory came over and hugged him while kissing his lips tenderly. "Let's go raise some hell, Hokee."

"You got it, sweetheart, but first, I need to visit the bus depot and grab my gun case. I'll be back shortly." Saying that, Hokee left the room and grabbed a taxi. Having the cabbie wait five minutes, Hokee dashed into the depot, got his case, then hurried back to the cab and hotel.

When he returned to their hotel room, he found Glory waiting, fully dressed, ready for war, welcoming him back with a warm hug. Hokee wore a pair of blue jeans with a dark blue long-sleeved denim shirt. His shoulder-length black hair was secured with a thick white headband featuring a sizeable blue turquoise stone carved in the image of an eagle landing with his talons reaching for some prey. The shining black eye of the eagle was a little bigger than the stone would usually accommodate, as it was the lens of a miniature camera with the electronics, including Bluetooth, enclosed in the thick white headband. Hokee wore his trademark black cowboy boots that matched a black leather vest. Today he looked all Indian with a severe shine in his eyes. They were the eyes of a dedicated hunter who would spare no mercy.

Extracting himself from Glory's embrace, he retrieved his gun case and removed the silenced 22 magnum he nearly threw away in the Sahara. Finally, he checked the clip to ensure it contained all nine shells, then checked to make sure there was one in the chamber. The 22 went into a

shoulder holster covered by his best. The silencer's added length would prohibit a quick draw, but Hokee didn't expect a wild west shootout. Then he put a fully loaded spare clip in a vest pocket. The trusty Colt 45, which rarely left his body, was snug in a holster behind his back. It was also fully loaded with one in the chamber. For today's excursion, he also carried a Fairbairn-Sykes knife in a soft leather sheath hanging down his back just below his neckline. The Fairbairn is a British-made knife with a thin seven-inch-long blade and is deadly in any close-quarters fight.

The hunter was now ready for battle.

Glory wore a loose black pantsuit. Today was not one to look sexy if she wanted to be taken seriously. Wearing little makeup that she didn't need anyway, with only a small gold chain around her neck, Glory appeared to be what she was, a professional investigative reporter covering stories for a leading New York television station. Leaving Hokee's side, she went to the dresser drawer and extracted a gray leather case holding a Globalstar GSP-1700 satellite telephone phone that could transmit pictures. The sat phone had a slight modification to include Bluetooth that linked to Hokee's miniature high-resolution video camera so that any images captured by the camera could be instantly sent via satellite back to New York. Another advantage of the sat phone was that it would still communicate via satellite when Hokee activated his phone jammer. A small clutch bag holding her identification, money and credit cards went into the gray case.

Hokee opened the door to their room and, holding Glory's hand; the two warriors left together to go forth and slay the dragons.

CHAPTER THIRTY-TWO

The Préfecture de police is one of a multitude of police buildings throughout the city of Paris. The Préfecture is the capital building for all 65 of the other police building in the city. It is six stories of gray granite Baroque splendor, more fitting a museum building than a municipal police headquarters. But then, this is Paris, a city not known to be shy of an elaborate display of opulence. For example, the towering sloped roof is decorated with sculptures of warriors on all eight corners of a structure divided by a stained glass-domed entrance hall full of world-class artworks.

Heading the National police force in Paris is the Police Prefect of Paris, Kylian Green. Kylian is only 5 foot 9 inches tall, much like Napoleon Bonaparte, with the same superior attitude. Today, he wore a tailored Italian suit made of the finest Egyptian cotton. His office suite was one of splendor on the 6th floor of police headquarters, with the Divisional commissioner of police stationed in the outer office as his watchdog.

At the Police Municipale level sits the Directeur principale de police, what Americans would call the Chief of Police. Monsieur Claude Laurent, the chief, was housed in a much less splendid office on the 1st floor with a matronly lady named Edith Sartre sitting outside as his gatekeeper. Claude is 45 years old and stands 6 foot one with a thick head of dark brown hair

streaked with gray cut short in military fashion. He is vain in appearance, always wearing tailored police uniforms but without the Napoléon complex.

Madam Brezing had a direct line to both men's offices. These lines were only used when the men desired a discrete visit to the mansion. Unbeknown to all but Madam Brezing and her security advisor, the madam collected videos from hidden cameras of all the influential men in France who visited the mansion at 999 Bd St. Germain. She had never used the videos to blackmail the visitors, but had them in case they might one day prove useful. Madame Claude, her substitute mother and teacher, taught her to prepare for the day when society or circumstances might require her to seek protection. Others might coerce today's friendly policeman to damage her and her business at some future time. It is always better to be prepared for the worst that could happen.

The Préfecture is on the banks of the river Seine, within view of the Notre Dame Cathedral. It is on the opposite side of the river from Madam Brezing's mansion, about ten minutes away.

CHAPTER THIRTY-THREE

Bd St. Germain runs about 2 1/4 miles in an arc on the Left Band of the Seine between two bridges-Pont De Sully on the East and Pont de la Concorde on the west. It features shops, restaurants, bakeries, and much more, including beautiful mansions like the one at 999 Bd St. Germain. The street is tree-lined and features many sidewalk restaurants. The boulevard is named after St. Germain-Pres church, the oldest church in Paris, with parts dating to the 6th century. The buildings on each side of the boulevard are typically 8 to 10 stories tall, giving the street the feeling of being in a tunnel. Madam Brazing's mansion is only six stories of white granite, but its fantastic Baroque architecture makes up for its diminutive size. Looking west down the boulevard from 999 Bd St. Germain, one can see the top of the Eiffel tower. Across the Pont de la Concorde bridge on the river Seine and a few short blocks away sits the Notre Dame Cathedral.

At eleven a.m., the sun was shining on a perfect summer day. Hokee and Glory had rented a car at the Concierge's desk and drove past 999 Bd St. Germain, Madam Brezing's mansion, to see if there were any police cars in the vicinity while looking for Captain Hobbs and the bus. The street was quiet, unnaturally so, as hundreds of people would typically stroll down the boulevard, viewing the magnificent shops full of expensive merchandise or

eating and drinking at one of the sidewalk cafes. Today there were very few people on the street; now, what could be the reason for that?

They saw no police cars in the vicinity and could not explain the stillness. It was eerie and unsettling, like this entire section of Paris had been declared off-limits. Sure, Madam Brezing expected somebody to come calling, but she didn't know whom to look for or when that person might arrive. Hokee had left no trace of himself along his back trail, and Brezing could not know about him or Glory specifically. Still, something had spooked everyone away from the area. Maybe it was the feeling of something terrible about to happen in the neighborhood. Hokee knew everything was a vibration at some particular frequency. It could be just that simple. Brezing and her mansion were emitting very negative vibrations that made people uncomfortable. Okay, even to Hokee, that thought seemed a little too much like the tin-hat crowd behavior, but whatever the reason, Hokee was not unhappy to see the streets empty. There was less chance of his cell phone jamming to cause a problem.

Captain Hobbs and his kiddie transportation vehicle were not yet in place, and Hokee didn't dare begin his assault on Brezing's mansion until the bus was nearby. Instead, they drove around the neighborhood for a few minutes, carefully avoiding passing past the mansion in case someone was watching the traffic from one of the many windows. It took nearly thirty minutes, but they finally spotted the captain as he parked a Renault Megane minibus about fifty yards down the street from Brezing's place. Just far enough not to be visible from the mansion.

Hokee parked their rental about the same distance from the mansion in the opposite direction, then proceeded on foot with Glory at his side. They hugged the inside of the sidewalk to be out of the line of sight from the mansion's windows for as long as possible. Getting close enough to be observed, they held hands like honeymoon lovers and walked down the sidewalk like tourists gawking at the magnificent mansions. Hokee studied the wires going to the mansion to determine which side of the building the telephone wires were on. This situation was their first bit of bad luck. The wires were on the opposite side of the building from the direction they were

walking, meaning they had to pass in front of the mansion to reach the wires Hokee needed to cut.

The only way to proceed was to continue walking as they had been, stopping briefly in front of the mansion as though observing its beauty. Hopefully, anyone watching would see two tourists walking the streets, admiring the views.

Hokee regretted his wardrobe, as his Indian look could place him in the same category as the missing Indian children. The coincidence would not go unnoticed. Too late now to worry about such things. It was time to get to work.

They continued walking, and as soon as they passed the far corner of the building, Hokee took off running, ducking below the windows to the spot where the telephone wires entered the structure. Then, pulling the knife from the back of his neck, Hokee cut the telephone wires, leaving the power lines intact. Then he rushed back to the front door, where Glory stood waiting. After activating the cell phone jammer, Hokee drew the 22 from its holster, then attached the silencer, holding it down by his leg while Glory rang the doorbell, hoping her image would confuse those inside about her intentions. It was not to be.

The door was opened by a huge bald man who looked like a sumo wrestler. He was wearing a soft black silk long-sleeved shirt that would cover a large cow. The shirt had a small white Fleur-de-Lys printed down the front in two rows. The sumo's pants were baggy white shorts and his feet were bare. A snub-nosed 9mm handgun pointed at Glory's head was in his right hand. In his large hand, the gun looked like a tiny toy. Hokee watched the man's eyes as they took in Glory, then as the sumo noticed Hokee standing behind, his eyes betrayed his intentions. Hokee focused on the man's eyes, then as the man's trigger finger started turning white to shoot, Hokee shot him in the head with the silenced 22 Magnum milliseconds before the sumo could finish pulling the trigger. Hokee rushed around a terrified Glory, heading inside to investigate the next level of threats.

Two guards wearing uniforms resembling clothes police officers might wear saw the door guard fall and drew their pistols as Hokee entered the sizeable open vestibule leading into the downstairs drawing room. Hokee wasn't sure they were not police officers on his brief glance at the threat. One of the guards stood at the foot of a broad white marble curved staircase, and the other guard was to the far right in front of two matching carved doors, which Hokee determined later led to Madam Brezing's private 5000 square foot suite. As the guards were bringing their guns into play, Hokee shot them both in the head, police officers or not. He wasn't about to let them get off a shot at him or Glory.

To Hokee's far left, in an alcove, sat an officer in the Paris Enforcement Corps, not someone in the investigation or security corps. This man was on a radiotelephone talking to headquarters. Unfortunately, Hokee did not expect an on-site police officer with radio communications back to police headquarters. Hokee's telephone jammer did not affect radio transmissions. Hokee marched over to the policeman and, grabbing the handheld radiophone, threw it on the marble floor, smashing it under his boots. Then relieving the man of his weapon, Hokee demanded, how much time before the cavalry arrived?

Stammering, the police officer responded in French, using words Hokee didn't understand.

Slapping the Major hard across his face, Hokee said, "**bullshit.** You speak English, probably better than me. Once more. Give me more Frenchie crap and you can join these other three," he said, pointing the 22 at the dead man by the stairs. "How much time before the others arrive?"

Fear flared in the man's eyes and he found it difficult to speak. Stammering, he said, "Ta... taah... twenty minutes, monsieur." He lied about the time, figuring that police commanders plus an army of police officers carrying automatic AK-47s would put this terrible Indian where he belonged, in a grave.

Hokee reached down with his left hand, grabbing the front of the policeman's tunic and jerking him to his feet.

"How many other guards are there in this house?" The heat in Hokee's eyes left no doubt about what would happen if the man refused to answer. "If you lie to me, you are a dead man."

Fearful of the wrath he saw in Hokee's eyes, the policeman choked out an answer. "Three, monsieur." The man would collapse if Hokee wasn't still holding on to his tunic.

"Are they police officers like those other two?" Hokee again indicated the man lying by the stairway, pointing at him with the 22.

"What? Oh no. Those aren't police. Madam Brezing had them wear a similar uniform to confuse you." Confessing this subterfuge seemed to give the policeman some strength.

Seeing that the man was showing signs of life, Hokee let go of his uniform. "What is your name, officer?" Hokee still had a fierce look that would not tolerate any more false steps by this officer or anyone else.

Seeing the fierceness displayed by his tormentor, the policeman stammered, "Ah... Ahn... André. André Crochet." To Hokee, it sounded like his last name was crow shay.

"Well, mister crow shay, I want you to bring all three guards to me here in the main room on the double with their hands in the air. If I have to go hunting, there will be a lot more dead people. **Chop! Chop!**" And Hokee pushed the man towards the open room.

The policeman never left the room but called out to the guards in French. As Hokee's silenced 22 hardly made any sound, these other guards were unaware that three of the number were already dead. Hokee assumed the policeman informed them of the situation as two guards came down the stairs and a third man exited from Madam Brezing's suite. The three guards had angry faces, but their hands were in the air.

Hokee pulled the Colt 45 from his waist, then put the 22 away. The 45 had a more menacing look. Then, making sure the three new arrivals got a good look at the Colt, Hokee went to them one at a time and took their guns. Each carried a 9mm Glock, the weapon of choice for NATO. "Now, lay down on the floor with your hand reaching forward." When the men just stood without moving, Hokee fired a shot into Brezing's thick wooden doors from the Colt, which sounded like a cannon. "**I MEAN NOW.**" The men immediately dropped to the floor with their arms outstretched. Hokee then took their firearms over to the table where he had deposited André's gun before addressing the policeman.

"André, I want you to go with my associate here," he said, pointing to Glory, who looked like a deer caught in the headlights. She had never seen that fierce look in Hokee's eyes or witnessed him killing anyone. "Bring down everyone from the upper floors. Don't miss anyone, or you will die. Do you understand?"

"Oui, oui, monsieur." The man scurried up the stairs, and Glory had to hurry to keep pace. They both seemed relieved to leave the room with the dead men and a fierce warrior.

It was at that moment that Madam Brezing entered. She had not heard the silenced shots that killed the three guards on the main floor. The Madam had been waiting beside the telephone to call police headquarters when the policeman stationed in the entrance alcove had rudely summoned her. Her suite was soundproofed behind the two thick solid Teak doors to isolate herself from the men and women who frequented the mansion. She had staff to deal with ordinary business affairs, keeping to herself as much as possible. After the rude policeman opened the door to her suite and yelled for her to come, the Madam wanted to see for herself what was happening. Then, seeing the dead guard outside the doors to her suite, she lost the color on her face and almost fainted.

Seeing the lady come through the doors, Hokee said, "Madam Sleazing, how nice of you to join us."

CHAPTER THIRTY-FOUR

To her credit, the lady straightened up and, speaking in crisp, accentuated English, responded to Hokee's address, not realizing at the moment that Hokee was purposefully insulting her. "The name is Brezing. Madam Brezing."

"Yeah, I know your name, miss Sleaze. You probably haven't learned that word before, so look it up sometime. Anyone trafficking in kidnapped people is garbage to me, and anyone trafficking in kidnapped children for pedophiles is pure evil. Even sleaze is too mild to describe your behavior. Come over and sit in your queen's chair." Hokee motioned towards the throne in which Madam Brezing conducted her auctions.

When the woman still stood by the door to her suite, Hokee barked, **"NOW. Dammit."**

Hokee's outburst, plus the fire in his eyes, convinced Brezing that the man was serious, so she timidly walked across the room to the high-backed gilt-laden chair. Her ears were still ringing from Hokee's loud shout.

Within seconds, they could hear footsteps on the marble staircase as dozens of girls, boys, young men, and ladies came into view. The youngsters looked like they were between the ages of five and eighteen, and the older adults ranged up to their mid-thirties. Hokee had assumed there would be women and men at least 50 years of age. He would ask about this later.

There was a few seconds gap before another group came down the stairs. This group was composed of muscular men and women who probably never smiled. They were the enforcers who imposed discipline on the enslaved.

Glory and André were the last ones down the stairs.

Hokee commanded, "Glory, turn on the phone and start sending pictures." Hokee then walked around the room, pointing his head at every young boy and girl. Then, turning off his phone jammer, he pulled a cell phone from his vest pocket and called Captain Hobbs. "Bring up the buss."

Speaking the Shoshone language, Hokee said, "please don't be afraid; I am here to take you back to your parents. Please step forward so I can see how many of you are still here."

Nine Shoshone girls and boys separated from the group and ran to Hokee.

"Glory, please see that these children are loaded onto the bus with Captain Hobbs, then come back."

Madam Brezing watched several hundred thousand dollars scamper out of the mansion. She didn't know what Hokee meant when he told Glory to send pictures, but it didn't sound good. As she sat in her chair, watching this mean-looking Indian order people around and seeing the three dead guards, she realized this could be the end of her business and possibly her life. She hoped the Police Perfect of Paris would soon arrive and place this wild man under arrest.

After the Indian children left the mansion, Hokee appraised the remaining enslaved people. It looked like a cross-section between Asia, Europe, and the United States. There were children and adults of several nationalities, races, and skin colors. Hokee asked, "how many of you speak English? Raise your hands."

About a dozen hands were raised. This group included some of the older men and women and more kids.

"How many of you would like to go home or find someplace to live where you would not be a slave?" The same hands went up. Hokee commanded, "Leave quickly and join the others on the bus out front."

Madam Brezing saw another giant chunk of money hurry out of the front doors.

Turning to André, Hokee said, "Now ask the same question in French." By this time, Glory was back inside, and Hokee said to her, "listen to André and make sure he asks the right questions. I want to know how many of those slaves remaining in the room want to stay here or how many would like to leave. So this right now is their chance to go home or wherever they desire." Hokee didn't think Glory spoke French, but perhaps André didn't know that yet."

Everyone stepped forward, so Hokee told André to tell them all to go out and get on the bus. "Glory, phone Captain Hobbs and ask him to take this load to the U.S. Embassy and drop off everybody except the nine Shoshone kids. Let the Embassy deal with sorting out the kids and what to do. I realize the bus will be crowded as hell, but I didn't expect Madam Sleaze to enslave this many people.

Glancing at his watch, Hokee saw that a little over six minutes had elapsed since he assaulted the mansion. If the policeman was telling the truth, he had about fourteen minutes before a large police force arrived. With the pictures of the children and Madam Brezing now safely in New York, he could breathe a little easier, but that didn't mean he was safe. He could still be arrested for killing, even if it was self-defense which André, the policeman, may not corroborate. Brezing would claim he was a cold-blooded killer.

Hokee handed Glory the 22 magnum pistol. A few months ago, he had taken her out into the lava flats and taught her how to shoot. "Glory, I need you to keep your sat phone alive and guard these prisoners. I cannot afford to have them interrupt me for a few minutes. Madam Slease and I have a little business to conduct."

Glory spoke for the first time since she had entered the mansion. "Hokee, dammit, you expect me to shoot somebody?"

"Only if they don't behave. Everybody, sit down on the floor and stay still." When nobody moved, Hokee put another bullet from the Colt 45 into Brezing's doors and probably the wall behind. The loud gunshot got

everybody hurrying to the floor. "Now stay there, or this beautiful lady will kill you." Then he gave Glory a big smile and walked over to Brezing.

Hokee grabbed an arm, pulling her to her feet. It was not intended to hurt, only to assert authority.

Being a small woman, Madam Brezing hardly reached Hokee's shoulder. She wore a floor-length royal violet silk dress that caressed her slender body like a glove. Her makeup was flawless, but the fear in her eyes betrayed any sense of confidence she wanted to project.

"Mam, you and I are going to visit your chambers. I believe you will find this most entertaining." There was an evil glint in Hokee's eyes that terrified Madam Brezing. She had every right to be terrified. What Hokee had planned was never on her agenda.

CHAPTER THIRTY-FIVE

Hokee marched Brezing into her chambers and gasped when he saw the splendor and luxury on display. Premier works of art, including original oil paintings and fabulous sculptures. Behind the pictures, the walls were covered with gold Lamay wallpaper. The black and white patterned marble floor was covered with some of the most beautiful hand-woven East-Indian rugs Hokee had ever seen. Everywhere he looked, there was a beautiful tiffany lamp on a teak table or an Italian crystal chandelier.

Inside the room, Hokee asked, "Okay, mam, where's your bathroom?" "Where's the bathroom?"

Brezing was confused. What was the word bathroom? Then she realized he meant the loo. "Ah, the loo."

"Yes, the loo; take me there now."

Hokee released her arm and let her lead the way into the loo. By now, he was past being impressed by the woman's sizeable opulent suite; still, the loo expanded his feelings of luxuriousness.

Hokee found a stack of soft Egyptian towels and, picking one up, handed it to the perplexed woman.

"I'll ask one question nicely, and if you answer truthfully, everything will be okay." Hokee had become quiet with an almost serene look, which gave Brezing confidence.

"Where is your ledger? I want to see your ledger." "Ledger?"

"Yes, the book where you record all of your transactions." Hokee still maintained a serene, almost peaceful look.

"I don't have such a legger... er, book." The madam watched Hokee to see if he would buy the lie.

Hokee reached behind his head and pulled the Fairbairn-Sykes knife; then, in a motion almost too swift to see, he lifted Brezing's hair and sliced off her right ear close to the scalp. He caught the ear as it dropped and laid it gently on the sink. Then took Brezing's hand with the towel and guided it to the side of her head."

The Fairbairn was so sharp that Brezing didn't feel the cut or the pain until she saw her ear in Hokee's hand. "**What,**" she screamed.

"Don't panic, lady. Hold the towel tight to your head to stem the bleeding. It's just an ear. If we put it on ice and get you to a good plastic surgeon in the next 30 to 40 minutes, he can sew it back on so your hearing will not be impaired, and you will barely see the scar, especially if you wear your hair down. However, if you lie to me again, the ear goes down the toilet. Lie to me after that, and you lose the other ear. Continue lying, and your nose comes off. Do I have your attention?"

"Oui monsieur." Brezing gasped, turning white with shock, and Hokee held her up as he guided her to a wall for support.

One more time, I want your ledger." Hokee's friendly, serene look was gone. Now his usually blue eyes had that dark black look opponents found terrifying. "Your book of transactions."

"Oui." With effort, Brezing stood straight and, holding a bloody towel to her head, left the loo with Hokee right behind. She led him through the kitchen with professional chef's workstations, through a library featuring a fireplace with hundreds of books with matching leather covers, and into her

security office with over a dozen television monitors featuring views of various bedrooms. Against one wall was an ornate secretaries desk with a fancy high-backed white leather desk chair. The front of the chair's arms and the top of its back were covered with wooden inlays covered in gold. The chair sat in front of the rolltop desk, which had carved gold filigree inlays along each edge. Brezing indicated to Hokee with her free hand he should lift the tambour door. Laying on top of the desk was a bound red leather ledger.

Hokee picked up the ledger and found page after page of neat vertical columns with names and amounts. There were several columns under French labels that Hokee couldn't read, with French names below. He assumed they were names of buyers, sellers, the enslaved people, and Brezing's transactions. Hokee tilted his head to photograph several pages before closing the ledger and stuffing it inside his belt.

Looking into Brezing's eyes with those black eyes of his and a deadly calm expression, he said, "only nine of the Indian children you purchased from Shabib Ghulam came down the stairs. You purchased eleven. Where are the other two?"

Brezing gasped and coughed. Blood was soaking through the towel, and she looked pale. I... I... sold them." She didn't want to admit this to that terrible, mean-looking man, but his fierce look would not permit a lie.

"Who purchased them?" Hokee's anger showed through his already wrathful demeanor.

"A man from Saudi Arabia, a prince." "What is this prince's name?"

"I'll have to look it up. Let me look at the desk."

Hokee stepped aside, and Brezing swayed over to the desk, showing the effects of shock and blood loss. Then, reaching into one of the desk's small compartments, she retrieved a small red leather-bound address and phone book. Hokee wondered about the red leather on the ledger and phone book, but that thought quickly vanished. It wasn't important.

"Show me his name and phone number," Hokee demanded.

Brezing looked panicked and reluctant to comply with this demand until Hokee picked up her ear from the sink, and it appeared like he was going to drop it into the toilet when she screamed, "**NON. NON.** I show you." She fumbled with the small book, tried to open it with one hand, and finally found the page she was looking for using her fingers. She pointed out the name and phone of the buyer. He was the one Hokee discovered later was the fake art lover, Prince Mohammed Bader Al Saud.

"Did he purchase both Indian children? Hokee asked with what sounded like a snarl.

"Oui." Brezing was reluctant to answer, but afraid Hokee would flush her ear down the toilet if she didn't comply.

Hokee laid her ear back on the sink, pausing for a moment, and asked, "What happens to the men and women who grow old? I didn't see anyone come down the stairs past age 35."

Brezing seemed relieved that this was his question. "I sell them to a Procurer."

"Is that like a pimp?" Hokee thought he understood but wanted to be sure."

"Oui." Brezing was about to say something else, but the sounds of those damn French sirens, *whoump, whoump,* could be heard faintly in the background. Brezing was gaining a bit of composure with a glint of glee in her eyes, *like now you'll get yours, you bastard.*

Hokee figured he could afford another thirty seconds. "Show me the videos you recorded of all the famous people who come here."

Brezing huffed like saying screw you, Indian when Hokee pulled his knife and was about to attack her other ear. "Non et arrêtez. **Stop! I show you.**"

On another wall was a large six-foot-tall picture of Napoleon. He was standing with his right hand inside his tunic. One of his classic poses while his left hand rested on the hilt of a gold-handled saber. Brezing went over to the painting and pushed a hidden button on the sword's hilt, allowing the picture to be moved inside six inches, then slid to one side,

allowing access to a hidden wall with slots holding hundreds of CDs. Hokee saw a red canvas bag on the floor holding several new CDs. The bag was the size of a large paper grocery bag with a white logo. Emptying the bag on the floor, Hokee scooped into it as many recorded CDs as the bag would hold, then took off for the front door in a trot. He wanted to get there before the police posse arrived with guns blazing. On his way out the door, he yelled back at Brezing. "put your ear on ice."

CHAPTER THIRTY-SIX

Back in the main room, Hokee was confronted with pandemonium. The cowed people on the floor were standing, and Glory was shaking like she was holding a jackhammer. The 22 was being waved around, but she was reluctant to fire the gun at anyone. Hokee pulled the Colt 45 from his waist, firing a shot into the ceiling.

The sharp, loud explosion and the black look on Hokee's face immediately got everyone's attention. Hokee's blazing fierce black eyes were those of a man who would not tolerate any disobedience. Speaking in a stern, loud voice, Hokee commanded, **"André, go outside right now and find out who is in charge. The top man. Tell him to come in alone, or I will start shooting people."** Hokee was lying, but looking into his eyes, you wouldn't know that. He then took the silenced 22 from Glory, putting it back in his shoulder holster. He kept the 45 in his hand to keep the crowd from getting any wild ideas now that the police had arrived. The room was deadly silent and Hokee could hear André speaking French to someone; he was nearly shouting. Another voice could be heard speaking much softer. A two-way conversation lasted almost a minute before André returned with the Directeur principale de police, the Chief of
Police. Monsieur Claude Laurent.

Chief Laurent wore his tailored police uniform with four gold bars on each shoulder. He had a sidearm in a gleaming black holster, but the gun was secured, not in his hand. "Major Crochet told me you wished to speak with me alone, monsieur."

"Yes, and to whom am I speaking," Hokee asked as pleasantly as possible under the circumstances.

"I am the Directeur principale de police, monsieur. I believe in America, you would say the police chief." Chief Laurent spoke flawless English with a charming French accent. To Hokee, he sounded like Maurice Chevalier in *Love in the Afternoon* with Audrey Hepburn and Gary Cooper. One of those old movies filmed back in the 1950s was a Hokee favorite.

"Well, Chief Laurent, we have a situation here that I wish to explain. You can see that I have killed three men," Hokee motioned to the corpses with the Colt, which he still held, "but if you look closely, they all either have guns in their hands or one lying nearby. I believe they were guards hired by Brezing. I shot them all in self-defense or to save my associate here, miss Gloria Bingham. Miss Bingham is an investigative reporter for WXTV, a major New York television station. Their news segments are broadcast worldwide."

"Excuse me, monsieur," the chief said, "but to whom am I speaking and why do I care about miss Bingham?"

"My name is unimportant, but you should know more about miss Bingham. Glory, please bring up the pictures on your telephone of Brezing and the trafficked slaves and show them to Chief Laurent?"

Glory took a moment to find the pictures, then went over to Chief Laurent. "You will notice, chief," Hokee explained, "several juveniles are in the photo. Every person in those pictures under the age of 35 is a trafficked individual kidnapped from their home and sold from one dealer to the next until purchased by Brezing. I have here," Hokee said as he set the bag of videos on the floor and pulled the ledger from under his belt with his free hand, "Brezing's ledger in which she lists every purchase and sale of these slaves."

"Looking somewhat shaken but still haughty, Chief Laurent asked, "what has that to do with me and the Paris police, monsieur? And how do you know they were trafficked, as you claim?"

"Nine children in those pictures are Shoshone Indian kids stolen from their parents on the Fort Hall Indian reservation in Idaho and sold to a human trafficker in Houston, Texas, of the good old U.S. of A. They were purchased from the trafficker in Houston by another trafficker in Mauritania, Africa. Brezing purchased the kids from the trafficker in Mauritania. I have been tracking those children from Idaho, and I recognized the Shoshone children immediately. You may have noticed that I contain a little Indian blood in my veins." Hokee couldn't suppress a small smile

"That, Chief Laurent," Hokee continued, "is how I know they are trafficked people. When given a choice, all of those slaves in the picture ran from this mansion for a taste of freedom they thought was lost forever."

Laurent was looking much less condescending. "And where are these people now, monsieur?" The chief couldn't say the words slave or trafficked. "Most are in the United States Embassy here in Paris, where officials can determine where they came from and how to get them back home."

Hokee knew what the chief was worried about, but those worries would worsen considerably in the next few moments.

"This ledger also lists the visitors to this mansion," Hokee continued with the devastating news to the chief, waving the ledger in the air, "and how much these visitors paid Brezing and who they met with in the bedrooms upstairs." Hokee was delighted to see that he had finally broken through the Frenchman's reserve.

"I'll take that book from you now, monsieur," Captain Laurent stammered, walking towards Hokee with his hand extended.

"Hold on chief, I'm not through yet," Hokee said, pointing the Colt in the chief's direction, although not directly at the policeman. Then, putting the ledger back under his belt, Hokee picked up the canvas shopping bag and tilted it in Laurent's direction so the chief could see that it was full of video cassettes.

"I am almost certain you did not know Brezing has hidden cameras throughout the mansion, including the upstairs bedrooms, and that she filmed every tryst by anyone of importance." Hokee shook the bag to emphasize his statement, "including sex with underage children. The word used to define people with this behavior is pedophiles. In every case, it is child abuse."

Chief Laurent looked as though he might be ill.

"Brezing has direct lines to the police department," Hokee said to emphasize his point, "possibly to your office and some other police officials. There is no way she could traffic in stolen people, including children, without the police knowing and pretending it doesn't exist, if not also taking part in those disgusting acts with children."

The chief studied the floor with great concentration and looked everywhere but at Hokee Wolf.

"Chief, please go outside and send your men back to their stations. Make any excuse you want, but I don't want a bunch of trigger-happy cops standing around with automatic weapons in their hands. Get rid of them."

Chief Laurent stood in the middle of the room next to Brezing's golden throne, like one of the famous statues lining the Paris streets. "Go now, chief," Hokee said with emphasis, pointing with his pistol.

Chief Laurent shuffled outside and had several conversations before the police officers left the area. Hokee thought it sounded like they feared the chief was being coerced, which was actually the truth, although not in the way they might have supposed.

Hokee could hear the police leave the area, and when the last officer was in a car headed back to their station, Laurent came back inside to face a devil whose name he didn't know or even wanted to know.

"Well, monsieur, what do you want to happen now?" He rightly assumed that removing the outside police officers was only the first of many requests this Indian madman would demand.

"Miss Bingham and I will leave shortly, and we don't want any nonsense about being arrested for murdering some of your delightful French citizens,"

Hokee said, pointing his pistol at the sumo by the front door. "I don't believe we can save Brezing, who was trafficking people, especially children, not to mention selling their bodies to anyone willing to pay the price."

Hokee thought for a minute and motioned for Glory to come over and take the bag full of videos. "Miss Bingham is doing an expose on human trafficking, especially the trafficking of children, which her station in New

York will broadcast to the world. There will be pictures of Brezing with the kids. Her collaboration with the Paris Police Department will probably also be exposed, but I believe the television news people can be persuaded to withhold specific names. Astute individuals may guess at some names, but without corroboration, their guesses will be just guesses."

Chief Laurent seemed relieved to hear this announcement. Whether his name would be found in Brezing's ledger, his picture on one of the videos, or perhaps some of his men who served under him, Hokee didn't care. If Laurent didn't know what was going on, he should have.

"Brezing sold two of the Shoshone Indian children to some Saudi Prince. I want those kids back. I have the ledger documenting their sale to the prince, but I have no contacts in Saudi Arabia. The Prince needs to bring the children back to Paris. The leverage we have is his picture here in the mansion with Brezing and the kids, plus the documented sale to him of minor children. We may not prove he is a pedophile, but we can confirm that he trafficked in stolen children. He is a human trafficker. I do not believe the Royal House of Saud would like that information to be publicized. You now know miss Bingham's credentials and what she can accomplish. Are you able to help me with this problem?"

It could be construed as blackmail, which wasn't Hokee's intent, but he wasn't eager to make the distinction clear.

Chief Laurent had to think about the situation for a moment. Whether the threat of blackmail was in his mind, Hokee couldn't tell, but the chief was considering Hokee's question.

"The city of Paris is usually entertaining several of the royal family," Laurent said. "How can I phrase this delicately? Many of the city's laws, such

as speed limits, age limits at certain clubs, and enforcement of gambling debts, to name just a few, are not respected by many princes and princesses. I am often called upon to mediate a dispute between a French citizen whose vehicle was involved in an accident by one of the Royals while speeding and possibly intoxicated. I might convince his Royal Highness to have the wayward Prince return your Indian children.

"Great. Miss Bingham, would you give the chief the number of your cell, please?"

Hokee waited while Glory found a pen and jotted her phone number on a business card provided by the chief.

"We'll leave now Chief Laurent. Please call miss Bingham when you have information regarding the two stolen Indian children. Oh, and Brezing may need a ride to a hospital. She seems to have lost an ear."

Chief Laurent had a puzzled look on his face as Hokee and Glory, breathing a sigh of relief, left the mansion as Glory looked at Hokee, "Brezing lost an ear?"

"Better you not ask honey before we get some alcohol into our systems."

Hokee didn't want to drive as he was on an adrenalin high, which had his nerves twanging like someone playing the bass drum on speed, but Glory seemed in worse shape. She was shaking and pale.

Glory's fear started when she looked into the eyes of that sumo killer who met them at the front door and she knew he was going to shoot her. Then that hole appeared in his head and he fell to the floor before the soft *phut* from Hokee's gun registered on her brain. She had always known that Hokee had killed before and he often confronted men and women who had to be put in place, but she had never witnessed such a black countenance and fierce look in her entire life. Her only experience with such raw power was watching someone in the movies, which was anger manufactured by an actor. Many movie performances were believable and even scary, but that wasn't the same as being in the same room with a man on fire who was honestly and sincerely terrifying. She could understand his anger at the people who trafficked children, making them sex slaves. Glory knew he had

to scare the shit out of everybody in the building to get their cooperation. And by God, did he ever, including her. She was still somewhat afraid to be in a car with Hokee, which was crazy; after all, this was a man she loved, didn't she?

Yeah, she could use a drink, maybe the whole damn bottle. Better not ask about the ear! God, that entire experience was terrifying. Not something to be repeated, ever again.

CHAPTER THIRTY-SEVEN

Hokee drove them back to the hotel, where he turned in the car. They returned to Glory's hotel room and the first thing Hokee did was fill a tumbler full of scotch over ice for himself and another one full of vodka over ice for Glory. Glory put the bag containing the videos on the floor, then taking the vodka from Hokee, sank into one of the suite's luxurious chairs. Neither one was speaking. Words seemed superfluous. They needed to chill. Hokee took a sip of the scotch, then set the glass down on the table with fresh-cut flowers supplied by the hotel.

Hokee put the ledger on a table next to the fresh flower arrangement, then laid his Colt 45 next to the ledger. After removing his vest, Hokee then removedthe shoulder holster with the 22 and laid them next to the Colt. Then, drawing his phone from a vest pocket, Hokee picked up his drink and collapsed in a chair next to Glory. Neither one had spoken a word after returning the car to the concierge.

Hokee took a big swallow of his scotch, then called Captain Hobbs. "Hello Hokee. How did it go at the mansion?

"Hi captain. No problems we couldn't handle. Have you been able to connect with Captain Jensen?"

'Yes, we are on the plane now, and Heather is boarding the nine Indian kids. Let me tell you, they are some frightened children, but Heather is working miracles to get them settled."

"I'm happy to hear that. Listen, captain, once the kids are on board, take off and fly to Pocatello. I'll have one of the sheriff's deputies meet the plane with a bus to take the children back to the reservation."

"What? Aren't you coming with us, Hokee?"

"We are missing two of the Indian kids and we're working on getting them back. They are not in France at the moment. I can't see having those nine children with you spending any more time away from their parents than is necessary. We're not sure when we will get the other two kids."

"Understand. Sorry we can't all be together, but we'll get these kids back to their parents."

"Thanks, captain, and thank Captain Jensen and Heather for me. Oh, the deputy who will meet your plane in Pocatello is Robert Belingsford; we call him 'Curly,' for the hair he once had, but he is now bald as a billiards ball."

"Okay, Hokee. If we don't see you again, it's been a pleasure, more excitement than we're used to, but a pleasure. Good luck."

"Have a safe flight, Captain Hobbs." Hokee broke the connection. He was never good at saying goodbye.

After a few vodka swallows, Glory was relaxing. "Are the children okay, Hokee?"

"Yes. Captain Hobbs said they were still frightened, but Heather was getting them calmed down. You heard me tell him to get them back home."

"Yes, and I appreciate that. I'm sure they are eager to see their parents."

"Listen Glory, I know you have been frightened out of your skin, but we cannot afford to get too comfortable right now. We may still face some danger."

"What are you talking about? I thought all we had to do was wait for that police guy, Chief Laurent, to call me with information about the two other Indian kids."

"We have these videos," Hokee pointed to the canvas bag, "which many people will want no one to see. And I don't mean just the local Paris police

or even the National police who are also in the city. I'm talking about the Paris government officials. I didn't bring that up with the police chief, but you and I both know that Brezing could not operate without government officials knowing what was happening at the mansion. These government officials will do everything they can to ensure those videos are never watched. And then there are the Saudis who could be even more worried about being exposed."

As Glory thought about what Hokee had just said, you could see the color drain from her face. "Oh, my God. Just when I thought we were safe." "We have some time, maybe an hour. It will take time for Chief Laurent to contact the right people and for them to decide on a course of action. My guess is they will storm the hotel with a swarm of special force police officers, what we call a swat team in America. They will want to get those videos before your television people in New York can watch them."

As Hokee explained his thinking, Glory took several large swallows of her vodka before slamming the glass down on a side table. "God dammit, Hokee, what have you got me involved in here? What are we going to do?" "We'll; we are going to relax for a couple of minutes, then go catch a taxi. "I'll explain my plan after you get packed. We have a few minutes, so let's not panic."

"How can you be so damn calm? Some people will try to kill us." Instead of shaking with fear, the vodka was working, and the lady was getting mad. A reaction Hokee was happy to see.

"Let's pack our things and get a taxi. I'll explain what I think will happen when we get someplace safe."

"I thought we were safe here," Glory complained. "Why do we have to move?

"Because Chief Laurent knows your name, and soon so will others. Let's get out of here as quickly as we can." Hokee didn't mean to sound anxious or gruff, but Glory thought he sounded both. Yet she didn't waste any time packing her two bags, as Hokee ensured both pistols were fully loaded. He had his small carry-on and the gun case ready and waiting when Glory finished.

"I don't want you to check out right now. Let's carry our bags to the taxi stand out front and act as if we've already paid the bill. The chances are the desk clerk won't pay any attention to our leaving."

"You're making me nervous, Hokee. I sure as hell hope you know what you're doing."

"Me too Glory. Me too." Hokee slung the gun case under an arm and picked up both of Glory's bags. He had Glory get the canvas bag with the videos and his small carry-on, and then they left the room.

No one paid attention as they exited the lobby, and they had the doorman signal the taxi driver at the front of the taxi queue. Before the driver could load their bags, Hokee put Glory in the front seat, placed all their luggage in the back, and then seated himself.

"Do you speak English?" Hokee asked.

"Yes, monsieur. But of course." He sounded almost offended; like, don't all taxi drivers speak English?"

Hokee studied their driver for the first time. He was a small man with a fair complexion, like an Englishman who saw little sun. The driver spoke English like a native Frenchman with an accent. Hokee was satisfied with his appearance. What Hokee didn't want was a driver from the middle-east who might have some connection to Saudi Arabia.

"We would like to visit the theater district. Do you know of such a place?"

"Oui, monsieur, I mean yes, sir." "Please take us there?"

Glory turned around in her seat, giving Hokee a questioning look. He held up one finger like, "wait, I'll explain it all soon."

The drive to the theater district took about ten minutes. Hokee paid their driver, then studied their surroundings. He asked Glory to signal another taxi and wait with it for him to return. Leaving Glory to watch their luggage, Hokee took off walking in search of a costume shop. He found one two and a half blocks away across the street. He went inside and spent twenty minutes before leaving with two large bags. Glory was waiting in the taxi with the luggage when Hokee returned.

"Let's see now," Hokee said, "Can you recommend a good hotel near the theater district?"

"Yes, certainly. The St. James is a splendid hotel, much like a Château. I believe you will be most comfortable there."

"That sounds perfect. Thank you." "De rien. I mean, you're welcome."

Five minutes later, they were deposited at the entrance of the St. James hotel.

Hokee gave their driver a substantial tip and turned to face the hotel. The St. James did not have anyone waiting outside to carry their bags inside, which made Hokee happy.

While Glory fumed at not being consulted in their arrangements, Hokee signaled a passing taxi to stop and pick them up.

This time Hokee let the driver open the trunk for their luggage and sat beside an aggravated lady who was losing her temper.

Before the driver took his place while they still had a moment's privacy, Hokee took her hand and said, "Look, Glory, we cannot leave a trail, or they will find us. Trust me for a few minutes. This whole exercise is how I make my living and stay alive."

"Okay, Hokee. Just don't get me killed."

Neither one knew how difficult, if not impossible, that would become.

CHAPTER THIRTY-EIGHT

Saudi Arabia

When Directeur principale de police, Monsieur Claude Laurent, returned to his office, he paid a visit to the Police Prefect of Paris, Kylian Green. After discussing the previous hour's events, Monsieur Green called King Salman in Saudi Arabia. King Salman, the current ruler of Saudi Arabia, may not be as powerful as King Abdullah, but at least in matters of the State, his influence is not questioned. As soon as he disconnected the call with the Perfect of Paris, King Salman had one of his servants locate Prince Mohammed Bader Al Saud.

With an angry voice, King Salman told Mohammed to get the two Indian children he purchased and immediately take them back to Paris, then return to Saudi Arabia quickly. They had many things to discuss, forestalling the damage they might expect from the videos taken from Madam Brezing's mansion.

After the prince left, the King summoned his security advisor, Prince Nayef.

"Our stupid Prince Mohammed got himself filmed trafficking in stolen children. We must get the videos in Paris recorded by Madam Brezing. They could damage our image in the world."

"Do we know who has the videos that Brezing filmed?"

"I am told that a lady named Gloria Bingham from a television station in New York City is with some Indian man who has the videos. Find the lady and you will find the man. Apparently, Brezing filmed everybody who interfaced with her stolen children, so there are many videos. An entire large bag full, I am told."

"Is there an address or a hotel where the lady is staying?"

"The French police are looking for the woman, checking all the hotels.

We will know where she is staying when you land in Paris." "What if the lady leaves Paris before I get there?"

"That should not be a problem. She will not leave Paris without the two Indian Children that stupid Mohammed is taking back to the city. He just left here, so he won't be in the air until he loads the children. If you go now, meet him at the airport and fly with him to Paris. Perhaps the best time to grab that Indian man and retrieve the videos is when he meets Mohammed's plane to get the Indian children."

"That sounds like a good plan, your majesty. I'll get a few top men to accompany me in case that Indian causes us any problems."

"I know I can count on you, Abdulaziz. The King said, "Allah Akbar," *God is great.*

"Allah Akbar," Nayef responded.

Paris France

Perfect Green and Chief Laurent started city-wide searches for Gloria Bingham in Paris. It didn't take long to discover she was booked into the Hotel Le Meurice. When police officers descended on the hotel, they found she was not in her room. She was still registered as a guest, so the officers settled in to wait for her return. It was still early in the afternoon, and they assumed she might have stopped at a café for something to eat or have a drink. They were not informed about her and Hokee's activities at Brezing's mansion. Instead, they were instructed only to keep miss Bingham and her male companion in custody until either Perfect Green or Chief Laurent arrived to assume control.

The afternoon waned and before long; it was early evening, and still no Gloria Binghan. The waiting police officers called their bosses for instructions. Then, using the force of their police powers, the officers instructed the desk clerk to provide them with a key to Gloria's room. The officers opened the room and discovered that her luggage was missing. They assumed the man had also been staying in the room, but there was no sign of his luggage either. Finally, after a hasty call back to headquarters, another city-wide search for the missing woman and Indian man was started

Every hotel within and around the city was contacted. Boarding houses and Airbnbs were visited personally, as many establishments would not divulge their guest's names over the phone. And finally, it was assumed that the man might have used his name to register for a room, and since no one knew his name, the vast police force was sent to visit every hotel in the city, regardless of its size or price range.

The police had good descriptions of both Hokee and Glory, as well as her name, but they could not find the couple. Then the police started looking for taxi drivers who serviced the Meurice hotel. After several hours, they found the driver who picked up the pair at the hotel. He described their visit to the theater district, where he dropped them off. The police officers discovered another taxi driver who took them to the St. James hotel. They were not registered at the Stl James or any other hotel. They did not have Hokee's name, but how many Indians could there be in the city? Unfortunately for the police department, the answer was too many. Finally, they discovered a taxi driver who picked the couple up with their luggage at St. James and deposited them at the bus station.

The police were almost sure the fugitives were on a bus, but could not find an agent who remembered selling them a ticket. Officers were assigned to get on every bus throughout the city, but they came up empty. Searching for a taxi that might have picked them up at the bus station proved futile. The couple had disappeared.

A detachment of officers was assigned to every train station, bus station, airport, and car rental office. There was no way these two people could leave the city without the police knowing. But they could not be found.

Chief Laurent was sitting at his desk trying to figure out a way to find the two Americans, when he remembered the man telling him the Indian children had been stolen from the Fort Hall Indian reservation in Idaho. He had his secretary, madam Edith Sartre, a matronly lady of 62 years who had been his gatekeeper and confidant for over 20 years, call the Indian Reservation and see who he should talk with regarding the stolen children.

It took Edith almost 35 minutes to discover that the reservation had a Police chief named Chief Wahvevah. It was still morning in Idaho, but the Chief was at his desk talking to Zoey when his secretary informed him he had a call from the chief of police in Paris, France.

Chief Wahvevah's chest puffed out to think that the Chief of Police in Paris, France, would call him. Chief Wahvevah already had an inflated opinion of himself, and receiving a call from France only added to his self-proclaimed grandeur.

"Hello, this is Chief Wahvevah, to whom am I speaking?" The chief was proud of the way he said 'to whom.' He thought it made him sound sophisticated.

"Hello, Chief Wahvevah? I am Chief Laurent of the Paris police department; did I pronounce your name correctly?"

Chief Laurent had a wonderful French accent, and Wahvevah practically swooned. Yes, Chief Laurent. That was perfect. How may I be of help?

"I understand that you have had a few Indian children stolen from your reservation over the past few months. Is that true?"

'Oh yes. But we caught the kidnappers and they are now in my jail."

Zoey had to shake her head at the chief's grandiose proclamations. He made it sound like he had caught the kidnappers and then claimed it was *his* jail.

"Did you hire a man to help locate the missing children by any chance?" Zoey could hear Chief Laurent's voice, and when he asked about a man helping to locate the missing children, she instinctively knew the chief should clam up, but the man's hubris knew no bounds.

"Oh, yes. Our council hired a private detective from Pocatello. I believe he is searching for the missing children as we speak."

"Would you know if this detective is in Paris, France, Chief Wahvevah?"

"I don't know where he is at the moment. He left here several days ago and did not tell us where he would be going. I suppose he could be in Paris if some Indian children were there."

"Would you be kind enough to give me the detective's name, Chief? I might have information regarding the children he is looking for."

Zoey was shaking her head no, trying to get the chief's attention. She knew better than to give out the name to someone you did not know, even if he claimed to be the Chief of Police.

"Oh, sure. That is Hokee, Wolf. He has an office in Pocatello and has quite a reputation for locating missing people."

"Well, chief, thanks for taking my call and the information. Goodbye." "Goodbye," Wahvevah answered, but he spoke to a deadline.

Zoey was distraught, but she didn't know how to reach the chief, so she shook her head with a sad countenance and left the room.

Chief Laurent now had a name for the large Indian with the frightening look, Hokee Wolf. He called Edith with instructions to give the name to the police officers searching for the missing couple.

CHAPTER THIRTY-NINE

Hokee had the latest taxi driver take them to the bus station where he previously had stored his gun case. They stood on the sidewalk until the taxi driver disappeared, then Hokee showed Glory his purchases.

For Glory, a black chador provided a full body cover and a Niqab for her head. The Niqab covered her hair and most of her face, leaving only the eyes visible. Hokee instructed her to visit a woman's restroom and dress while he watched their luggage. Glory returned a few minutes later, and no one who knew her would recognize the investigative reporter from New York City.

Hokee had Glory wait with the luggage while he took his package and the gun case inside to put back in a storage locker. Then he visited a men's restroom to dress in his new clothes. The cowboy boots were replaced with moccasins. It is doubtful that muslin men wore cowboy boots. The moccasins were not leather dress shoes, but they should do.

Hokee had a black dishdasha that covered his entire body so he could keep his regular clothing and both pistols. For his head, he had a red turban under which he stuffed his long black hair. He had a full-face beard secured with spirit gum and a pair of glasses with a clear lens in a large black frame. There was nothing in his appearance to suggest a mixed-breed Indian.

Instead, his naturally dark complexion stressed his Mideastern look. Then, returning to Glory, she had to look twice before recognizing Hokee Wolf.

Now suitably dressed, Hokee signaled for a new cab. This driver was a black man from England who spoke with a cockney accent. Hokee was almost sure the man could not understand any American Indian language, so Hokee asked the man to take them to Hotel Madrigal, speaking English with a Shoshone accent. He hoped it sounded to their driver like a Mideastern accent.

"Glory, take out your phone, turn it off, and remove the sim card." When she looked at him with a question, he barked, "**now!**"

The Madrigal is a low-budget hotel with rooms for around $150.00 a night. Hokee had done a little search in the men's room after donning his new clothes. He wanted something that would fit the budget and look of a middle-class Mideastern couple visiting Paris for the first time. Coming from the bus station would support that idea.

Now came the tricky part. Paris hotels must get their visitor's passports when they check in for a stay. Of course, Hokee still had Aliem's passport and Am ExpressCard, but Glory's passport would not match a Mideastern woman or Aliem's. Now came the time for bluster.

They carried their luggage inside a spacious lobby with a wide decorative metal spiral staircase leading to the second floor. Hokee walked up to the front desk, where he met a smiling French lady wearing a name tag, Lina. Lina wore a knee-length pale blue dress with the Madrigal name and logo stitched in white threat above her name tag. She appeared to be about 60 but wore it well. Hokee guessed when she made herself beautiful to go someplace lovely, she could pass for 50.

Fumbling to reach Aliem's passport and credit cards were part of the act. Smiling as though he had just won the lottery, Hokee handed Lina the stolen passport and credit card.

"And the lady's passport, monsieur?"

Speaking in guttural Shoshone, Hokee tried to explain that women where he came from did not have passports. This pronouncement was made with much arm and hand movement, as though he was using body language to convey the message.

"How did you enter Paris without her passport?" Lina almost seemed embarrassed to ask the question.

Reverting to broken English with a solid Shoshone accent, Hokee explained, "Customs say hokay. She your lady, you keep. No problem."

Regaining her composure, Lina said, 'well, if Customs said hokay, I guess she can stay under your passport."

Bowing to show his gratitude and respect, Hokee said, "Merci."

Lori handed him a key to 44, and the number confused Hokee, so he asked again in broken English with a Shoshone accent, "first flor?"

"Oui, right down this hall," she said, pointing. Do you need help with your luggage?"

"No. All rites." Hokee bowed again and picked up Glory's two luggage cases, leaving her to handle his small overnight bag and the bag of videos.

Room 44 was only a few doors down a wide hallway carpeted in a rich green pattern with white flowers. Setting one of Glory's bags on the floor, he used the key to open the door to their room.

As soon as they were in the room with the door shut, Glory removed her Muslim clothes, giving Hokee a sour look. "Is this the only costume you could find for me?' she scolded.

"Hey lover, you must admit, the French police will not be looking for a Muslim couple in a budget hotel. I hope Lina at the front desk doesn't call the police to report a woman without a passport. I don't believe she will. It is against the law for her to let you stay without a passport, but since I gave her mine and you are my property, it should be okay."

"What do you mean, I'm your property, and how could you give her your passport? The police may figure out that a name like Hokee Wolf might be that murdering Indian they are trying to find. And you didn't have a passport when you stayed at the Four Seasons or Le Meurice."

"Relax honey. The muslin women are considered property. I could even kill you, and it wouldn't be murder if you were a muslin woman. Which you're not, so I can't kill you. And I didn't give them Hokee Wolf's passport. I took a passport and credit card from a man who tried to kill me. And no, I didn't kill him. He may report them both stolen, but I doubt the

information will reach France since it was in Mauritania. And you registered at both hotels. I was a visitor, not a guest."

"You are good at this subterfuge crap. I would never have guessed it, although now that I think about your beautiful home and all the artwork, I should not have been surprised."

"Yeah, I hung around with the theater crowd when I thought I'd be an artist. They taught me a lot about costumes and makeup. I don't have to use that information much, but it always comes in handy."

"I can see that. And thanks for making me feel safe. How long will we stay here?

We can't turn our phones on because the police can use GPS to find where we are staying. They don't know my name yet, so my phone should be okay to turn on and check with Laurent about the flight schedule for the kids. It shouldn't take over two days. Possibly sooner.

Their days of fun in the City of Lights were about to end.

CHAPTER FORTY

Chief Laurent, the Paris Chief of police, wasted no time calling the Paris Police Prefect, Kylian Green. After learning the name of Hokee Wolf, with a home and office in Pocatello, Idaho from Laurent, Monsieur Green again called King Salman in Saudi Arabia with the latest information about the man they believed was holding the videos from Brezing's mansion. King Salman hastily called Prince Nayef, his security man, now on his way to Paris.

Nayef was told that Chief Laurent in Paris was using the considerable powers of the police department to locate Hokee Wolf and the missing videos. But they were having trouble, and perhaps mister Wolf's Pocatello office would know his location. Knowing that the King was expecting results from his security chief and the damage those videos could do to the entire Kingdom of Saudi Arabia, Prince Nayef called his senior security advisor, a disgraced mercenary killer named Waylon Dankworth from England.

Dankworth stood six-foot-six and weighed 250 pounds of hard muscle. A former commander of SAS special forces, the Special Air Service unit that is England's most formidable fighting organization. It is recognized worldwide as one of the best highly trained forces. Dankworth is at the top of the world's most dangerous and efficient killers list. Unfortunately, his lust for underage boys caused him to be disgracefully booted out of his service to the Queen. The Kingdom of Saud was happy to gain his services.

Using underage boys for sex is not an uncommon occurrence in the kingdom.

Prince Nayef, operating primarily within the palace, protected the King and all the royals. While Dankworth reported to the prince, he maintained order on the outside, covering the entire kingdom. This responsibility often kept him away from the court, where he had to rely on his judgment without conferring with the Prince. Still, he kept the prince informed of his activities and decisions.

Six senior trained fighting men reported to Dankworth, one of whom was also a retired officer from the SAS special forces. Like Dankworth, Reginald Wilson was a killing machine without a conscience. Dankworth left with Wilson for Pocatello, turning over the responsibility of protecting the kingdom to Fayez Ghazali, his number two man who had trained with the U.S. special forces at Camp Blanding in southern Florida. Dankworth and Wilson flew in a G650ER, one of the fastest nonmilitary planes in the world with sufficient range to make Pocatello, Idaho, without stopping for fuel. Pocatello does not have a customs official at the airport, so the two men from Saudi Arabia counted on American goodwill to allow them to disembark and investigate Idaho State University for one of the royals. Their convenient cover story.

While en route to Paris, Nayef did some quick calculations in his head. His Paris flight would land in approximately two hours, but he would gain one hour, almost six p.m. local time. Dankworth's flying time in the Gulf should be nearly twelve hours, meaning it would be about six a.m. Paris time when he arrived in Pocatello. Paris is eight hours ahead of Mountain Standard time in the United States, so Dankworth would land at approximately ten p.m. Pocatello time. Too late to investigate Hokee Wolf's office, but perhaps the information needed could be obtained from another source. If not, Dankworth would have to wait until the following day to visit Wolf's office. That meant that Nayef would need to spend a whole night and day in Paris before possibly getting the location of Hokee Wolf. Unless

Chief Laurent was successful in finding out where Hokee Wolf was staying, but Nayef had little faith in that option. Oh well, Paris was not a bad place to hang out. Prince Mo would just have to tend to the Indian brats while the Prince and his four chosen guards visited Paris.

Now that he had a name and a description of the man he was seeking, Chief Laurent was confident that his battalion of police officers would locate the half-breed bastard. Before long, his legion of searchers discovered Hokee had stayed at the Four Seasons with a woman named Gloria Bingham, although Hokee was not listed as a guest. Then he stayed at the Le Meurice with the same woman again as a guest, but that was another dry hole. Where was the bastard? Big Indian men accompanied by a beautiful blond woman did not disappear, but the couple could not be found. Hopefully, the Saudis in Pocatello would have more success locating the whereabouts of the man and woman.

CHAPTER FORTY-ONE

The next day, Hokee activated his phone and called Chief Laurent to determine the status of the two Indian children being delivered from Saudi Arabia.

After getting through Ms. Sarte, his gatekeeper, the chief came on the phone, but not before alerting his staff to begin an immediate search for the caller's location.

"Hello, this is Directeur principale de police Laurent. To whom am I speaking, please?"

Hokee thought the chief might be stalling. There was a considerable delay before the chief came on the line. His secretary, or lady Friday, surely told him it was Hokee Wolf calling. Anticipating a phone search, Hokee and Glory were strolling outside the city's NEUILLY SUR-SEINE district. An area Hokee learned was heavily populated with Muslim immigrants.

"Hello chief Laurent. This is Hokee Wolf, and I'm calling to learn the arrival time of the children from Saudi Arabia."

"Ah, Monsieur Wolf, how nice to hear your voice. I hope you are enjoying our beautiful city."

This response confirmed Hokee's suspicion. The chief was definitely stalling.

"Why yes, chief, the lady and I find your city most hospitable. And so safe. My goodness, your police force is so active. They seem everywhere. And now to my question, what about the Indian children?"

"We intend to make Paris safe for its citizens and many visitors, such as yourself. It is pleasing to hear such a report from tourists like you and Ms. Bingham. If there is anything we can do to help make your stay more comfortable, I hope you will let me know. If you tell me where you are staying, I will ensure the officers in your area are extremely diligent."

"God dammit, chief, quit with the bullshit. Where are my kids?"

There was another long delay before the chief answered Hokee's query. "I'm sorry, Monsieur Wolf, but there has been a delay with the flight from Saudi Arabia. The children are scheduled to arrive in Paris sometime tomorrow. I don't know the exact time. If you give me your phone number,

I'll tell you the precise time and place for the exchange as soon as the information becomes available."

"That's okay, chief; I'll call you tomorrow." Hokee then disconnected the call, immediately turned off his phone, and removed the sim card.

"Keep a sharp lookout, Glory. The police may have gotten a fix on my phone. So let's catch a cab and get out of this area before they arrive. I don't want them to suspect we are disguised as Arabs."

Chief Laurent's communications officer hurried into the chief's office. "I'm sorry, chief. The best we could do was determine that the caller was near the NEUILLY SUR-SEINE repeater. The call ended before we could get an exact location."

The chief soon had several officers in the area canvassing everyone they could encounter, flashing pictures of Glory and Hokee, which they had downloaded from the internet. No one had seen the American couple. Even though he was a large man, Hokee's long black hair and dark complexion would not appear unusual in the community, but Glory, with her blond hair and good looks, would stand out like a pine tree in a forest of aspens. Yet no one would admit to seeing the beautiful lady or her long-haired companion. There is considerable friction between the police officers and the Arab community, particularly the Muslim faction. Hence, Chief Laurent was not particularly surprised that his officers could not elicit any information regarding Hokee and Glory.

Laurent knew the Indian children were somewhere in Paris, being attended to by someone from the royal palace. He neither knew nor cared where, as Prince Nayef had assured him that the man called Hokee Wolf and his companion would not live to see the children. When Hokee and Glory approached the area designated as the transfer location, three of Nayef's guards, proficient killers with sniper rifles, would be stationed in remote spots with a clear shot at the couple. Goodbye Americans, and goodbye to the palace threat.

CHAPTER FORTY-TWO

After receiving a call from Hokee, Curly met Grant's plane at the Pocatello airport. He had borrowed a sheriff's prisoner van to haul the nine Indian kids back to the Fort Hall Indian Reservation. Heather had spoiled the kids on the flight home, giving them all the hotdogs and ice cream they could eat. When they left the plane, they were all happy and laughing. Heather stood at the bottom of the stairs, hugging each child as Captain Hobbs ushered them to the plane's door one at a time.

The scene at the Fort Hall police station was one of tears and joy mixed with disappointment from the parents whose children had not been returned. Curly reassured both sets of parents that Hokee was getting those two children back and they should be home soon. He was relieved to deliver the children and return to Pocatello. After turning in the sheriff's van, Curly started for home before realizing he had not checked in with Hilda for a few days. But first, he had to visit Hokee's place.

He had made it a daily habit to check in on Shilah and relax on Hokee's large shaded porch. Curly wasn't too sure if the wolf was finding sufficient rabbits or squirrels to eat, so he usually tossed him one of the rabbits from the porch refrigerator. Since the fridge also had a copious amount of beer inside, Curly felt it was his duty to help reduce the load. So, helping himself to a bottle of Jim Dandy, a local microbrew favorite, he relaxed in one of the big homemade easy chairs. Curly didn't know that Hokee had deliberately loaded the fridge with beer for his friend, as Hokee almost always drank scotch. Because only a couple of rabbits remained in the refrigerator, and since he didn't know how long Hokee would be away, Curly made a mental note to stop by the rancher where Hokee bought his rabbits for Shilah and buy a few more.

It was getting towards quitting time for Hilda, so Curly decided to pay a visit to Hokee's office and make sure everything was okay instead of just making a phone call. Hokee had seemed a little worried about Hilda when he left to find the missing children, so Curly reluctantly left the easy chair and drove back to Hokee's office. He could have called Hilda on the phone, but a visit seemed more in order, and if Hokee called again, he could at least tell him he had visited the office personally and checked in on his secretary. As a deputy sheriff, Curly had been exposed to some gruesome sights, but walking into Hokee's office, he almost lost control of his emotions. Hilda was lying unconscious on the bloody floor in front of Hokee's desk. Her practically naked body was covered with blood from a hundred knife cuts on her arms, legs, and torso. Her left breast was sliced open, and her face was beaten into a bloody pulp.

Curly immediately felt for her pulse, and while she was still alive, her pulse was weak. He immediately called for an ambulance and paramedics to arrive quickly. A lady was dying from blood loss, and they had little time. While waiting, Curly searched for something to cover her body. Her clothes were nearby but had been cut into shreds as it appeared they were cut off from her body. He had a blanket in his cruiser but was reluctant to leave Hilda lying there alone. Glancing around the wrecked office, he noticed a colorful serape Hokee kept as a reminder of his past draped across the back of his office chair. Curly grabbed the wrap and draped it over Hilda's body. He did not know how she could still be alive with all the blood she had lost, and with all of her cuts, he did not know how to staunch any further blood loss.

Fortunately, an ambulance and paramedic crew arrived in less than three minutes and the team immediately started an IV drip to replenish the liquid in Hilda's body. Next, they wrapped her body tightly in yards of gauze to stem the blood flow before lifting her onto a stretcher for a ride to the hospital. Curly remained in the office to see if he could find out what had happened. Afterward, he would go to the hospital to check Hilda's status. There was nothing more he could do for her now; at least she was in the care of professionals.

The office was a complete wreck. Papers were scattered everywhere. The drawers on Hokee's desk had been removed and emptied, then thrown across the room. Pictures were torn off the wall and smashed, leaving shattered glass everywhere. It looked like a tornado had swept through the room, leaving nothing untouched.

Hilda's office looked the same. Obviously, whoever had visited Hokee's office was looking for something, and they had beaten and cut up Hilda to learn whatever it was they wanted to know. The only thing Curly could think of was they wanted to know where to find Hokee Wolf, and of course, no one knew the answer to that, especially poor Hilda. Curly learned from Hobbs and Jensen at the airport that the Indian children were being held prisoner in a Paris mansion before being rescued by Hokee. The other two missing Indian boys were in Saudi Arabia and Hokee was also working to find them. Where he was at this moment, no one knew.

Curly tried calling Hokee and could hear the phone ringing, but it was never answered. There was nothing Hokee could do for Hilda wherever he was; still, Curly thought he should know about his office and the visitors who were probably still looking for him. With that thought, Curly decided a discrete look around outside would be in order.

There were two ways to enter Hokee's office. First, an outside stairway on Clark, a side street, led to the upstairs and a hallway providing access to a dozen different businesses. Midway through the hallway was another stairway leading downstairs to a foyer with access to the bank and the other outside sidewalk. Curly took this hallway, and after looking out of the glass doors in front to see if anyone was lurking around outside, he left the building.

Anyone watching Hokee's office would probably be under the trees in the large lot across Clark Street from the bank. This lot was three-quarters of an acre of undeveloped property covered with Douglas pine and oak trees directly opposite the outside stairway to Hokee's office. Many locals working in the surrounding buildings parked their cars in the convenient lot. Several great spots to wait and watch were practically invisible from the stairway to Hokee's office. Curly stood at the corner of the bank and studied the tree-studded lot down the block and across the street. After several minutes, he observed two men in a new Cadillac Escalade parked between two large oak trees. Their vehicle was barely visible, and the men were hard to see. After studying the scene carefully for several minutes, Curly could see that the men's attention was focused on the stairway across the street. Nothing illegal in their actions, but definitely suspicious.

Curly walked around the block in the opposite direction, returning to his vehicle. Then, on a whim, he drove into the lot from the opposite side and got the license number of the Escalade. After calling it in, he learned the vehicle had been rented a few hours earlier at the Pocatello airport by a man with a Saudi Arabia passport and driver's license. That these men were from the same place Hokee was looking for the two missing Indian boys was beyond a coincidence. Okay, enough proof. These guys meant trouble and were undoubtedly the ones who had tortured and nearly killed Hilda. But unfortunately, until Hilda regained consciousness and could identify the men, there was nothing Curly could do except be alert to their actions. It was times like these when he wished Hokee was here to take charge. Not concerned with the niceties of the law, Hokee would be all over the Cadillac and its occupants, taking names and kicking ass. Until he returned, Curly would monitor the men and their actions.

CHAPTER FORTY-THREE

Hokee waited until the following day to call Laurent back and find out about the two Indian boys.

Knowing it could only be Hokee calling him on this private number, Laurent answered, "ah, monsieur Wolf, I was hoping to hear from you today. The children landed at the de Gaulle Airport only a few minutes ago. I should have a meeting place for you in the next few minutes where you can pick them up. Would you like me to call you back on this number?"

"That's okay, chief. I'll call you back in thirty minutes." Hokee disconnected before they could trace his location.

Hokee smelled a rat but, at the moment, felt powerless to address the issue. Until he had a location and time, all he could do was wait. Glory was ready to strangle Hokee for getting them into this mess, although she knew there had been no choice, and he had kept them safe. They only left their hotel room to purchase food at a convenient local market, which they ate back in their room. It was all this damn waiting that jangled one's nerves, and Hokee's fear of a trap did nothing to soothe her nerves.

Hokee called Laurent back from a taxicab, figuring that the chief could not get a good fix on their location if they were moving.

No greetings, just "monsieur Wolf, thanks for being so prompt. The children will meet you in one hour in the lobby of the Four Seasons hotel, which I believe you are familiar with, no?"

"Yeah, Laurent, I know the dump. Will you be there to bid me a fond farewell?"

"But of course, monsieur. I'll see you soon." Hokee disconnected, saying nothing more.

Hokee had the taxi cab park around the corner and down the block from the Four Seasons. "Glory, I must check out this meeting place before picking up the kids. I would like you to stay in the cab and watch our luggage. But first, drop by the bus depot and pick up my leather case, then come back and park here." Hokee avoided saying the word gun case in case their French cab driver understood the English word.

"Hokee Wolf, you have got to stop scaring the shit out of me. Why do you have to check out the meeting place?

"Glory, I'm pretty sure the kids were here yesterday. They have been stalling, and I don't know why. I haven't been able to figure it out. I suspect an ambush, so I want to check it out."

"If you get yourself killed, I'll never forgive you, damn you."

To the cab driver, Hokee said, "would you drop me off on avenue George fifth, about two blocks up from the Four Seasons Hotel?"

"Oui, oui, monsieur."

Hokee repeated his message for Glory to have the cab back at the same location as he left to inspect the hotel scene. He was wearing his dishdasha and long beard with his hair bundled up under the red turban. The oversized glasses with large black frames neatly hid his face, making him unrecognizable. After waiting a few minutes for Glory to retrieve his gun case and return to their parking spot, he walked down the side street and entered the Four Seasons from the same doorway he had used to escape the hotel security guard a few days earlier. Then, as he walked down the ornate hall past the pictures of French royalty, Hokee had to suppress a grin. He had read enough French history to know the whole ruling lot was a bunch of sick, power-hungry sex fiends, much like the man who had purchased the Indian boys.

In the lobby, Prince Mohammed sat with the two Indian boys, one on either side. He was chaffing with a scowl at being assigned child-sitting duty. No one else seemed to be in the lobby, including the desk clerk. Looking out of the windows in the front door window, Hokee could see Chief Laurent and two Mideastern gentlemen standing on the curved driveway by the door, engaged in conversation. One of the men was pointing at the top of a building across the street, but from his angle, Hokee could not see where the man was pointing.

Recognizing this as an opportunity from the Gods, Hokee walked up to the man sitting with the two Indian boys.

"Are you Prince Mohammed?" Hokee knew a prince was the man who had purchased the boys; Brezing had pointed out the man's name in her ledger.

Why yes, I am," the prince answered in a haughty voice. Talking to Muslim men who were obviously not Shiite was beneath him. He knew the man was not Shite because the turban was all wrong. "And who are you?"

"Chief Laurent asked me to get you out of the lobby. He doesn't want to have the boys see what happens to Hokee Wolf and that woman, Gloria Bingham." Hokee thought throwing in the chief's name along with those of the proposed victims would add credibility to his story.

"Where are we to go?" Mohammed asked, seeming reluctant to move. "Please hurry, your highness. We have little time." Hokee was desperate to get the prince out of sight before Laurent and those other men came inside the hotel.

The prince just sat, looking confused. Hokee continued, "I've been asked to hide you temporarily. Just please hurry, your highness. There isn't much time." Hokee almost pleaded.

Reluctantly, the Prince rose from his seat and angrily grabbed one arm from each of the Indian boys; he jerked them out of their seats before dragging them with him, following Hokee down the hall. When they reached the side hall leading outside, Hokee stopped the Prince. He put his hands on both sides of the Prince's head, then gave it a hard jerk, nearly twisting his head backward, breaking his neck. He hated pedophiles, particularly wealthy spoiled royals who thought they were better than

ordinary people. Then he addressed the two Indian boys in their Shoshone language, assuring them he was the good guy who rescued them from their jailors. Speaking to them in their own language worked like magic. He told them he was Hokee Wolf in disguise, a name the boys recognized that further put them at ease.

Laurent had stationed police officers in the hotel and on the streets, but no one paid attention to the dark-skinned Muslin-looking man holding hands with his two dark-skinned children. The American killer did not have children, and he certainly was not a Muslim. Hokee hated having both hands tied up, holding on to the Indian boys as he wanted his gun hand free, but the boys seemed anxious and afraid. Holding hands with the man they had heard about and who their hero helped reassure them they were safe.

Back on the street, Hokee retraced his earlier route with the Indian boys happily walking by his side. Reaching the cab, he loaded himself and the two boys, instructing the driver to take them to Charles de Gaulle Airport. He did not know how he would get them home, but at least the boys were safe for the moment. Glory could not stop gushing and hugging the boys.

Satisfied with placing the three snipers with silenced rifles, Chief Laurent and Prince Nayef returned to the hotel lobby to await the arrival and demise of Hokee Wolf. Getting gunned down in Paris by an unknown gunman was not unheard of in the City of Lights, and Laurent would be happy to bury this troublemaker in the pauper's graveyard.

The lobby was empty, with no sign of Prince Mohammed and the two Indian boys. The chief had instructed the hotel staff to take a one-hour break, leaving the lobby unattended. There was no one around to provide information about the missing trio. The two men were trying to figure out what to do when a woman's scream had them rushing down the hall. They found Prince Mohammed with a broken neck and no sign of the Indian boys. Laurent knew who was responsible, but how Hokee had accomplished the deed remained a mystery. There were police officers hidden everywhere, watching for the big Indian, but no one had seen a thing. The only person in the area was the Muslin man with his kids, who was barely noticed or remembered.

It was doubtful that Prince Mohammed would be missed back at the royal palace. He was an embarrassment to the Kingdom and better off dead. Still, getting killed in Paris didn't bode well for the chief, primarily since he handled the royal's safety and was responsible for killing Hokee Wolf. Hokee had disappeared, and a royal was dead instead. The Police Prefect of Paris might have to choose a new chief.

CHAPTER FORTY-FOUR

Hokee had a problem. There was no way to fly with his weapons unless they were in a locked gun case shipped with the luggage. Hokee was unwilling to part with his trusty Colt 45, and while the other weapons were expensive, they could be replaced, but what to do with them at the airport? The only solution was to leave the airport to find a shop selling weapon carriers in Paris, a city not particularly gun-friendly. Finding a comfortable kiosk in which to relax and have something to eat within the vast confines of the de Gaulle airport was easy. The airport seemed endless. They found a McDonald's, which made the boys happy, and Glory appeared relieved to settle down and rest in an area that made her feel safe.

Reluctant to leave the boys and Glory at the airport while he searched for a gun case but equally hesitant to drag them back into the city, Hokee ordered a coffee to drink while considering his problem. Glory was busy attending to the children, so Hokee borrowed Glory's satellite phone to call his office and check in with Hilda. He was surprised to hear Curly's voice. Curly would not be answering his office phone unless it was an emergency. Either Curly was in his office or had his phone calls transferred to another number.

"Hello, Hokee; thanks for checking in." You could hear the sarcasm clear across the Atlantic.

"Sorry, Curly, we've been a little preoccupied, but I believe things have settled a bit. What's the emergency?" Hokee thought Curly sounded frantic, but his and Glory's life hadn't been a damn picnic.

"Someone tore up your office and beat the crap out of Hilda. They cut her up badly. She's out of emergency and expected to live, but it was close. I found her barely alive, lying on your office floor. Both of your offices are a wreck."

"Damn. I knew this job was going to be trouble. I saw it in the sweat lodge. Are you sure Hilda is going to be alright?" Curly could hear the concern in his friend's voice.

"Yeah. Pretty sure. She ain't gonna be pretty for a while. They beat the crap out of her face. She was tortured. I believe they were trying to find out how to locate you."

"Christ. What to say? Hell, I'm sorry, but I had to take this case. We've got the last two kids, but I'm unsure how to get home. I'm working on the problem. Do you have any leads or any idea who might have been responsible?"

"Yes, I do. I am a deputy sheriff, you know." Curly enjoyed making his friend sweat out the information, even though it was a difficult situation.

"Well, do I have to fly back to Pocatello and beat it out of you? Hokee wasn't in the mood for fun and games.

"Nah, and I'm sorry for being such a pissant. I know these are tough times. Two Saudi Arabian men are parked under the trees in that lot across Clark Street. They seem to have a fascination with the stairway leading up to your office. I couldn't get a good look at their faces without exposing myself, but I'm pretty sure they are responsible."

"Saudi Arabia? Yeah, that fits. One of the royal pedophiles is the one who bought the Indian kids. Glory is threatening to expose the whole rotten kingdom with a bunch of purloined videos from a mansion we raided. I'm sure the King is desperate to prevent that from happening. They know we're in Paris, but they don't know where. They were probably trying to find that out from Hilda. Can you prevent them from leaving until I return?"

"We can try Hokee. Do you have any idea when that might be?"

"Not at the moment, but it should be sometime tomorrow if we're lucky. I'll try to get us out of here at the earliest possible moment. I'll call you with the flight time as soon as we have a flight."

"Okay. I'm sorry about Hilda, Hokee. I was probably over at your place playing with Shila when it went down."

"It's not your fault, Curly. If you were present, they might have worked on both of you. I'm glad that you saved her life. Give her my respects and make sure she gets the best possible treatment. Money is no object."

"Oh hell, Hokee. You don't even have to say that. But, of course, I'll see that she is treated like a queen."

"Thanks Curly. I'll call you soon. Bye." "Bye Hokee."

Glory had been listening to Hokee's end of the conversation and knew something terrible had happened. "What is it, Hokee? What happened?" She knew the two of them were in danger here in Paris, but back in Pocatello?

"Someone, probably two men from Saudi Arabia, tortured and beat up Hilda. Curly found her barely alive, but they saved her life. She was out of emergency care, but Curly said she'll be a long time recovering. I guess they destroyed her face."

"Oh Hokee, I'm so sorry. Poor sweet Hilda. You knew she was carrying a torch for you, didn't you?"

"Yeah. It's a long story. Her husband was a police officer who was killed by men who were after me. I made sure he was taken care of financially, but she seemed in a perpetual state of mourning, so I brought her into the office to give her something to do and help take the sadness away. I have been aware of her feelings for a long time but have kept it strictly business between us. This situation will make it difficult, as I need to spend some time helping her recover."

"Why would two men from Saudi Arabia torture your secretary?" "Curly doesn't know, nor do I, but we both suspect they were trying to locate me and thought Hilda might know my location. I had Curly monitoring her, but he was at my place taking care of Shila when the men found Hilda alone in the office. We suspect the royal family doesn't want those videos Brezing took made public. I'm pretty sure they were planning on killing both of us when we went to the Four Seasons to collect these two," he said, indicating the two boys cuddling up to the pretty lady.

"Do you think they will wait for you to return to Pocatello?" Glory sounded worried, with a catch in her voice.

"God, I hope so."

When Glory looked at Hokee, she saw the same frightening, fierce dark look in his eyes he had when he shot the big doorman at Brezing's mansion. The look frightened her, and she was glad his anger was on someone other than herself. Yet, even though she could feel the heat from his emotions, he seemed in total control. He couldn't hide his feelings, but he was their master.

Hokee stood up as though leaving, then decided to check in with Grant to check on the plane and crew. After introducing himself, he was immediately transferred to another number.

"Hello, this is Hokee."

"Hokee, my God, but I'm happy to hear your voice. This is Captain Hobbs. Are you still in Paris?"

"Richard. What a great surprise. And yes, we are still in Paris. Why are you answering Grant's phone?

"Grant was unhappy that I left you in Paris, even though you ordered me to bring the other Indian kids back home. Grant ordered me to fly right back and not leave until you were on my plane. I hope you still need a ride." "Your timing couldn't have been better. We have the two other boys, and I've been trying to find a way out of Pais that wouldn't get us killed or arrested. So where are you exactly?"

"We're flying over the big pond, about four hours from touchdown. Are you at de Gaulle?"

"Yes, The DCG Terminal. I suppose you will land at general aviation?" "Yes. Hold on while I pull up a map. You are at the north end of de Gaulle across the A1 freeway from the general aviation terminal. There is plenty of time for you to reach the terminal before we arrive."

"Captain, I assume you will need to refuel before flying back to Pocatello or New York?"

"Oh yeah. This baby flies a long way on a tank full of fuel, but not across the pond both ways. Why do you ask?"

"I need you to listen carefully. Please land and refuel, then call me when you are at the terminal ready to leave."

"Okay, Hokee, Sure. We should call you in roughly four and a half hours."

"Great, I'll talk to you then; bye, captain." "Bye Hokee.

Hokee disconnected the call and faced an impatient Glory. "Well, are you going to tell me what's going on, or do I have to guess?" The lady was not happy.

"Please be still Glory. Could you give me a couple of minutes? I have to concentrate." Hokee closed his eyes and seemed to fall asleep, but Glory knew he was just going deep inside to find answers to a perplexing situation. Hokee was gone for over five minutes before he opened his eyes and gave Glory a big smile. "Sorry, honey, but I had to think through our problem.

Please go to that information desk down the hallway and get us an airport map. "I'll watch the boys and explain everything when you return."

"Okay, buster. But you damn well better not hold anything back." Then, with that said, she kissed him on the cheek and left to get the map.

CHAPTER FORTY-FIVE

After Glory returned with the maps, Hokee studied them for several minutes before looking up and catching Glory's evil eye.

"Okay, here's what I believe is happening. I'm almost positive that the police department here in Paris can listen in on our phone conversations. Every major advanced country and large city on earth has spies in all the other developed countries, and technological secrets don't remain secret for very long. It is no secret that the U.S. has been listening in on our conversations for several years." Hokee took a breath, but before he could continue, Glory interrupted.

"But Hokee, there are millions, maybe even hundreds of million calls at any moment. Nobody has enough people to listen to that many calls."

"You are right, Glory. But with the advancement in computers, every call can be monitored and recorded. Storage space is cheap. The little thumb drive has gigabit memories. The computer is programmed to listen for keywords. If a particular word or phrase is picked up, an alert sounds and a live operator comes online to listen in and playback the conversation. If you are a person of interest and they have your cell phone number, they can listen to every call you make or receive. You can bet your next promotion that the Paris police department has both of our cell phones on constant alert. Every word we speak is being listened to, even right now. That's why I'm now turning off my phone and removing the battery and sim card. I assume your phone is also disabled."

"If that is true, they already heard everything you said to me." Glory seemed perplexed.

"Yes, but I said nothing they don't already know. Now we can talk privately. I don't believe the bad guys can hear us through the P.A. system."

"Okay, Hokee. What's up with Captain Hobbs?"

"When Grant learned we were still in Paris, he sent the plane and crew back to pick us up. Captain Hobbs was told he wasn't to return until he had us on board."

"Well, that helps solve some of your problems. So what's up with having him call you after he is refueled and at the terminal? Why not just meet him there?"

"I might as well tell you. I didn't want our conversation overheard," Hokee nodded toward the Indian boys, "but there is no way to hide the truth at this point. Chief Laurent had an ambush prepared for us back at the Four Seasons. We were not supposed to leave there alive, especially with the two boys. I killed Prince Mohammed and left his body in the hallway. Laurent knows our plane is returning to Paris and that we will board at the general aviation terminal, courtesy of my phone conversation with Hobbs. I now have to figure out a way to get us on the plane and in the air without getting everybody killed."

"Oh, well then. And here I thought it might be something serious." Glory couldn't keep the wicked smile from reaching her eyes.

"Yeah, I know. A walk in the park." Hokee had to smile at his beautiful companion, who could make light of a serious situation.

"So Hokee, how many have you killed here in Paris so far? A rough count will do, you know, 50 to 100 or 25 to 50.

"Well, gee. Let me see now; it's hard to keep track when I'm next to a ravishing beauty."

Glory nudged him in the ribs with her elbow. "Okay, wise guy. How are we going to get out of this mess? Did you come up with a plan while you were sleeping a while ago?" She couldn't keep the grin off her face.

Hokee nudged her right back, careful to be gentle. "I'm afraid the killing business isn't over just yet, Glory. I've got to find a kiosk that sells binoculars. Will you be alright here with the boys for a few minutes?"

"Sure. Okay with you boys, if you hang out with me for a few minutes? By the way, what're your names? We've been so busy I forgot to ask earlier." "Etu and Chesmu." The boys blurted out simultaneously, eager to talk with the pretty lady, and it sounded like Esmu.

"Okay, one at a time." Glory had to smile at their eagerness. "You first," she said, pointing to the oldest-looking one.

"My name is Chesmu; it means charming and witty. Do you like it?" "Oh yes. It's a pretty name, and it fits you. You are undoubtedly charming. Now, what's your name? She said, pointing at the other boy. "My name is Etu, and it means the sun, but full of confidence and personality. I hope you like it."

"Etu. What a pretty name, and you don't seem to lack confidence."

Hokee stood and, looking at the trio, said, "well, I think you guys will be okay for a few. I'll be back shortly." He leaned over and gave Glory a quick kiss on her lips before walking away.

Chesmu said as Hokee disappeared into the crowd, "he's my hero. Did you know he lived on our reservation when he was a little boy?" Chesmu seemed to swell with pride when he talked about his hero.

"No, he never told me about those times. What's it like, living on the reservation?" And just like that, Glory had the boy's full attention.

Hoke didn't have to walk far before finding an electronics store selling everything from iPhones to Motorola hand-held radio units. The store also had a dozen or more binoculars priced from fifty dollars U.S. to several thousand. Hokee settled on Zeiss Conquest HD 8x56 Binoculars for $2100.00. He liked their low-light-level performance characteristics. When returning to Glory and the boys, a coy smile showed the Indian lads had been filling her head with stories they heard about his reservation days—a subject he had avoided discussing with the television investigative reporter.

They still had a few hours to wait for Captain Hobbs and Grant's plane, so Hokee took them for a stroll through the large terminal. The boys were fascinated with everything, including the immense sculptures hanging from the ceiling and the beautiful artwork on the walls. This experience was their first exposure to commercial airline terminals, as their previous flights had all been on private airplanes. Hokee took his time strolling with frequent stops to explain some of the more abstract sculptures. They were barely back in their seats when he received the call from Captain Hobbs. Hokee had put his phone back in order several minutes earlier, anticipating this call.

"Captain Hobbs, please get a phone from one of your colleagues and call me back on this number. Hold on a second, Glory, please dig out that satellite phone and give me the number." He then gave the number to Hobbs before disconnecting.

While waiting for Hobbs to secure another phone, he took the phone from her hands, then asked, "Glory, please go find that information kiosk you found earlier and ask them to order us a long-stretch limousine. The longer, the better, and tell them to hurry."

Glory hurried off to do as he had asked when the satellite phone buzzed. "Hokee here, is that you, Hobbs?"

"Yeah, Hokee. I am on Heather's cell phone. What's going on?"

"The French police have my phone number and are listening to my conversations. I'm on a satellite phone, which they will have some trouble tapping into, and they don't have Heather's number. Now tell me exactly where you are."

"We're parked about 150 feet from the front door, door four, of the general aviation terminal."

"Okay, great. Which direction is the plane facing relative to the taxi runway?"

"About ninety degrees from the main taxi lane."

"Taxi lane. I got it. Now, Captain Hobbs, I would like you to get the plane headed directly towards the taxi lane and have your engines burning, ready for an immediate takeoff. Have the stairs down and Heather at the door ready to seat the Indian boys.

We'll be there in about five minutes. Will the control tower give you grief if you head off without permission? We need to be in the air immediately after boarding."

"They won't be happy, and unless a plane is landing, it shouldn't be a problem. The general aviation runway isn't usually very busy. The de Gaulle airport discourages general aviation."

"Okay, get ready, and you may hear some fireworks."

CHAPTER FORTY-SIX

Hokee handed the satellite phone back to Glory, who came rushing up with information that the limousine would wait for them outside in the loading zone.

Grabbing one of Glory's luggage cases and his gun case, Hokee gave his overnight bag to the largest Indian boy to carry, which made him feel important. You could see his chest poke out, and a big grin splashed across his face. Glory grabbed the bag with the videos before handing the other Indian boy their sack of treats for the plane, making him equally proud. Then, grabbing her other bag, she followed Hokee to the limousine.

The limousine was a large white stretch Mercedes Benz that looked a block long. Their driver was a dapper little French man wearing a dark-tailored suit and a red beret with a smile nearly a yard wide and beautiful blue eyes. The two side doors were open, and the driver tried to take their luggage, but Hokee intervened, telling him the luggage could ride with them as there was plenty of room.

"Take us to the general aviation terminal quickly." Hokee slipped two hundred-dollar bills into the driver's hands to ensure he got the point.

"Oui, monsieur. Quick."

As they approached the general aviation terminal, Hokee could see Grant's plane already headed out towards the taxi lane, and he could hear the engines roar, even inside the limousine.

"Pull up next to the stairs by that plane, please," Hokee instructed their driver, pointing towards the white G650. The limousine's windows were dark except for the two front windows and the windshield. Those inside the limousine could see outside, but no one outside could see inside, providing privacy for the VIPs who regularly travel using luxury vehicles. Hokee had requested a stretch limousine for this very purpose.

The limousine stopped about twenty-five feet from the steps leading into the plane, but Hokee held up his hands, preventing anyone from getting out of the car. He pulled out the Zeiss binoculars purchased earlier and began scanning the surrounding buildings. It took a couple of minutes before finding what he feared he would see. Perched near the top of a parking garage 500 feet away, with the muzzles of their guns resting on top of the parking garage wall, were two snipers waiting for them to exit the limousine. All you could see of the snipers were their heads and gun barrels. It looked like their weapons were pointed directly toward the limousine. If they were in a regular taxi with only front and rear seats, the snipers could fire into the back seats with a high probability of hitting anyone inside. But the stretch limousine with blacked-out windows prevented the snipers from knowing where the passengers were sitting. The men with guns had to wait for Hokee and Glory to exit the vehicle before they could shoot them.

Looking at the two Indian boys, Hokee said, "boys, do you see that plane over there with the stairs leading to an open cabin door?" He pointed out the plane."

Both boys answered, "yes, Hokee."

"Good. When Glory opens the car door, you run like the dickens to those stairs and get on the plane. Okay?"

As he spoke to the boys, Hokee pulled the Browning Hell's Canyon X-bolt from the gun case. Glory's eyes took in the scene with the gun, but she understood why it was necessary and didn't comment. When he packed the rifle back in Pocatello, Hokee wasn't sure it would be used, but now he was

glad to have it with them. It was already loaded, so he jacked a live cartridge into the firing chamber and flipped off the safety.

"Glory, I need you to get your luggage ready to take off. Give my overnight case to one of the boys. Now move back from the window nearest the front seat so you are well out of the way, then reach forward and lower that front window about two inches when I give you the signal. Then get ready to open the door when you hear me shoot; as soon as you hear my first shot, open the door and run with the boys to the plane."

To Glory's credit, she said nothing and asked no questions. Instead, she could see Hokee's determination and confidence in his actions from previous encounters with the forces of evil.

Hokee went to the rear window and got ready. Then said, "now, Glory." The passenger compartment's front window went down, and Hokee watched through the binoculars to see what would happen. The two rifles in the parking garage immediately trained on the dark front window as it was lowered. Both snipers fired simultaneously. Bullets shattered the window Glory had lowered, plowing into the seat where she would have been sitting if she had not moved back as instructed. The snipers used rifles with noise suppressors, but when the front window shattered, Hokee hit the switch, dropping the rear window. Then, sticking the Browning's barrel out of the back window before the snipers could adjust their aim, he found the snipers in his scope and fired two rounds at the men in the parking garage.

The Browning did not have a silencer, so Hokee's shots sounded like claps of thunder echoing around the general aviation area.

The Browning is one of the most accurate guns made, and Hokee is an excellent marksman, but his shots were hurried and he wasn't sure if he hit either man. Only their heads had been showing, but at least temporarily, nothing but gun barrels were visible on the top of the wall. Glory had the door open as echoes of the shots Hokee fired were still bouncing around the complex. The boys were off and running with Glory, swinging her luggage before the echoes died away. Even if he didn't hit either man, it would take them a few seconds to relocate the limousine and its passengers in their rifle scopes. Hokee took ten seconds to break his gun down and put it in the gun case before opening his door and sprinting after Glory. The Browning was

an expensive weapon and Hokee was reluctant to leave it behind. He left five hundred dollars on the seat to pay for the damage to the limousine.

Heather had the two boys moving back towards the seats when Hokee entered the cabin. Then, pulling up the stairs, he yelled, "**get us out of here,**

Captain." The stairs were barely folded inside when Hokee slammed the door shut and lurched back to find a vacant seat as the pilot released the brakes, thrusting the plane into a quick start down the taxi lane.

When he saw the ground disappearing below, Hokee got up from the seat he had collapsed into and went up to the cockpit.

"Captain Hobbs, great job, now make a beeline for England at your maximum speed. I'm not sure if Chief Laurent can order the French military to shoot down a private civilian airplane, but let's not take any chances. I might have pissed them off back there."

"Ya think?" Hobbs had a lopsided grin with traces of fear still lingering in his eyes. He had heard Hokee's rifle shots even above the roar of the airplane's engines.

"Yeah, I know—just more fun for my friends in the life and times of Hokee Wolf. But, seriously, thanks to you, Captain Jensen, and the lovely Heather, you guys more than likely saved our lives. It wasn't so much the French as the house of Saud who was calling the shots. The kingdom doesn't want to be disgraced. Even if it means a little murder here and there."

They passed England with no sign of pursuit by the French, so Hokee relaxed for the first time in many days. Then, reaching over and taking Glory's hand, he asked, "I suppose you want to go to New York and work on the human trafficking story?"

"You know I have to see this through Hokee. But listen honey; I promise to visit Pocatello and the beautiful Shila as soon as we put this series to bed." "Okay, I better go up front and tell Captain Hobbs before we get too far across the pond, as he calls it,"

Back at the Charles de Gaulle airport, a disgraced Chief Laurent could now look forward to an early forced retirement. With one dead sniper and one with a severe head wound, Prince Nayef still had no CDs, which news would not be well received by the King back in Saudi Arabia.

Chapter Forty-Seven

Captain Hobbs taxied the plane to the JFK International Airport general aviation terminal to drop off Glory, and Hokee got off the plane to help Glory with her luggage and the bag of CDs.

They both walked into the terminal building so Glory could sit down while waiting for the television station limousine she had called for from the plane. Giving Hokee a big hug, Glory said with a wry smile, "well, Hokee, you sure know how to show a girl an exciting time. I am almost afraid to spend time with you, as one never knows when some madman might seek you out for revenge." Glory was only half jesting as, in her mind, she could still see the Sumo doorman pointing his gun in her face.

"Yeah, I know Glory. But you must admit you would find life dull without all the excitement you get when we're together."

"Hell, Hokee, a little dull would never kill me. Traipsing around with you is another matter." Then, as she spoke, Glory wrapped her arms around Hokee, giving him another hug and a big kiss. "But I wouldn't have it any other way, lover. Keep a light burning the porch cause I'll be showing up in a few days to make sure your life is miserable."

"God, I hope so; Shila really misses you, you know," he said with a big smile. "When you're putting the series about human trafficking to bed, call me if you have questions. We never really talked much about Mauritania or Houston. I'm reasonably sure the Houston police will have pictures of the cages in the warehouse Teeten used to store his prisoners. With a little pressure from the right people in New York, you should have access to those pictures and possibly pictures of Teeten and the ship the Ghulam boys used to transport the trafficked people to Mauritania."

"I will definitely call you," Glory said. "There are too many unanswered questions. The series is important and hopefully, we can shed some light on a very dark subject."

"Good luck with the series, Glory. I know luck doesn't have much to do with it, only your hard work, but when I hung around with the theater crowd, the phrase was, 'break a leg.'"

"I know that one. I never understood how that replaced good luck, but I'll take it. I'll miss you, Hokee, but I'll see you soon." With that, she gave him another big kiss before saying goodbye.

"Goodbye, for now, beautiful; see you soon." Hokee gave her a big smile as he turned and went back to the plane.

Going into the cockpit, Hokee asked Captain Hobbs, "do we need more fuel to make it to Pocatello?"

"Not for this baby," Hobbs replied, patting the control column. "We've only used about half of our fuel."

Hokee found his way back to the two Indian boys, who were soaking up the grand adventure of traveling with their hero in a private jet. Heather was nearby and told everyone to buckle up because we're going to take off soon. They had about four hours before touching down in Pocatello and Hokee wanted to spend some of that time meditating. After a few minutes in the air, Hokee asked Heather if she would pour him a little scotch. Seeing that the boys were occupied with some game Heather provided, Hokee carried his drink forward to be alone.

Settling into one of the oversized recliners, Hokee shut his eyes to relive his last sweat lodge experience before leaving for Houston. He remembered the faces of evil that had worried him about the forthcoming endeavor to

locate the missing Indian children. Then, reviewing the faces in his mind, Hokee recognized the men in Houston and Mauritania. With a bit of difficulty, he could see the faces of the people in Paris, particularly Madam Brezing and the large sumo man who answered the door as he shoved a pistol in Glory's face. There were several indistinct images in his mind in which the sense of evil was dominant.

Seeking clarity, Hokee began shamanic breathing exercises to cleanse his mind and help him focus on the evil feelings he could remember but could not see clearly. It slowly dawned on him that the indistinct images were the men from Saudi Arabia, including the ones he had seen in Paris and those who had beaten and cut up Hilda. When doing the sweat lodge, he could remember the frightening sense of evil and the many faces twisted by its power. He also remembered leaving the lodge shortly after encountering this terrible power. His body needed water, and he needed to regain his energy. Unfortunately, he had to leave this session before seeing all the faces. His one indistinct image was of a large man. Hokee could not get a fix on the man's face or how many others might be with him.

It felt like only a minute had gone by when Heather came by and picked up his mostly forgotten drink. "We're about to land, Mr. Wolf," she said playfully. "We wouldn't want to spill this expensive scotch."

"My lord woman, are we really in Pocatello? And let me have a swallow of that scotch before you dump the rest in the sink."

"Yep. We're just about to land. You seemed so peaceful that we all kept quiet so you could rest.

"That was very thoughtful, and I appreciate that, plus all the help you have given me on this little adventure. You're probably looking forward to getting home and a little less excitement."

"Well, it hasn't been dull. A little frightening at times, but I'm grateful for the experience. I hope you'll use Grant's plane again soon so I can spend a little quiet time with Idaho's number private investigator." Heather had not wholly given up on spending some alone time with Hokee.

"Grant has been generous with this plane and the fantastic crew, which means you and the pilots. I'll be coming to Nampa soon to thank Grant personally. If you and those pilots up front are available, I would like to buy you all a great dinner."

"That would be welcome, Hokee. I'll look forward to seeing you soon." Heather left to take her seat as they were almost on the ground."

Once on the ground and they had taxied to the general aviation terminal, Hokee thanked the crew for their kindness and help on this mission. Then, giving Chesmu his overnight bag, Hokee grabbed his gun case, took Etu's hand, and guided the boys off the plane. It was a short walk to the parking lot where he had left the Explorer. Hokee would have preferred to visit Hilda in the hospital first, but there was nothing he could do to ease her pain, and the boys needed to be driven back to the reservation. Without a second thought, Hokee loaded the boys into the vehicle for a ride to Fort Hall.

When they had cleared the airport, Hokee called police headquarters at the Fort Hall Indian reservation.

"Hello, this is Zoey."

"Zoey, I'm so happy you answered the phone. This is Hokee. I have Etu and Chesmu with me, and we're about 40 minutes from the police station. Please notify the parents so they can be on hand to welcome the boys home?" "Hokee, how wonderful. That means you have returned all the kidnapped children. You really are the world's best private investigator." "Let's not get carried away, Zoey. I was just lucky. See you soon." Hokee disconnected the call before Zoey could respond. He knew the girl was infatuated with him and didn't want to encourage her. Continuing the conversation might have been misconstrued on her part. Better to nip her feelings at the start.

Before they reached the reservation, Hokee dug out his wallet and gave each boy two hundred dollars. "Here, boys. Take this money and buy some new clothes."

The boys had been dressed up like little Lord Fauntleroy by Prince Mohammed, totally unsuited apparel for the reservation. The shine in their eyes said it all, but each boy stuttered a "thank you, Mr. Wolf."

The parents and half of the reservation were on hand to welcome the boys back home. Zoey tried a private conversation with Hokee, but as soon as the boys were back with their parents, he returned to the Explorer and headed back to Pocatello to visit the hospital.

He also had a date with Curly and two men he was eager to meet. Hokee had spent a lot of time figuring out how he wanted to handle their meeting.

CHAPTER FORTY-EIGHT

Hilda looked like a mess. Her right eye was still swollen shut and the rest of her face was mottled with purple and black bruises. Both arms and legs were swathed with bandages covering almost every inch of skin and a large dressing was on her body. She was awake and tried smiling when Hokee entered the room.

"Oh my God, Hilda. I'm so sorry the damn mission caused you so much pain. Is there anything I can do for you until you get out of here?"

Hilda's voice croaked when she spoke. "It wasn't your fault, Hokee. You had to take that case. Did you get all the children back to their parents?"

"We sure did, Hilda. Grant provided an excellent crew who were a great help. You may not have known, but I had to call Glory to help with the rescue. She is back in New York with videos showing Paris officials molesting underage children. Her station is doing a series on human trafficking, emphasizing kidnapped children. That is a nasty evil part of our society Hilda, and I feel just awful that it caused you such grief. I know it isn't much comfort, but we put many human traffickers out of business."

"Will we be able to watch the series Gloria is doing?"

"It's a local station, not one of the major networks, but I'm pretty sure one of the big guys will want to broadcast the series; it's a major human interest story. If not, Glory will send us a copy."

"You'll let me know, won't you?"

"Hilda, my sweet lovely Hilda. I'll be here daily to monitor your situation and bring you the latest news. I'll let you know when the series airs, and maybe we can watch it together. My next visit is with Curly and the men who did this to you."

"Oh, be careful, Hokee, those are big, mean men."

"Don't worry Hilda. I have a plan for dealing with those guys. They won't be hurting any more innocent people."

"You'll let me know, won't you?"

"You betcha. Relax and get better. I'll be lost without you in the office to keep me focused. I'll see you tomorrow Hilda." Hokee gave her a warm smile as he turned to leave.

"Goodbye, Hokee."

Hokee's next stop was to his home and Shila. The wolf was so happy he almost knocked Hokee over as he stood up after getting out of the Explorer. It would be difficult to say who was the most joyful man or wolf. Hokee ruffled the hair on Shila's head and neck while giving his best friend a big hug while Shila's tail beat on Hokee's leg. "Okay, big guy, ready to help me round up the bad guys?"

Shila didn't know what Hokee said precisely, but it was clear to the wolf that his master included him in his next adventure. Then, when Hokee opened the rear door, Shila jumped in like his tail was on fire.

Driving back towards his office, Hokee called Curly. "Deputy Belingsford,"

"Good heavens, Curly, I almost forgot you have a last name." "Yeah, Hokee, I have a mother too."

"No kidding. And all this time, I thought you were delivered in a warm fuzzy blanket by a big bird."

"Listen, wise guy; ya don't mess around with a deputy sheriff. I'll have to arrest you and throw your skinny butt in jail."

Ignoring the taunt, Hokee continued, "You might have wondered why I am disturbing your afternoon nap, deputy Belingsford."

"Well, yeah, I wondered a bit. But when I heard you were on the line, I figured out pretty quickly that you need my help to get your butt out of a jam."

"All too true, Curly; where are you now?"

"I'm about a block down from your office, sitting in an unmarked car at the side of Clark Street, watching the men who beat up Hilda."

"Great. I'll see you soon.

Curly was not in his sheriff's uniform, but wore faded blue jeans with a purple Grateful Dead T-shirt and a red ball cap featuring a four-leaf clover on the front. Hokee slipped into the passenger's side of the unmarked.

"Hi, partner," Hokee said. "I'm happy to see that the bad guys haven't killed you yet."

"Yeah, me too," Curly responded. "I gotta tell ya that waiting on you to get here wore me out. You can't imagine how badly I wanted to waste those bastards. I know a deputy sheriff isn't supposed to talk that way, but you and I have done some dirty deeds together, so I imagine a little honesty wouldn't damage your high opinion of me."

"I totally understand the sentiment, and I appreciate your waiting. I'm not sure I could have waited after seeing what those Saudis did to Hilda."

"It wasn't pretty Hokee. I feel so bad for Hilda. If I had gone to your office first instead of visiting Shila, I might have been able to prevent the attack."

"And you might have gotten butchered as well, Curly. Neither of you expected trouble like that from some foreign men. I thought there might be some trouble later after I returned home, but not while I was in Paris."

"What?" You played house with Glory in Paris while I've been roasting my butt watching the bad guys. What kind of friend are you, anyway?"

"Yeah, it was unconscionable of me to play around having fun while you were here babysitting. If only you could have been in Paris dodging assassins while wearing Arab robes and headdresses to avoid getting caught by the police while I was sitting in the shade drinking a cold beer, we could have both been happy."

"Sorry, Hokee. I guess you guys didn't have a picnic either. It's so damn easy to get caught up in our dramas that we forget others might have an even worse time. Do you want to tell me about it?"

"I will, but first, let's take care of business. What restraints do you have?"

"The sheriff's bag is in the back seat. I've got two sets of handcuffs and about fifty flex cuffs. What do you have in mind?"

"I want to sneak up to their vehicle, then poke my 45 in their faces. Then you come in from the other side to stand guard while I tie them up in restraints. I'll take several of your flex cuffs to get started tying them up; you can help me finish the job securing them. I believe a trip to the McCammon hole might be in order."

"I like the way you're thinking, Hokee. I believe ole Neter, that evil, rotten satanic priest we dumped in the hole could use some company."

"Yeah, I believe you're right, Curly. I'm not sure how many virgins that old fraud threw into the hole, but maybe enough that the three of them can each have one."

"There are probably at least three, but you and I both know that when those girls went into the pit, they were no longer virgins."

"I'm sure you're right, Curly. My only question is whether to kill these bastards before we toss them in or let them take the long fall down the bottomless hole somewhat conscious?"

"I vote we cut them up a little so they get a feel for what they did to Hilda, then toss them down the hole." Curly had a grim look on his face when he made this suggestion.

"Okay, let's not hold up the party partner. We don't want to keep the bad guys waiting. Shila's here and wants to help."

CHAPTER FORTY-NINE

Hokee pulled the Colt 45 from the holster on his hip and held it beside his leg. He thought about sneaking up to the automobile the two men from Saudi Arabia were sitting in, but decided the direct approach would be quicker and have the same result. Curly and Shila trailed a few feet back and off to the side, so it wouldn't look like an ambush.

The late afternoon sun was warm, and the sky was azure blue, a hue only seen in a lava field desert where the air is clear and not a lot of vegetation to color light reflected from the ground. The tree-covered lot across the street from Hokee's office provided shade and a little cover as the two men and dog crept towards the Cadillac Escalade.

Dankworth and Wilson, the two contractors sent by Saudi Arabia's security chief, Prince Nayef, to locate Hokee Wolf, were bored and half asleep after watching an empty stairway for many long hours. Nayef had called Dankworth after Hokee left Paris on a private airplane with new instructions to kill that *damned bastard*. Nayef assumed Hokee was on his way home with the two Indian boys and wanted his men to accomplish what he had failed to do at the airport.

Unaccounted for by the watchers was the stop in New York for Glory, Hokee's trip to the reservation delivering the boys, and a subsequent visit with Hilda and then his home to get Shila. The hours added up, and the men watching the stairway had grown tired and complacent. They didn't have a picture of Hokee because the only time Nayef had seen him, Hokee was dressed as an Arab. Chief Laurent had provided a description, so the assassins had a general description, but after days and hours of watching nothing, boredom took its toll.

Hokee walked behind the trees, shielding him from view by the men sitting in the car until he was almost to their vehicle. Curly and Shila trailed a few feet behind, waiting for Hokee's signal. When he was twenty feet away, Hokee strolled the rest of the way to the driver's side car door window, which was down so Dankworth could enjoy some fresh air. Hokee was almost to the car door when Dankworth noticed the man approaching his window. Too late, he saw the Colt 45 pointing at his head.

"Neither of you move an inch."

The voice was loud, forceful, and commanding and froze both car's occupants.

Getting their attention, Hokee stayed just out of arms reach or a swinging car door.

"Now, both hands on the car roof - palms up, RIGHT FUCKING NOW, both of you."

The command took Dankworth and Wilson by surprise. They had been relaxing, almost half asleep, when a big man with a deadly serious expression commanded their attention with a pistol pointed at their heads. Both men were highly trained and skilled in all aspects of fighting. If either man found one second to respond, they had access to the knives behind the back of their neck; guns were resting by their sides and hands so quick and powerful they could render an opponent helpless in less than a second. But with a Colt 45 pointed at their heads in the hands of a genuinely menacing man who was just out of reach, they slowly raised their hands to the car's roof.

"Palms up."

Both men did as ordered. Each believed that a moment would come when they would get their chance. No matter how slight the lapse of concentration by the man with the gun, they could move like lightning with lethal consequences. These men believed that no one else on earth had their proficiency or training. So it was just a matter of time. For now, they would go along with the command and wait for their chance.

Curly drifted up to the passenger's side door with his service revolver, an S&W M&P9 9mm in black anodized steel. A truly nasty-looking pistol. "Curly, don't get too close. I have a feeling these bad boys have some special training. Just stay out of arms reach but keep your gun pointed at their heads with your finger on the trigger. If they so much as twitch, Curly, shoot. Do. Not. Wait.

The men looked at the sheriff's deputy after Hokee's statement. Satisfied that Curly had the men covered, Hokee slipped into the Navigator's back seat as their heads turned towards Curly. The 45 was in his right hand, so when the men felt the disturbance and turned their heads back toward him, they looked down the barrel of what must have looked like a black cave.

"Heads pointed forward. Right damn now!"

As their heads pointed forward, Hokee shot out the rear-view mirror so that Dankworth, who sat in the driver's seat, couldn't see what he was doing. Then, tying two of the flex cuffs together, Hokee wrapped the ties around Dankworth's wrists, tying his hands together. Finally, Hokee cinched the cuffs tight, so there was no way Dankworth could wiggle his hands free.

Hokee slipped over behind Wilson and repeated the procedure, tying Wilson's wrists together. Tying more flex cuffs together, Hokee slipped a noose around Wilson's neck, then tied the noose to Wilson's wrists behind his head, pulling the wrists as far backward as possible. This was a procedure Hokee invented years ago while dealing with some nasty bikers he couldn't trust to behave. The beauty of this procedure is that the person with his wrists tied behind his head cannot pull his hands forward without choking himself, taking the subject's hand entirely out of play. Hokee repeated the procedure on Dankworth before slipping back out of the Navigator using the same door he entered.

Hokee called Shila to stand by him when he opened the driver's side door next to Dankworth. Then, standing five feet away, Hokee ordered, "Okay, mister, turn sideways on the seat and put your feet on the ground. Curly, be sure to watch the guy on your side. If he twitches, kill him."

Dankworth glared at Hokee with a face distorted by hatred, while snarling like an angry lion. His eyes were two dark holes full of menace that seemed to say, *just wait, asshole, you'll get yours.'*

"Turn sideways and put your feet on the ground–NOW!" Hokee barked.

As though waiting for a break or a chance to act, Dankworth slowly swung his legs around, then put his feet on the ground.

"Okay, mister, now on your knees." Hoke stopped yelling. He decided if the bastards wouldn't cooperate, he'd just shoot them.

Dankworth was not ready to comply with this order until he looked into Hokee's eyes. What he saw there compelled him to drop onto his knees. There was no doubt in Dankworth's mind that this half-breed bastard was ready to shoot him in the head.

"Now walk on your knees forward five feet, and I mean now. You can probably see that I'm ready to put a 45 slug in your head."

"Oh, you bastard," Dankworth spoke for the first time in a voice laced with venom. "You don't have any idea who you're dealing with. You are so dead. My people will hunt you down to the ends of the earth if I don't get you first."

"Thanks for the lecture; now, walk on your knees." Hokee was hoping to see fear in his prisoner's eyes, but all he saw was hatred and anger. It seemed like his prisoner believed it was only a matter of time before he could act and free himself. Then, once Dankworth was away from the car, Hokee approached him from in front and grabbed his head, pulling him onto the ground. With his hands tied behind his head, Dankworth hit the ground with his cheek, cursing Hokee, using every black word he could remember.

"Shila, come here, boy. I've got a job for you."

Shila came bounding towards Hokee with a smile on his canine face. It seemed like he was thinking, "okay, it's about time you let me help."

Directing Shila to Dankworth's head, Hokee said, "Shila, if this man moves his head even a little, tear out his neck."

Shila settled in front of Dankworth's head, close enough to snap his large jaws on Dankworth's neck if he twitched.

"Get the filthy beast away from me." Dankworth was clearly afraid of the wolf. Hokee's gun worried Dankworth, but for the first time, Hokee saw fear in the man's eyes.

"He will leave you alone as long as you lie still. Now slowly lower your feet to the ground. Slowly."

Once Dankworth's feet were on the ground, Hokee said, "I believe you have special training and know how to use your legs. Remember that any false move and the wolf will tear your throat out."

Hokee stayed well back from Dankworth's feet as he fashioned another loop in the flex ties for the man's legs. He slipped the noose over Dankworth's feet and bound them together as tight as he could. Then, taking more flex cuffs, he pulled Dankworth's feet up towards his back and secured them to the ties on Dankworth's arms. Now pulling his arms forward or lowering his legs would cut off the oxygen to his head.

Satisfied that the man was no longer a threat, Hokee told Shila to watch him, then went around the car to Curly's side. Hokee helped Curly secure Wilson the same way he had secured Dankworth.

With the two men trussed up like thanksgiving turkeys, they began searching the bodies, where they learned the men's names and that they were British citizens.

"Well, hell, Curly, we've got ourselves a couple of Limeys. Commander Waylon Dankworth was discharged, and Officer Reginald Wilson is retired. Both were members of the Special Air Service, England's most potent special forces unit. And looking at their service identification, they are a couple of really nasty men. I wonder why they're working for the king of Saudi Arabia."

"Maybe they like young boys, and that's their primary goal. I believe pedophiles are more accepted by the Arabs than the British."

"I suppose you're right, Curly. Wonder what the biggest draw was, the King's money or the young boys."

"Let me check the car for their weapons while you search the boyos."
"Oh sure. The deputy gets the cushy job while letting the peons do the dirty work. But I don't mind giving our boy's a close inspection. I spotted some guns on the front seat, but I'm pretty sure they have a second gun

stashed, probably on their ankles, and you know, no respectable special forces man would leave home without a serious knife."

They found two Glock 17 pistols with double-stack magazines holding 17 rounds of 9x19mm Parabellum shells. Each man had Sig Sauer P230 strapped to his ankle, and both carried Fairbairn-Sykes knives down the back of their necks. This knife has a long, slender double-bladed stiletto-type blade the men held in custom leather sheaths.

"Man, look at those knives, Hokee. I wonder which one carved up Hilda?" Curly was angry enough to stomp the men's heads into the dirt.

While Hokee and Curly, with some help from Shila, captured and bound their two prisoners, a gawking crowd had collected on the sidewalk, preventing any gratuitous damage to the Saudi Arabia killers by either Hokee or Curly.

Leaving Curly and Shila to watch over their prisoners, Hokee left to get his Explorer, which he backed up as close to the prisoners as possible.

"Okay, Curly, we've got to load these men into the back of my Explorer." Hokee locked the guns and knives in the glove box to accompany his impressive collection of confiscated weapons.

"I'm sorry, Hokee," Curly said as Hokee came to help pick up one of the prisoners, "I should have said something sooner, but I was busy trying to figure a way to hurt these bastards. Let me get our sheriff's pickup. It's just around the corner, and it will be easier to load these men."

"Hey, good idea. I wasn't looking forward to stuffing them into my Explorer."

Hokee drove his Explorer out of the way so Curly could park close to the two men. They lifted Dankworth into the truck first. "My God, this limey is heavy," Curly said as he grunted and pulled the man into the bed. Wilson was a little easier, but neither man was easy to handle, given how Hokee had them trussed.

Curly's Chevrolet 4x4 had an extended cab so that Shila could ride in the back seat. When everyone was loaded into the pickup, they took off, leaving a confused crowd on the sidewalk

Their next stop was the McCammon hole.

CHAPTER FIFTY

After leaving the highway near the McCammon Hotel, Curly headed east on a paved road, which turned into a bumpy dirt road and finally a rough trail. It didn't appear that anyone ever visited the hole.

"I wonder if anyone ever comes out to this hole anymore?" Curly was thinking out loud as he backed the pickup as close to the hole as possible.

"It sure looks abandoned," Hokee responded as he let Shila out of the back seat. Shila seemed delighted to be allowed to run around and explore.

"You aren't worried that Shila will fall into that hole, are you?" Curly asked Hokee.

"Not that wolf. Probably any wolf. They're much too canny to fall into a trap like that."

"Well, are you going to do the cutting, or is it just me?" Curly asked. "Curly, I would like to torture these men in ways that might even make you squeamish, but I've been thinking, and my spirit guides are chattering so loud it feels like my head is about to explode. If we torture them, we're no better than they are. It damages our souls. Forget about what we do to them; it hurts us more. Let's dump them in the hole and let them torture themselves on their way to hell."

"I hear you, ole wise one, and reluctantly agree with your guides. Let's dump em in the hole and go have a drink."

"You men are making a big mistake," Dankworth yelled. "You do not know what they'll do to you yanks."

It wasn't clear who he had in mind that would do the damage. The police in Paris, or his boss, Prince Nayef? Hokee didn't know about Nayef and wasn't afraid of the Paris police.

Wilson, who had finally determined they could not free themselves, yelled, "it was all Dankworth. He's the one who cut up the lady. Please let me go, and I'll get Nayef to forget about you."

Dankworth recognized they were in the hands of experts and was determined to go out like a man. He said, "Shut up, Reginald, don't act like a baby."

Wilson hated to be called Reginald, but couldn't keep his trap shut. "Yeah, well, ain't you the big bloody bastard? You're the one who kept insisting that woman tell us where her boss was, even after we were sure she didn't know."

While the two men were talking, Curly lowered the tailgate and began pulling on Wilson's legs, as he was the closest to the back. When only his shoulders were still on the tailgate, Hokee grabbed him under the arms and walked him to the edge of the bottomless hole with Curly. "On three Curly," Hokee said. "One, two, and three." They swung Wilson's body with each count and tossed him into the hole on three. They could hear Wilson scream for several seconds until his head connected with a protruding rock deep down the hole.

"What in the bloody hell was that?" Dankworth asked.

"That hole over there, sir, is known as the bottomless hole. Before today, the last one we know of to do the endless fall was a man much like yourself, except he liked to do it with virgin girls. We figured you and your buddy would be good hole mates." Curly couldn't help but grin at his little speech. Hokee and Curly grabbed Dankworth, pulling him out of the pickup's bed. Lile before, Hokee took the shoulders and Curly the feet. Dankworth was too proud to beg and had not planned on making any other noise, but

couldn't refrain from telling Hokee and Curly their days were numbered. And when thrown into the black hole, he screamed for a long while.

"It doesn't sound like he hit anything, Hokee. You don't suppose he is still alive down there, do you?"

"I seriously doubt it, Curly. It would be nice to think he would spend a few weeks starving to death, but I'm pretty sure the fall killed him at some point."

"Come on Shila, let's load up and go get that drink Curly promised."

"Hey, I said let's go have a drink; I didn't say I was buying. Besides, I did all the driving."

"Hear that Shila. Just like a corrupt sheriff's deputy to weasel out of buying drinks. We'll have to dip into our retirement fund to buy the man a beer."

"Beer hell. I've worked up an appetite for a real drink. I'm thinking of Old Crow.

"Well, at least it ain't a Shirley Temple," Hokee said, stroking Shila's neck.

FINALLY

Eight days later, Hokee pushed the buzzer on Hilda's front door. Her three-bedroom black rock house blended into the hillside on a lava bench west of Pocatello. The views from her home included the entire city below, stretching from Idaho State University in the south and disappearing into the farmlands to the north. White stepping stones led from the crushed rock driveway to a bright red door. Bright yellow Floribunda rose bushes decorated both sides of the steps leading to a broad-shaded porch.

Hilda's face bore faded black and purple blotches from the beating she had taken, but the smile on her face when she saw Hokee was all he needed to know she was recovering. Her loose-fitting rose-colored sweater hid any scars or bandages she undoubtedly still carried.

"Oh, Hokee, please come in," she said, opening the door.

"Hi Hilda, I should have called, but I got this video package from Glory in the mail today, and I wanted to share it with you before heading home. Is this a good time, or should I come back another time?"

"This is a good time. Is that Glory's expose on human trafficking?" As Hilda talked, she stood aside, letting Hokee enter her living room.

Hokee took a moment to notice the well-organized room. A plush tan Berber carpet was complemented by a dark brown sofa and matching easy chair. Across the room from the couch was a modest 48-inch television screen resting on a black TV stand. Blond lamp tables on each side of the sofa held black lamps with white cloth-covered lampshades. There were what looked like original paintings featuring different birds on each wall. It wasn't a fussy crowded room Hokee was used to seeing in the houses of lonely widows. "Yes," he answered. "I believe this is the first installment. I thought the series would be picked up by one of the major networks, but Glory called to let me know they all considered exposing the French government too controversial. I suspect our government had a hand in suppressing the major networks. Thankfully, Glory's television station didn't share their misgivings."

"That's too bad. I know you and I both paid a price to disseminate this information to the public. It seems like such a disgraceful comment on our society that such evil may continue."

"It's big money Hilda, and money means power. I'm sure our rulers in

D.C. are getting their share. You notice I didn't say our servants or representatives."

"I noticed, and yes, we now have a ruling class. Here, give me the CD and I'll put it in the player."

Glory's station did a reasonably decent job with their presentation. They showed pictures of the Houston cages and one of Teeten taken in front of a pen, pushing a child inside. Hokee wondered if that picture was photoshopped or an actual photo. There were plenty of graphics detailing the problem. And, of course, the station had plenty of heartbreaking images of Mauritania, the squalor and open slavery. Fortunately, there was no mention of the good Samaritan who killed a bunch of bad guys and freed the enslaved people in Houston. Nor were the several other people Hokee killed in other places mentioned. Hokee was happy Hilda didn't have to hear how many people he had removed from the game of life. But, as in chess, the Knight sometimes has to rescue the pawns.

The first installment ended as Glory entered Paris looking for pedophiles. Glory looked beautiful throughout the exposê, and she did an Oscar-worthy performance presenting the information. The performance ended with a teaser for the next show. It was the look of fright in Glory's eyes as she faced the pistol held by the Sumo doorman to Brezing's mansion. Hokee didn't realize until he saw that teaser that the camera Glory had was taking pictures of her as she filmed the scenes unfolding in front.

After saying goodnight to Hilda, Hokee headed home, thinking along the way of Glory's promise on the phone to visit Pocatello just as soon as she wrapped up a few things in New York. He smiled to himself. The wrapping up business would probably drag on for a long time. Glory was a city gal, while Hokee was a private investigator and part-time shaman. He couldn't see himself in the Big Apple, and he couldn't see Glory *anywhere* in Idaho, let alone Pocatello.

Now he was ready for a soak in the cold water of his underground river to wash away the stink from his body. Then another sweat lodge to cleanse his body and mind. Hopefully, this would eliminate the remaining poison from his soul.

Turning down the long driveway to his place, he thought, *well, I've still got Shila.* As his thoughts turned toward the cave he called home and his waiting friend, he decided that having a wolf for a companion wasn't all bad.

AUTHOR'S NOTES

Hokee's brutal treatment of human traffickers and pedophiles may shock Hokee fans, but the ongoing slavery and abduction of young children is a blight on our civilization. Those who prey on the weaker members of society deserve no mercy. It is no secret that slavery exists in every corner of the planet, including the USA. The world needs more Hokee Wolfs to help cleanse this abomination from our pack. Annihilating several thousand otherwise friendly native Americans is also a blot on humanity.

I was born and raised about ten miles from the Bear River Massacre and 80 miles south of the Fort Hall Indian Reservation. A blacksmith in Preston, Idaho, living near the massacre, spent his weekends searching the sandy hills around the massacre site, collecting arrowheads, cannon balls, tomahawks, and spear points. His frame-mounted collection covered three entire walls of his spacious house, and I spent many hours of my youth studying his displays. Even then, I could not help but feel sorry for what otherwise 'civilized' members of society would do to other human beings. Unfortunately, we still see this behavior against those of a different color or religion.

ABOUT THE AUTHOR

Clark is the author of several thrillers, including *Hokee Wolf I* and *Hokee Wolf II*, and one romance. His books have all received 4+ star reviews from fellow authors and readers around the world. He lives in Utah with his wife Kim and their mixed breed shepherd Quigly.

NOTE FROM CLARK VIEHWEG

Word-of-mouth is crucial for any author to succeed. If you enjoyed *Hokee Wolf III*, please leave a review online—anywhere you can. Even if it's just a sentence or two. It would make all the difference and would be very much appreciated.

You can contact me at clarkviehweg07@gmail.com

Thanks!
Clark Viehweg

We hope you enjoyed reading this title from:

www.blackrosewriting.com

Subscribe to our mailing list – *The Rosevine* – and receive **FREE** books, daily deals, and stay current with news about upcoming
releases and our hottest authors.
Scan the QR code below to sign up.

Already a subscriber? Please accept a sincere thank you for being a fan of
Black Rose Writing authors.

View other Black Rose Writing titles at
www.blackrosewriting.com/books and use promo code
PRINT to receive a **20% discount** when purchasing.

www.ingramcontent.com/pod-product-compliance
Lightning Source LLC
Chambersburg PA
CBHW050159120726
47903CB00002B/687